FACES OF MUSIC

25 Years of Lunching with Legends

by Mr. Bonzai

THOMSON
✳
COURSE TECHNOLOGY
Professional ▪ Technical ▪ Reference

Publisher and General Manager, Thomson Course Technology PTR: Stacy L. Hiquet
Associate Director of Marketing: Sarah O'Donnell
Manager of Editorial Services: Heather Talbot
Marketing Managers: Heather Hurley and Kristin Eisenzopf
Executive Editor: Mike Lawson
Senior Editor: Mark Garvey
Marketing Coordinator: Jordan Casey
Project Editor: Jenny Davidson
Thomson Course Technology PTR Editorial Services Coordinator: Elizabeth Furbish
Interior Layout Tech/Cover Designer: Stephen Ramirez

ISBN: 1-59863-024-5
Library of Congress Catalog Card Number: 2005929802

Printed in Canada
06 07 08 09 TC 10 9 8 7 6 5 4 3 2 1

Thomson Course Technology PTR, a division of Thomson Course Technology
25 Thomson Place
Boston, MA 02210
www.courseptr.com

Dedication

For Keiko,
the one and only

Foreword

Given the chance to interview rock stars, record producers, filmmakers, humorists, and other icons of popular culture, most of us would probably fall into the temptation of asking the Grand questions that we'd hope would draw out the Definitive stories.

Not Mr. Bonzai. He prefers instead to beguile the likes of Brian Wilson, David Lynch, B.B. King, Timothy Leary, and Frank Zappa with interrogations that may seem naive on the surface, but in the end get right to the heart of what makes creative people tick.

In a similar way, Mr. Bonzai's photographs show us a different view of their subjects than we're used to seeing. He brings a freshness, a sense of innocent wonder to his craft, as an artist who breaks the rules to explore his own unique vision.

Together in *Faces of Music*, these words and pictures reveal a rare bond between the author and his subjects, and they make the reader feel invited to the party.

Paul Verna

Author, *The Encyclopedia of Record Producers*

About the Author

A native New Yorker, **Mr. Bonzai** is a graduate of the University of California at Irvine, with a B.A. in English and a minor in Art. After college, he was a writer/performer in the improvisational Praxis Theater, and co-founded "Strangemouth," a radio comedy group which broadcast live in the U.S. and Canada. As Creative Director of Canada's top-rated CHOM-FM, he served as announcer, writer, and producer. Upon his return to the U.S., he managed Lyon Recording Studios, also operating as inhouse producer, engineer, and announcer.

Since 1980, Mr. Bonzai has written over 1,000 articles for magazines in the U.S., Europe, and Asia, including over 500 interviews with leading musicians, artists, directors, producers, engineers, and media figures. He has published two books: *Studio Life: The Other Side of the Tracks* and *Hal Blaine and The Wrecking Crew: The Story of the World's Most Recorded Musician.*

An award-winning photographer and writer, Mr. Bonzai's work has appeared in *Rolling Stone*, *The New York Times*, *The Los Angeles Times*, *Billboard*, *Mix*, *EQ*, *Sound & Recording*, *Daily Variety*, and *Hollywood Reporter*, among numerous others. He lives in Hollywood with his wife, the sculptor Keiko Kasai.

Acknowlegments

In addition to all of the subjects in this book, Mr. Bonzai would like to thank…

Tozen Akiyama, Michael Alexander, Rocky Araki, Neil Aspinall, Asao Atsunori, Robert Benchley, Sarah Benzuly, Peter Brown, Capitol Recording Studios, Jordan Casey, Chogyam Trungpa Rinpoche, Conway Recording Studios, Ludwig Coss, Jenny Davidson, Claris Sayadian-Dodge, Karen Dunn, Kristin Eisenzopf, *EQ* magazine, Jeff Evans, Mal Evans, Albert Fox, Glenwood Place Recording Studios, Edward James Goggin, Jerimaya Grabher, Bernie Grundman Mastering, Laurie Gorman, George Harrison, Annie Heller-Gutwillig, Henson Recording Studios, Michael Herring, David Hockney, Greg Hofmann, Heather Hurley, Blair Jackson, Sarah Jones, Enid Kaspar, Tom Kenny, Judi Kerr, Shinji Kurihara, Mike Lawson, John Lennon, Curt Lyon, Norman MacCaig, Paul McCartney, *Mix* magazine, Megan McLean, Ocean Way Recording Studios, Sarah O'Donnell, Yoko Ono, Jim Pace, George Petersen, Rick Plushner, Martin Porter, Pro Sound News, D. Whitney Quinn, Stephen Ramirez, Record Plant Recording Studios, Hillel Resner, Penny Riker, Lisa Roy, David Schwartz (founding editor of *Mix* magazine), Sound City Recording Studios, Sound Factory, *Sound & Recording* magazine, Terry Southern, Ringo Starr, Heather Talbot, Mark Turnbull, Kamran V, Trici Venola, Paul Verna, The Village, Christopher Walsh, Alan Wedertz, Frank Wells, and toppermost thanks to the Housekeeper, Mrs. Dorothy Jarlett.

Contents

Introduction

This is how the lunching started…

On September 29, 1967, I stepped through the open gates of John Lennon's estate in Weybridge, Surrey, south of London. I didn't know what to expect, but I felt that I had some valuable information for John concerning Alpha brain waves and meditation which I had gathered while working on a project back home at the University of California. I also had some ideas about films and music and art. Most of all, I appreciated John's sense of humor and wanted to meet him. I had a few days free before going north to the University of Edinburgh in Scotland.

As I approached the house I passed a full-scale, brightly painted circus wagon that could have come right out of *For the Benefit of Mr. Kite*. The housekeeper stuck her head out of a second floor window and asked, "Are you looking for John?" I replied yes and she explained that he was sleeping and asked if I could come back later.

I returned to the train station, had a pot of tea, and then made my way back to John's house. The housekeeper greeted me at the front door and told me that he was still sleeping, but thought it would be all right if I waited in the garage. She brought me some tea and biscuits and I sat looking at the Rolls Royce. The limousine was absolutely outrageous. Bright yellow, almost gold, with framed paintings of flowers on the door panels. After about an hour, the Beatles' manager Peter Brown came to the garage door and asked who I was and what I was up to. I told him and he said he would speak with John.

Within a few minutes John Lennon walked up to me as I stood politely in the doorway of the garage. I looked at him in his green linen suit with tiny mirrors embroidered in an Indian fashion. I turned around to show him his portrait, which I had embroidered on my jacket, with two tiny sequins for his eyes. I said, "You can't do this, can you?" He replied, "What?" I said, "Meet John Lennon." He shrugged and said, "No, I suppose not. C'mon in the house—just having breakfast."

I was shown to a sofa and looked out on the scenery as John sat at a kitchen table eating eggs and fried tomatoes. He was eating alone, so I grabbed my bag and notebooks and joined him. I told him about the brain wave experiment I had managed at UCI, and spoke about meditation, rock-and-roll light shows, and my idea for a Zen western. As he finished eating he said, "We've got to head into London to do the David Frost program. Would you like a lift?"

John, Peter, and I walked out to the waiting limousine. The windows were blacked out and there was even a telephone. We drove a short distance to another house and George Harrison came out and jumped in. John introduced me and said I was from California and on my way to study in Scotland. The discussion once again turned to meditation and as we drove, George took my journal and drew a diagram of the different levels of consciousness. He suggested that I read *Autobiography of a Yogi*.

It took about an hour to reach London. The limo was a standout on the roads, and I remember a fellow on a bicycle craning his neck to get a look and almost falling off his wobbly bike. John and George were leafing through a script for *Yellow Submarine* and discussing the project that would come to light within a year. George had been talking with Eric Burdon and told John that Eric wanted to take the Animals to China. John laughed and said, "He'll never get in."

To me, this was fantastic. Just the four of us. But then we pulled up to the TV studios and it was pandemonium. It had been only a few months since the release of *Sgt. Pepper*, and with Beatlemania in full swing there was a mob of screaming girls and fans waiting.

John and George jumped out of one door and were ushered through the crowd by a team of security guards. I left my bag with my journals on the back seat, and Peter and I jumped out of the other door. He grabbed my arm and pulled me through the crowd. Lucky for me, because if I had been separated I would have become anonymous and lost in the mayhem. We entered the auditorium and climbed to the very back top row to watch The Frost Programme.

During the show, John was asked about meditation and paraphrased what I had spoken of just two hours before at his home. He explained that there was a parallel between sleeping and meditating. As you don't know the moment you fall asleep, only the moment you wake up, you also don't know when your meditative state wavers and only become aware when you regain the meditation.

When the show finished and the crowd left, Peter took me down to the stage and introduced me to David Frost. Then we headed back to the limo, where I had left my bag. We all climbed in and nobody told me to leave, so I just shut up and watched the nighttime scenery roll by. We were heading towards St. John's Wood and the EMI Studios. As I sensed we were nearing our destination, I remember nudging John and raising my eyebrows as if to say, "May I come along?" He nodded yes.

We entered the large Studio Two, which had a staircase leading up to the control room that looked down on the large recording area. Up in the control room I was introduced to George Martin. I don't remember the engineer Ken Scott, but you'll learn why later in this book. Ringo was reading a Beano comic book and fiddling with a radio tuner. Neil Aspinall, later the managing director of Apple Corp., was there and also the Beatles' "roadie," Mal Evans. Paul arrived a little later in a full-length black fur coat. Mal went off to get fish and chips while the evening's work was planned.

I heard a rough mix of "I Am the Walrus" played back and bits of "Fool on the Hill" and "Your Mother Should Know," plus the beginnings of "Cry Baby Cry" from the *White Album* (1968) and "Mean Mr. Mustard" from *Abbey Road* (1969). At one point, I followed John and George down to the main room where they sat on the floor with guitars. George was helping John to work out a guitar part and explained to him that it was a waltz beat he was using.

The fish and chips arrived. I was quite hungry, having not eaten since my biscuits in the garage, and this was my first introduction to that mainstay of the English diet. John asked if I would like some sauce and I asked if it was for the fish or the chips. He said, "I don't know—for the paper if you want." After the quick meal and some joking around, they immediately went back to work.

This entire experience was like a waking dream. I was the only outsider and every few minutes I would mentally pinch myself and marvel at what I was witnessing. I tried to be invisible, but when there was a break in the workflow, I would occasionally inquire about things that I heard. After a playback of "Walrus," I asked George about a phrase I couldn't quite make out in the background vocals. He said it was "Everybody's got one." After the song was released, the rumor was that they were singing "Everybody smokes pot."

Back up in the control room, the experimentation with "Walrus" continued. Ringo tuned the radio to what I later learned was the BBC Third Programme. It was a serious play being broadcast live and this caused a lot of interest and merriment. The console had big shifters that looked like gear shift knobs, and it was John who seemed to be running the show. Snippets of the play were blended in and out, live off the air. Later that year, I was up in Edinburgh reading Shakespeare's "The

Tragedy of King Lear" and had the strange sensation that it was familiar material. It is Act IV, Scene VI that ended up in "I Am the Walrus."

As the evening rolled towards midnight, I thought I should excuse myself to catch the last train to Wimbledon, where I was staying with friends. I didn't want the session to finish in the middle of the night and find myself standing on a dark street needing a ride. I was exhausted from running on adrenalin for about 16 hours. I wished them a good time in India and asked if they would autograph my journal. They happily agreed and John asked me what he should write. I said, "Oh, just something witty and intelligent." He wrote, "Here is something witty and intelligent. Having a wonderful time, John." Paul added, "That goes for me." George wrote "Good Luck for Edinburgh University," and Ringo, "Love and Best Wishes."

That week in London I saw two concerts, Frank Zappa and the Mothers of Invention at The Royal Albert Hall, and The Jimi Hendrix Experience at The Royal Festival Hall. Within a few days I was in Scotland studying Elizabethan theater, Romantic poetry, and writing my own poems in a class taught by the Poet-in-Residence, Norman MacCaig.

. . . .

During the school year I sent letters, drawings, and photo-cartoons to John and Peter Brown. On May 30th, 1968, I got a letter from John's assistant, Peter Shotton (who was in John's first skiffle band). It read, "Anytime you're in London just ring the office and I know John will be pleased to see you." And so I did.

I first stopped at the Apple offices on Wigmore Street. John introduced me to Yoko Ono and explained, "I found him in my garden with my face on his back." While hanging around I overheard John talking on the phone about Stanley Kubrick making the next Beatles' film, *The Lord of the Rings*. I asked who John would play and he said, "Frodo, I suppose." I brought up the subject of Tarot cards and John gave me two pounds to buy him a deck. We also spoke of Tibetan Buddhism, as I had recently visited the Samye Ling monastery in Scotland and met with Chogyam Trungpa, Rinpoche, who would years later become a teacher to Allen Ginsberg.

I asked if they were recording and John said, "Well, probably. Would you like to come by?" I said yes, of course, and he took one of Neil Aspinall's business cards and on the back wrote, "Please let this man David in" and signed it.

I visited EMI Studios once again for my second recording session. Paul wasn't present, and John once again seemed to be running the show for what would become *Revolution 9*. Studios One, Two, and Three were being used and there were tape loops of different lengths being prepared. I spent most of the time following John and George around as they raided the vaults for obscure tapes that could be chopped up and looped. One of them was a school examination tape, hence the very clear and serious reading of *Number nine*. I was also in one of the smaller tape machine rooms where tapes were strung up, reaching perhaps ten feet long with spools and pencils used to keep them rolling through the tape playback heads. Ringo showed me how to do my first tape splice and edit, an art which is no longer needed in the digital age.

I listened to John as he spoke to George Martin. "Well, what we need is a mic going all the time with sounds and reactions so we can use them whenever we want. All of our best stuff was never on tape. We'd be working and really getting into something and then we'd go to the studio and go, "1, 2, 3" and it wouldn't be the same."

In the course of the evening I heard a bit of the song "Revolution," but when the single came out I was surprised to hear the fast version. In my notebook I wrote down "Black bird flying into the night." George was pumping away on a harmonium, Ringo was banging away on the drums. John called out, "Give us any beat ya got, Ringo!" Tapes were being played at different speeds, going backwards and forwards. By this time, I was completely hooked on life in a recording studio.

Before making my exit in the early morning hours, I said goodbye to John and expressed my hopes that I would see him again and perhaps have something to offer in the future. He wished me the best in my studies at the University and encouraged me to stay in touch.

. . . .

Back in California I finished up my studies and got my degree in English, lucked out in the draft lottery and wasn't called up to explain my conscientious objection. I co-founded an improvisational theater troupe which morphed into a radio comedy team. I worked as a radio DJ, learned audio production techniques, made thousands of tape splices, did some TV work in Canada, became a recording studio engineer, hosted a weekly nightclub talent show, and sold my first story to a new magazine called *Mix*.

This stroke of good fortune prompted me to move to Hollywood, where I began this lunching with legends. Pink's famous chili dogs and Chianti with Leonard Cohen. A pot of tea with Mose Allison in a teahouse looking out over the city. A Japanese obento lunchbox with Hans Zimmer. A sumptuous vegetarian feast with k.d. lang in the gardens of the Chateau Marmont. Room service in a swank NYC hotel with Bruce Swedien and his wife Bea. Coffee and pastries with George Martin and his manager John Burgess at the Mondrian Hotel. Fried chicken and boysenberry pie backstage with Ray Benson. Pastrami on rye at Dupar's with Carmine Coppola. Beer and pizza with The Firesign Theatre. Wine and cheese with Danny Korchmar. Martinis with Ray Manzarek and his wife Dorothy. Shabu-shabu with Danny O'Keefe. Cheeseburgers with Danny Saber. Sushi rolls with Max Weinberg. Tuna tacos with Graham Nash and Nate Kunkel in Hawaii. Edamame and ice cold sake with David Lindley. Chicken soup and matzoh balls with Don Was at a roadside diner…

Getting hungry? Dig in.

Mr. Bonzai
1 August, 2005
Hollywood, California

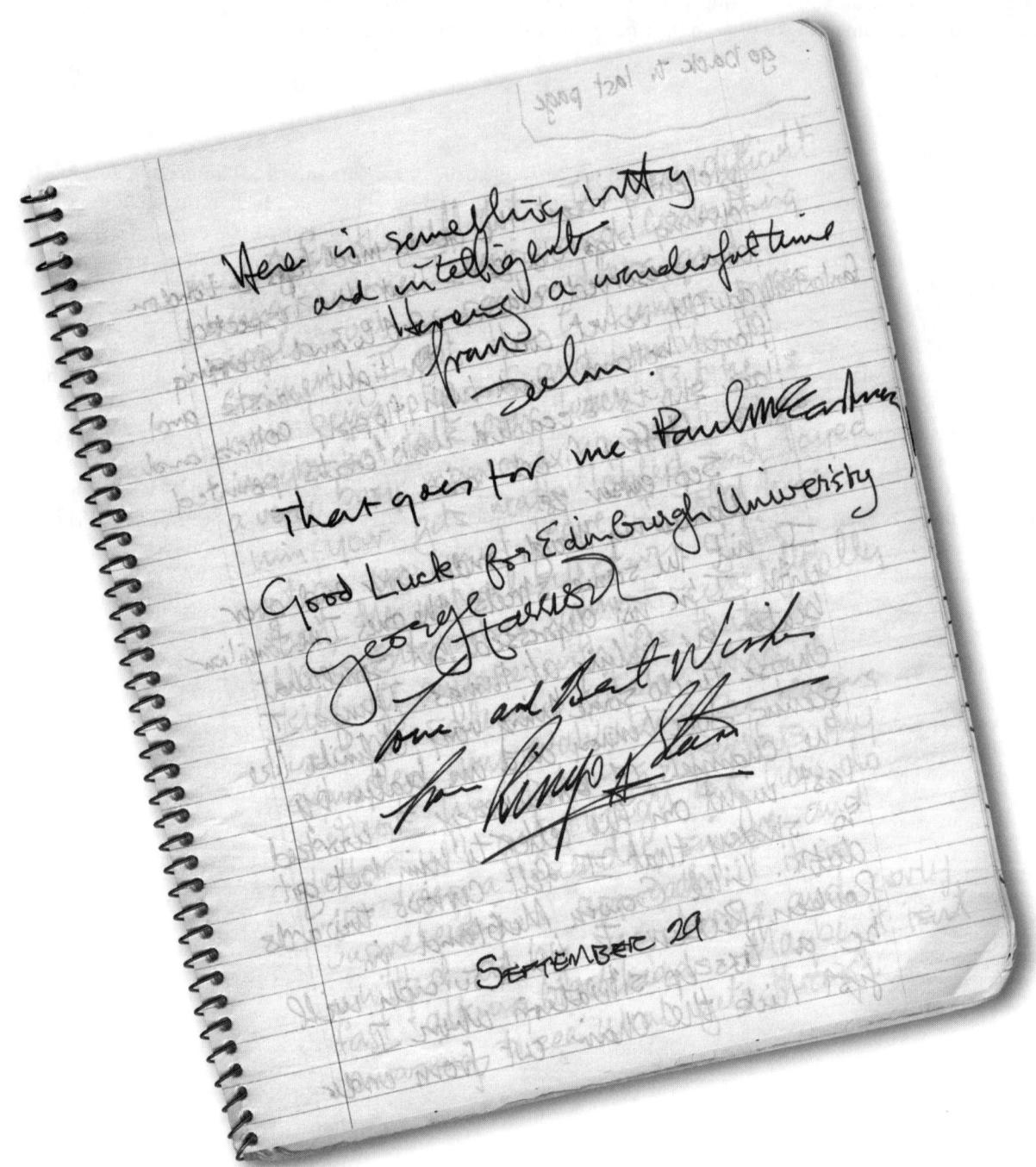

Here is something witty
and intelligent
Heres a wonderful time
from
John.

That goes for me PaulMcCartney

Good Luck for Edinburgh Univeristy
George Harrison

love and Best Wishes
from Ringo Starr

SEPTEMBER 29

Gary Adante and Stevie Wonder, Wonderland Studios, LA 1986

Gary Adante

Gary in Wonderland   1986

XXXXXXXXXXXXXXXXXXXXXXXXXXXXXXXXXXXXXXXXXXXXXXXXXXXXXXXXXXXXXXXXXXXXXXXX

How did a 20-year-old kid end up in the Stevie Wonder camp?
Well, you see, I was born a poor black child myself [laughs]. Actually, I was working at The Record Plant, going through the whole procedure of becoming an engineer: go-fer, janitor, and then assistant engineer. For some reason, people had faith in what I was doing and I started engineering very quickly. I was mixing Billy Preston and working with bands like Rufus, and I was also assisting Steve's engineers. When they split up, I was the next in line. I really admired him, liked him, and we got along pretty well. We've been working together ever since *Songs in the Key of Life*.

What have you learned from working with Stevie?
Patience, and I've obviously learned his style of production.

Is it different from most other artists' workstyles?
I think it's very different. His way of working is very spontaneous. Lately, though, we've moved into nearly total synthesized recording. Steve does a lot of programming at home now and quite often we just go into the studio, press a button, and it just goes. The overdubs are still pretty spontaneous. We go for a sound, an idea—he never pre-plans. It's an interesting way of working—he leaves a lot of the magic to the time.

Stevie certainly gave you a lot of credit at The Grammys®. What do you think he's learned from you?
I don't know. I know he's been really patient with me—we were both young when we started working together.

That's funny—I tend to think of him as born mature.
He seems that way a lot, but if you spend enough time with him, you realize he's as much of a kid as most people in the entertainment business, if not more so.

You must have been at The Record Plant in the wild and wacky days.
Yeah—there was one night when I think it was Paul McCartney on drums, and Ringo, too. John Lennon and Harry Nilsson were singing. A Record Plant engineer was playing bass, and there was Bobby Keyes and Klaus Voorman. All these people playing instruments that they didn't normally play, and Steve called me from a hotel he used to stay at on Hollywood Blvd. I picked him up and took him to the studio, took him in and sat him down at the Rhodes. It was just a mad recording scene, roll after roll, with people saying it was a Second Coming. It'll never happen again, because the musicians in the room were just amazing. But after a while, I heard this, "Gary, Gary!" It was Stevie screaming in the midst of it all for me to come and rescue him. It was pretty chaotic, with people looking for a song that everyone could play. That was about the time that we were talking about working together. I was kind of glad to get out of the room anyway.

John Alagia and Liz Phair, The Village, LA 2005

John Alagia

Gentleman in Charge

2005

What was the first song you wrote?
It was called "Take It Easy," and it was a variation on the folk song "Kumbaya." I recorded it when I was 12 on a little 2-track cassette machine with sound-on-sound.

Did you feel all along that music would be the ruling force in your life?
I wanted it to be, but I thought it might just be a pipe dream. But from the age of nine, I was absorbed in music, and I thought that you could spend a lifetime exploring it, maybe more.

How did you get involved with Dave Matthews?
I started going down to some clubs in Virginia and recorded their shows. At that time, Dave was just interested in refining his sound. So they brought me into the studio to help finish up some of those recordings. Every once in a while, Dave would come up to my house and record some new ideas, which he would then take back to the band. I wasn't thinking so much about the possible commercial success as I was about how important and how wonderful this music was. We'd sit around with a couple of guitars and he'd be pouring out all these little musical ideas that would eventually become some of his biggest hits, like "Crash," "Too Much," "Crush," "Stay," and so on.

Why did you decide to work with Liz Phair?
I gravitate toward the strong songwriters and do my best to help them communicate to the listener. I have a lot of respect for Liz—she's really individualistic, and has her own distinct way.

How did you meet John Mayer?
I heard a demo and not only was he a monster guitar player, but he could write beautiful songs. We started talking about making a record, and we drew up the list of songs. We did the basic tracks in eight days and then finished it up at my studio in Maryland. *Room for Squares* was done top-to-bottom in 28 days. We also did some more mixes with Jack Joseph Puig at Ocean Way in Hollywood.

Advice for getting a good start in the music business?
Don't jump into this business to be popular. Don't ever try to make what you're working on popular music—just follow what you have in your head and your heart. Don't follow trends. Make the music you want to make, and hopefully people will listen.

5

Steve Allen, LA 1983

Steve Allen

"This Could Be the Start of Something Big"* 1983

What are the musical influences in your life?
I am a melody freak. Consequently, I'm almost always annoyed these days when I see a modern musical. I was over-joyed several months ago when I saw *Showboat*, because that score has, as I recall, eight great melodies. Today, the average musical has no great melodies. It may have other musical virtues, maybe great music for dancing, but where the hell are the melodies? I love the great composers, like Jerome Kern, Sigmund Romberg, Victor Herbert, Cole Porter, Irving Berlin. These people are gods to me. They had the gift of melody.

Is that what is missing in modern popular music?
We're talking about a matter of degree, and every so often a lovely song does come along. Henry Mancini gave us eight or ten lovely tunes. Burt Bacharach gave us eight or ten lovely songs. Jim Webb—six or seven terrific songs. Anthony Newley, The Beatles—six or seven terrific songs. Michel Legrand is my favorite contemporary composer. Anyone who wants to know how to do a musical should see *The Umbrellas of Cherbourg*. It's pure opera from beginning to end and yet any nine-year-old can enjoy it. It's not arty or over the heads of people, and there is one glorious melody after another.

If you were suddenly stranded on an island with no audience, but you had a piano…
If I had a piano, I'd be perfectly happy—I'd eat the piano—no, but I'd be perfectly happy because 90% of my piano playing has never been heard by anyone but me. It happens here in the house or wherever I may live. I'm addicted to piano. I have to have a piano the way you have to have food or sex or liquid or alcohol. I must experience the piano fre-quently. Whenever I am in a situation where I can't get at one for a few days, I actually start looking for pianos, the way a guy would start looking for a fix or a drink. So, if I were under a palm tree with a piano, forgetting the fact that from the moisture the piano would be out of tune, I could be very happy, because I love to play and I love to hear the stuff. I'd rather hear Oscar Peterson play—if he was on the island that would be even better.

Would you consider yourself eccentric?
In some ways, yes. In certain ways, at least, I perceive myself as a very normal, average person, but I recognize in other ways that I'm peculiar. One way would be in what I do professionally. I didn't plan to do 14 things for a living, but I guess the fact that I do is odd. I certainly joke and horse around more than the average person.

* music and lyrics by Steve Allen

Mose Allison, LA 1992

Mose Allison

What has been the most important contribution to your livelihood? Is it the records?

No, it's singing the songs and working in clubs that has kept me alive. I never made any money on my records. The only money I made from records was from the mechanical licenses when Van Morrison, or The Who, or the other artists recorded my songs. According to the record companies, my records have never made money. After 30 years, a few of them may have made it out of the red.

Well, what's the key to your success?

The key to my success is the fact that I will get to play again this week [laughs]. I like playing, and I like what I'm doing. I'm fortunate. Throughout my career, I've run across super-talented people all over the world—and you'll never hear of them. They were never able to make a living, or they gave it up. I know that there is an element of luck, and I've persevered. I've kept at it and no matter how sentimental and silly it is, I still keep trying to play well. I keep trying to do a good job. In fact, I've got a line that I haven't used yet—"I'm just a sentimental slob. I even try to do a good job."

You look like you're in a trance when you're playing…

I enjoy it, and it's a challenge if you're trying to do it like I think it's supposed to be done. It doesn't do itself. Sometimes it seems real easy and those are the sets when it's all worthwhile. Now and then, you start a set out, and for no reason that you can figure out, no way you can predict, nothing you can do to ensure that it will happen—but everything starts clicking right away. It's as if it's happening of its own accord—you have control, but you are not forcing anything. I call it the "Spime."

What's that?

Spime is my word for space-time. People are always talking about the Space-Time Continuum, so I figured, look—you need one word for that. That's the Spime. When you get into the Spime, that's when you feel the flow of things, and there is no effort involved. It just happens.

Photo with Julius Wechter courtesy of Hal Blaine.

Herb Alpert (left) and Julius Wechter, Sunset Sound Recorders, LA '60s

(L-R) Herb Alpert, Brian "Big Bass" Gardner, engineer Alan Meyerson, Bernie Grundman Mastering, LA 1999

Herb Alpert

Top Brass

◇◇

72 million records, 5 albums in the Top Twenty at one time, 3 albums in the Top Five. Do you know the secret?
Well, the timing was right. And the songs were good. The sound was good—I listen to those records, and they're still good. I made them with joy in my heart. I didn't make them because I thought I could sell X amount of records. They were done with love and care—not that that is the ingredient for selling a lot of records, but it was the way I worked. I didn't overthink things.

I studied with a great teacher in New York. He didn't play trumpet, but he taught the physics of playing the instrument. I learned how you actually make the sound. He broke it down from a totally different point of view. The conclusion is that the trumpet is a reed instrument. The lips are the reeds and they make the noise. The lips vibrate and you hold this piece of brass—he called it a piece of plumbing. It doesn't matter what you hold in front of your mouth to amplify the sound. Essentially, you are the instrument. He broke the process down to explain how the actual vibrations work. Once I started to understand that, I stopped fighting the instrument.

Who was this teacher?
Carmine Caruso. He also likened the musician to the athlete. All you have to do is sync the body muscles to move in time, like the football player running through tires, or a boxer hitting his punching bag. The boxer gets the groove, the rhythm going, which allows him to get his groove going when he is in the ring. My teacher had these calisthenics that you do on the horn which have nothing to do with music; they have to do with syncing your body muscles to move together at the same moment. Once you start looking at the horn from that point of view, it takes on a new life.

Why did you pick the trumpet?
I liked the sound. And you could probably do a psychological study on trumpet players. I don't know if it's a need to be the center of attention, but I think we need to be heard (laughs). The trumpet is not one of those instruments that you can hide behind. You hit a couple of clams on the horn when you're playing in a section or a small group—it's really heard. Before the electric guitar was cranked up, the trumpet player was the guitar player of yesteryear. He got all the women, too.

(L-R) engineer Rich Costey, Fiona Apple, producer Jon Brion, Brooklyn Recording Studio, LA 1999

(back row, L-R) engineer Tom Biller and assistant engineer Tom Banghart

Fiona Apple

Not a Pawn   1999

XXXXXXXXXXXXXXXXXXXXXXXXXXXXXXXXXXXXXXXXXXXXXXXXXXXXXXXXXXXXXXXXXXXXXXXXXXXXXXXXXXXXXXXX

What do you think of your producer Jon Brion?
I absolutely love him, as a person and as a musician. He's very understanding, and he has the best taste. He's heaven to work with. How easy it is to take for granted the talents that he has. I look back at the time I played the songs on the piano at my house for Jon, and then when I began working with him in the studio—it doesn't even seem that he has to think about it. He just follows the music. He has an ear that allows him to suddenly play things. But he will exhaust himself working on something to get it just right, until you think he will pass out. And then he comes up with something that is absolutely key to the song. And he's a great friend. He's such an important part or my life as a musician.

What is different about your second album?
Because of changes in me personally, and also because of working with Jon, every element has been taken to the highest degree. It is more confident, and less self-conscious. Jon has his genius and his visions, and will go and go and never stop and play everything that comes into his mind. He can do so much. It's easy to discuss and take apart the song and its structure. But it's not only that he wants to make a good record—he wants to make a record that the songwriter intended. He knows that I will be going out to play this.

Looking forward to going out on the road?
Yes, I am. I will have my regular band and techs, and I love them.

Name for the album?
It's a very long title, from a poem I wrote during the last tours. Short title: *When the Pawn…*

Were you encouraged as a child to express yourself?
Yes, but I didn't want anybody to know. My parents encouraged me to play piano, but I didn't tell any of my friends. If you are 12 years old and play the piano, I knew what they would think. I couldn't stand the idea that people would think I was writing stupid things, because I wasn't. It was too important to me to have anyone thinking about it. I just didn't want anybody to know.

Did you think this would become your life?
No, not at all. I never thought about it. I never gave thought to what I would do when I grew up. And when it came along, I didn't have to weigh it against anything else.

(L-R) George Massenburg and Peter Asher, Conway Recording Studios, LA 1997

Peter Asher, LA 1992

(L-R) producer Peter Asher, Heart's Ann and Nancy Wilson, John Kalodner, engineer Nathaniel Kunkel, Ocean Way Recording Studios, LA 1997

Peter Asher

Star Powers

XXXXXXXXXXXXXXXXXXXXXXXXXXXXXXXXXXXXXXXXXXXXXXXXXXXXXXXXXXXXXXXXXXXXXXXXX

How did the duo of Peter and Gordon materialize?

We started singing together when we were at Westminster School in London and then continued when I entered University. After playing for two or three years at parties and clubs, we got offered a record contract.

How did you discover James Taylor in the early Apple days?

Well, going back to the Peter and Gordon days, one of the bands we had backing us was called The Kingbees. The lead guitar of that band was Danny Kortchmar, and we became great friends. Even when our tour was over, we remained in touch. I used to visit him when I was in L.A. He's a wonderful guitar player, and since then, as I'm sure you're aware, has become a very skilled record producer and made tons of hits of his own with Don Henley and others. Anyway, "Kootch" was later in a band called The Flying Machine with James Taylor. He and James had known each other since they were about 12 years old, and had a duo when they were kids.

When The Flying Machine broke up, James decided to go to London and seek his fortune. Kootch gave him my number, and he called and asked if he could play me a tape of his. He came by my house that evening with a tape of "Something in the Way She Moves," "Something's Wrong," "Knocking Around the Zoo," and all sorts of fantastic songs. I was knocked out and said, "Listen, it so happens I've just started working for this new label—I'd like to sign you to the label and produce your record." He said okay and we did it. It all fell into place very easily.

How do you get along with such a wide assortment of people?

I don't know. I tend to like working with people who have a fairly special kind of voice—one hesitates to use the word unique, but in fact, when I think of Cher, Diana Ross, Linda Ronstadt, James Taylor, Natalie Merchant—the thing they all have in common is they are very distinctive vocally and musically, and have a definite style of their own. I like that and I find it easy to work with. When I get asked to work with somebody, and they say, "I can sing anything," that puts me right off. It's like saying, "I can sound like anybody."

I really like people who have a sound of their own, and a clear idea of how they sing and what they want to sing. And I really enjoy helping them to get it the way they want it, and the way that I think will sound the best. I don't mean to imply that I don't contribute musically myself, because I do—but I do so with the aim of putting the voice and the song in the best possible setting, rather than creating something independent of that. Yes, I do seem to get along well with the people I work with.

Joe Barresi, Sound City Recording Studios, LA 2000

Joe Barresi, Sound City Recording Studios, LA 2000

(L-R) co-producer/mixer/engineer Joe Barresi, Queens of the Stone Age members Joey Castillo, Josh "Baby Duck" Homme, Troy Van Leeuwen, and mastering engineer Brian "Big Bass" Gardner. Bernie Grundman Mastering, LA 2004

Joe Barresi

Engineer of the Stone Age

2000

Do you know any interesting business tricks?
This is a very small industry. Karma comes back around.

What was your most ridiculous experience in a recording studio?
I'd have to say making The Melvins' *Stoner Witch* record with Gggarth was quite an experience. We did some pretty stupid things on that one—made the assistant engineer dress up in an Elvis costume for three weeks, miked Gggarth's dog's mouth as we tickled his belly (the dog's belly that is) and flew in the sounds he made—backwards—underneath a track. We recorded a reamped vocal with two PZMs taped to a pair of kick drums in a huge tunnel that had an amp blaring from within. And loads more nonsense!

Who is the most amazing artist you've worked with?
I love certain elements of every record I've worked on. Bauhaus was amazing—watching them in a room together for the first time in 15 or more years, come up with a new song was brilliant. Making the Fu Manchu album, *King of the Road* was a lot of fun, too. We did it out in the desert in 13 days—start to finish. Those guys are such a great band. It was really effortless.

What makes a great producer?
Someone who has a clear vision of how a song or a record should be. Someone who can help an artist realize their goals by providing a creative environment, free of all the craziness that goes with the making of a record.

What's wrong with the music industry?
Basically, you've got A&R/label people who change jobs more often than their underwear. Artist development is equated with Britney Spears getting implants, and not a genuine concern about how to build a band's musical career. Being a great engineer or musician isn't as fashionable as having an enormous computer with the latest editing software. There is a serious lack of people who actually know how to make records these days.

Any advice for getting a good start in this business?
Always give 100% to whatever you do. If you agree to do a job, whether it's as a runner, assistant engineer, engineer, whatever, then do it to the best of your ability. That's all anyone can ask of you. Good work is always noticed and appreciated. Also, never do anything just for the money. With the crazy amount of hours you have to put in doing this, I'd definitely rather work on something that I enjoy than suffer through a session that I don't particularly dig but pays better.

Jeff Baxter, LA 1986

Jeff "Skunk" Baxter

Guitar Maestro   1986

XXXXXXXXXXXXXXXXXXXXXXXXXXXXXXXXXXXXXXXXXXXXXXXXXXXXXXXXXXXXXXXXXXXXXXXXXXXXXXXXXXXXXX

Is the guitar your main form of expression?
If your main instrument is the one where you have the widest vocabulary, then sure, it's the guitar for me. But when you sit down with a computer and sequencer and a bank of synthesizers and samplers, it's hard to say what instrument you're playing. I started out playing piano as a kid, and learned harmony, theory, counterpoint. This has been invaluable in my use of the guitar synthesizer.

You grew up with electronics?
Yeah, I've been a diode head since I was getting shocked taking apart radios.

When did you have your first taste of fame and fortune?
As a teenager, I was making $300 a week as a studio session player, but the first real money came with a band called Ultimate Spinach in Boston, '67 and '68. I was quite amazed that we played for people and they liked it. I had the world's loudest, biggest guitar amplifier, built by Pete Atrainer. He built this 1000-watt monster with no knobs, just an on-off switch and a standby switch. My god, it was outrageous—had four fans. This was during the psychedelic era and it was hard to tell who was more psychedelic, the band or the audience.

After that, I played with Tim Buckley—a wild man, and a helluva songwriter. And I was with Jimmy James & the Blue Flames, before he came back as Jimi Hendrix. We were just kids sluggin' away at the Café Wah, all looking for gigs and playing together.

What was your essential contribution to Steely Dan?
Creating musical tension—being facile enough on the instrument to interpret. I really loved the songs, and some people have kindly referred to my style of guitar as "oblique." In some ways, recording was like building a model airplane. Every time you fit a piece in, maybe you sand it a bit, alter it slightly until you feel it fits not only the entire picture, but also the individual lines.

What about The Doobie Brothers?
Well, they were well on their way before I joined. I got involved because I was with Steely Dan and we toured a lot with The Doobie Brothers. I was with Steely Dan from the beginning and there was a time when I was with both groups—touring with The Doobs and making records with Steely Dan.

(L-R) Don Was, Terry Becker, Randy Jacobs, Brooklyn Recording Studio, LA 1997

Terry Becker, A&M Recording Studios, LA 1998

Terry Diane Becker

Human Touch

1998

◇◇

How did you get started as an engineer?
I came in by the back door after giving up a career as a professional dancer at 23. I had learned how to count music and intricate time signatures, as all good dancers do, and enrolled in The Institute of Audio Research in 1974.

Why has this work consumed your life?
I can't think of anything else I'd rather do. I really love it. It's like an itch that you have to keep scratching.

How do female artists react to a woman at the console?
I've worked with a lot of women artists and it's been great. I feel that they have an innate trust in me. Occasionally, I'll kick everybody out of the studio when doing vocals. Just me and the singer.

Is there such a thing as the "feminine touch" in engineering?
I don't know. I'm a pretty gentle person, and I think that puts people at ease and allows the artist to do the job better. At the same time, I am concerned with getting really beefy, kick-butt tracks.

What did you do for "The Last Waltz"?
I worked on the studio side of the project for the 6-sided album, almost exclusively with Robbie Robertson. There were 20 engineers on the project, but I did get a mix of "The Last Waltz Reprise" on the album. I also worked with Richard Manuel on his vocals.

Which came first, the music or the musician?
I think that music has always existed in nature—the percussion of rain, the rustling of branches in the wind, the voices of animals. When people get together, it's our nature to make music.

What was your most hysterical experience in a recording studio?
I was an assistant for a session with two famous female singers, and it was the first time they had met to do a duet. At the end of the first verse, the first singer held the note for about 20 bars. Not to be outdone, the second singer tried to go further. She was exhausted because she had just come off tour, and reached to the depths of her energy. She held the note, tilted back, and passed out on the floor.

Any advice for getting a good start as a recording engineer?
There is so much computer recording and home studios, I would suggest learning how to record a lot of people in one room all making music at one time. It's all about great songs and great performances—and that requires humans.

Walter Becker, LA 1990

Photo courtesy of Walter Becker.

Walter Becker

Steely Man

Did you feel early on that you would be a musician?
I didn't really feel that I was going to be a musician until I started listening to jazz when I was eleven. That's when I got interested in playing. My father got himself a hi-fi and he had a Dave Brubeck record. It was recorded live, so it didn't have so much of the weird time signature stuff. Just a blowing thing, and Paul Desmond was incredible. I listened to this over and over again until I knew every note, every solo. I thought it was the greatest thing in the world.

What have you learned from Donald Fagen?
I learned so much from Donald over the years. I think it would be impossible to work with somebody, the way that he and I work together, without learning something almost every day. When I started working with Donald, I watched him and got the idea of how you could play piano and write music—which I can just barely do now.

I also learned a tremendous amount about harmony and songwriting from Donald—the ways of constructing songs. And I think there were many things that we learned together. Having an ongoing writing collaboration process is a great growth experience. If it works, it accelerates your trial and error tremendously. You have someone there to say, "Yeah—that's great," or "Failure." You come to a consensus more quickly.

Such great images, but in some cases, I can't figure out what's going on…
Me neither, sometimes [laughs]. We ended up with these fragmentary effects, just because they had to be so concise, and we were trying to avoid the same story over and over again. It's hard to write a successful song that's not a love song, or one of the seven types of pop songs that have been written to death.

Yes, I think there is a Steely Dan territory that no one else has touched.
Or would even want to really [laughs]. I always figured it was like some little side street. There was something wrong with it, or nobody was there. So, we got this little shop there, and we built up our little trade.

Do you know any business tricks that would be useful to those struggling to save their butts in the music business?
Hmmm. You know, it's just not my long suit. Our motto has always been: "Lose money on every deal; make it up in volume."

Seems like you're sittin' pretty these days.
It would be easy enough to just sit back and enjoy life, which I did for a while. But I'm actually happier when there is some sort of struggle. Most of the people I know in the arts, and in music, feel like that. We need something—a big boulder to push uphill.

Photo of Ray Benson in his studio courtesy of Cramden Coach Corp.

Ray Benson, Austin, TX 2000

Photo of Ray Benson with his awards by John Carrico ©2000

Ray Benson, Austin, TX 2000

(L-R) Music critic Marie Goggin, Ray Benson, Mr. Bonzai, Knott's Berry Farm, Anaheim, CA 1998

Ray Benson

Designated Driver

What is the history and the greatness of western swing?

Western swing is music that was a hybrid from the Southwest starting in the late '20s, and it was pioneered by Bob Wills and a guy named Milton Brown. They had a band called Milton Brown and his Musical Brownies. These were wacky guys—the main instrument of the western band was fiddle, and then this Hawaiian guitar thing.

You got to understand that in the '20s and before, the population was about 70% rural. The fiddle was the lead instrument, and if you were a cool guy and wanted to get the girls, you played the fiddle. These guys were fiddlers in the country mode, but Bob Wills said it all changed when he heard Bessie Smith. And then he discovered vaudeville, ragtime, Dixieland, and swing. He went, "Wow—this is young people's music, this is dance music." They combined it with their fiddling heritage and formed this western swing band. Before that, Bob had played with a medicine show as a black-faced fiddler.

He was directly influenced by an old guy named Emmet Miller and His Georgia Crackers. This is the guy I call the missing link in American music. Emmet was a white guy who did black-face vaudeville stuff, sang like a black man, and did the original version of "Lovesick Blues"—which was a big hit for Hank Williams 30 years later. He also did "Anytime," and in his band was Tommy Dorsey, Jimmy Dorsey, Jack Teagarden, Gene Krupa, and some other great luminaries. Emmet sang in a kind of falsetto and also yodeled. Bob Wills said he got his inspiration here, and Jimmy Rogers also got his yodel from him. There's the history of country music right there.

How did you get hooked on this music?

Well, shit, it was 1968, and I heard it and really liked it. I enjoyed western music—Buck Owens, Merle Haggard, Hank Williams. I was playing rock-and-roll and folk music, and as a kid I had played in square-dance bands. When I was eleven, I started a band with my sister and we played folk music, doing songs by Woody Guthrie, The Carter Family. Then came rock and electric guitars, and jazz. I played tuba in a marching band, bass fiddle in the orchestra, sang in the choir. And I could read music, so I got jobs through high school. When I heard Bob Wills, I bought a cowboy hat and started Asleep at the Wheel to play country rock and country music. When I heard Bob I realized I could wear a cowboy hat and play jazz! [laughs]

What's the best thing about being 6 foot 7?

You can stand at the back and still see the parade.

What's the worst thing?

Airplanes.

Stephen Bishop, LA 1984

Stephen Bishop

Charming Guy with Guitar in Animal House

What is your public image?

People have a tendency to slot artists. They know me from "On and On," and "It Might Be You" from *Tootsie*, which has sunk me deeper into the MOR well.

How did you make the big leap from San Diego to Hollywood?

It was a very big leap. I first moved to Hollywood when I was 18, in 1969. The first time I had actually been here was in 1966 with my group The Weeds. We were a combination of The Beatles, The Stones, and The Buffalo Springfield, all rolled into one. I started writing when I was 13 and had amassed about 26 songs by the time I was 15. We came up to record in this guy's living room. We recorded all day and night. Some recording studio this guy had—he was in another room and he'd come out and say, "Okay, go!" and then he'd run back to his room and press the button. I was just thrilled.

What comes to mind when I mention Barbra Streisand?

I met her very early in my career. She was looking for songs for *A Star Is Born* and I was invited up to her house. I sang in the living room for Jon Peters, and she appeared on the balcony wearing this incredible robe. She was tanned; she looked like a total star. She took my breath away. And she said, "Stephen, was that you? I thought the record player was on—you have the most incredible voice." She sat there with me and I played over 30 songs. She was so complimentary and the big living room made my voice sound great. I drove home in my little Volkswagen that night thinking, "Boy, am I hot shit!"

John Belushi?

Asshole, little kid, great guy, and I miss him. I really do miss him—it's sad.

Who is the most amazing talent you've worked with?

Art Garfunkel. He is one of the finest record makers, as far as innovative records go. All his records have new little things.

What was your worst experience in a recording studio?

I was doing a string date for "Looking for the Right One" on the second album. I get nervous when I do string dates because they're so expensive—$6,000 an hour, or something like that. Thirty musicians are out there with Marty Paich conducting, and we're just about to roll when someone spilled a nice sticky Coca-Cola into the board. We were delayed while they cleaned up and dried the console with hair dryers. So if anyone says the song turned out kinda sugary, they'll know why.

Hal Blaine, LA, circa 1970

photo courtesy of Hal Blaine.

Hal Blaine, 2004

(L-R) Drummer Chad Smith and Hal Blaine, Palm Desert, CA
2004

Hal Blaine

The Midas Beat 1984

Why did you end up as a drummer?
I started with some doweling from an old rocking chair that I used for drumsticks when I was eight years old. I always knew I would be a drummer. When I was 13 we moved to California and I started my own little band. We got our first jobs playing for five bucks a night and a free chicken dinner.

Did you have any formal training?
In 1949 I moved to Chicago and attended the Roy Knapp School of Percussion. It was Gene Krupa's alma mater, Louis Bellson's—a lot of great drummers went there. While studying, I worked at nightclubs backing strippers from eight at night to four in the morning. It was strictly sight reading and a great training ground.

How did you break into the big time?
I moved to LA, started playing with some groups, and through a series of events I met Tommy Sands, the teenage idol, and started working with him. A month in Vegas with Patti Page led to three years on the road with her. When Elvis got out of the service, I got a call to do drums for *Girls, Girls, Girls* and a whole string of his movies. I recorded with Sam Cooke, Dick and Dee Dee, The Olympics. That led to Phil Spector and all the early "wall of sound" hits. I became the original drummer with The Tijuana Brass and made the first of my Records of the Year.

Why were you at the center of all this activity?
Because I had a sound. I tuned to a midrange and got a very fat tom-tom sound—boom, boom, boom, not a ticka-ticka-ticka. It created a new sound on records that was identified with the West Coast. I also designed The Octoplus, the drum kit with the massive tom-toms that drummers use today. Before that, drummers were using four drums, sometimes five. I had eleven. Listen to The Carpenters, The Byrds, The Beach Boys, Jan and Dean, The Monkees.

I was strictly a side man brought in for the recording sessions. We made 35 dollars in the afternoon while the groups made $35,000 that night. But there were no animosities. Dennis Wilson, for instance, and I were very good friends. Dennis was a fine drummer—for the stage, but he wasn't really a great recording drummer.

What's the secret of being a top session drummer?
It's experience mostly. Knowing what to play on a record as well as what not to play. With experience you don't have to think about it—it becomes second nature. At this point I must have recorded close to 35,000 records.

Any advice for aspiring drummers?
There are no losers, only winners who give up too soon.

Tchad Blake, LA 1997

LA 1997

Tchad Blake and Neil Finn, Sound Factory, LA 1998

Tchad Blake

The Binaural Man

XXXXXXXXXXXXXXXXXXXXXXXXXXXXXXXXXXXXXXXXXXXXXXXXXXXXXXXXXXXXXXXXXXXXXXX

What are your best sounding records and why?

In the pop category, I'd say *Colossal Head*, Los Lobos—it sounds big, tough, and 3D. In the field category it would be *Signs of Sardinia* by Gesuino Deiana. It's my best binaural effort.

Why are you obsessed with binaural recording?

I just love what it does in my head to listen. It's such an underused technology, I can't believe it. Besides, I also love the travel and interaction with people I meet.

Could you reveal one of your recording secrets?

No secrets here. I'm pretty straight ahead in my recording. The mechanical filters might be the most unusual thing. I haven't seen anybody else do that.

What's a mechanical filter?

Pipes, tin boxes, rubber tubes—anything I can put a mic into and alter the response of that mic.

Do you have any secrets of mixing?

Not really, but for those starting out—when getting sounds, mixing, or tracking, listen to everything, or as much as you can, together. A common error is to get a great kick sound, then solo the snare, then the overheads, etc. It's best to have it all in, right from the start.

Why did you become a recording engineer?

I got a job in a studio thinking I could record my own stuff after hours for free, which I did a little of. The problem was that I'm not a very good composer and just didn't write very much. So the job won out.

Any advice for getting a good start as an engineer?

Don't listen to people who tell you what you can and cannot do, or should or shouldn't use. It's wide open. You can use just about anything to record everything and should.

If you were a musical instrument, which would it be?

A Hohner Bravi Alpini harmonica. They always sound as if they're having the greatest time.

What is your role when you produce?

It's different with each artist. I like a sense of abandon in the studio, and I try to work fast, not getting hung up on things that won't be remembered six months on. I don't usually think things out beforehand. Spontaneity. I like to jam.

Martin Böhm, Vienna, Austria 2001

Martin Böhm, MG Sound Studios, Vienna 2001

(L-R) Martin, Nina, Eva Böhm, Vienna 2001

Martin Böhm

Vienna Legend

Why did you become an engineer?
When we started touring with our band, nobody really took care of the sound seriously, so I took over the responsibility and found out very quickly that this was what I wanted to do. I'm far better as an engineer than I was as a musician.

What did you learn from George Massenburg?
Be a genius. Have golden ears. This man is really far away. What really fascinated me was the fact that everything he does, he does 100%, even if he is playing PS2 with his son. And old is not necessarily good, in terms of equipment. He is the only man I know who is top on both the creative and the technical side.

What did you learn from Ed Cherney?
Keep your nerves. We were mixing a Rolling Stones live show with a ridiculous schedule. For me it seemed impossible with what we had on tape. He managed to finish it off right on time in a very straightforward way. And although he never looked back, the two-hour show was completely matching from start to end. He just knows what he is doing.

How was it working with Bono and The Edge?
What an experience. Both guys are so musical. We did an acoustic version of "Stuck in a Moment," Daniel Lanois producer. Both guys were coaching each other while they were recording. Very straightforward. They really understand the trademark U2. And Dallas Shoe, who's worked for The Edge for 17 years as guitar tech, provides the guitar sounds so fast that it never breaks the musical flow.

Who were your engineering heroes when you were getting started?
Bruce Swedien first made me aware that good engineering can really make the difference. I always liked the old big band recordings that he did. But that was long before I decided to become an engineer. Later I really liked George Massenburg's work with Earth, Wind and Fire, and others.

Do you know any interesting business tricks?
Always charge slightly less than your client will expect.

What do you listen to while you're driving?
To the engine of my 360 Modena.

What makes a great producer?
Make the artist shine in his or her most individual way.

Any advice for getting a good start in the recording business?
Be as focused as possible.

LA 1992

LA 1992

(seated L-R) The Doors' Robby Krieger, engineer/producer Bruce Botnick, producer Bones Howe, The Doors' John Densmore; (standing L-R) engineer Allen Sides, arranger Pat Williams. Ocean Way, LA 1997

Bruce Botnick

Laying Down Doors   1992

XXXXXXXXXXXXXXXXXXXXXXXXXXXXXXXXXXXXXXXXXXXXXXXXXXXXXXXXXXXXXXXXXXXXXXXXXXXXXXXXX

When did you have your first professional gig?

After high school, I got a job at Liberty Records recording studio, 1961. I worked for two-and-a-half years for free, as an assistant. I went for the food, I cleaned floors, I operated the tape machines. I was an apprentice, and I learned about microphones and how to cut disks. I worked my way up to solo engineering, and did my first records with groups like Jan and Dean, The Ventures.

Let's hear about your first session with The Doors.

Well, I was doing work for Elektra Records. I had done their first rock-and-roll record with the band Love. This record and the next album, *Tim Buckley*, were produced by Jac Holzman. Through Jac, I met Paul Rothchild, then head of A&R and their main in-house producer. Since The Doors were an L.A. band, and Paul was out of New York, Jac Holzman asked that I be involved. They just booked the studio for a week and that was the first album. We recorded the album in seven days.

What was your first impression of Jim Morrison?

He was a pretty normal guy—an upstanding Irishman.

How did you swing it as producer of The Doors?

Basically, we just went into the studio to do "L.A. Woman." After all the years of making records with Paul Rothchild, The Doors had gotten to the point where they didn't want to be produced anymore. Paul was getting tired as well, without that enthusiasm of the first or second record. Besides that, it was more a matter of capturing things by this time. It evolved to the point where they wanted to do it on their own, so I suggested that we just do it together. They asked where we should record, and I thought we should do it in their rehearsal hall. It was a comfortable place to work, and I brought in the equipment and we recorded the album in seven days, same as the first album.

Is there one person who guided your early years more than anyone else?

Ted Keep, the mixer at 20th Century Fox. He was friends with Sy Waronker, whose son Lenny is now president of Warner Bros. Records. When Sy started Liberty Records he brought Ted Keep along and they opened their own recording studio, because in those days all the labels had their own studios.

Ted was great, because he was cantankerous, opinionated, and really knew what he was doing. He had the very first transistor board in the business. He built it himself. Ted gave me enough rope to hang myself, which I liked a lot. I'd watch him and then I would try, and then compare. I'd make mistakes, and I'd play my work for him and he'd tell me, "It sucks. Why are you wasting my time?" Then I would fight even harder.

Jon Brion, Grand Master Recording Studios, LA 2005

The Paramour, LA 2003

With Fiona Apple, Ocean Way Recording Studios, LA 2003

Jon Brion

Indestructible

Do people have the wrong impression of Fiona Apple?

That is definitely the case. It's just an impression based on what they saw on TV, when she was on an award show making a speech about the world being bullshit. She looks like a mess of trouble, and the songs on her first album are about terrible things that happened to her. People assume that she is a dark and negative person—but as you can see that is not the reality at all.

She's extremely bright. If something upsets her, she feels it acutely, but she also describes it acutely. She is not what most people would think of as the "difficult artist." She is not a diva, and she is open to ideas, and it is not a dark soap opera. She treats everyone well, and there is no feeling of a ladder of command common to many recording situations. With many projects, there is almost a class system in the recording studio, but not this one. After all, making records is supposed to be a creative working environment—most of us do this because we didn't want typical jobs that mirrored the way society works.

Was there much pre-production?

Nope. The way it worked was Fiona asked if I would like to do the record. She decided that she wouldn't play me anything until she had written the whole album, and had written all the lyrics out by hand, and had made a booklet for me. I went over to her house and sat next to an upright piano. She said she wanted to play the entire album and then we could talk afterwards. I tell you—good songwriting is the best pre-production in the world. Good songs are pretty much indestructible.

Van Dyke Parks contributed to Fiona's first album. What is the essential value of Mr. Parks?

I came to Van Dyke the way many have, through his Beach Boys work. I bought a book about making the *Smile* album, went out and got the record and was floored by the scope and span of the work. So rewarding. It's a complete world you enter with Van Dyke.

What music would you like played at your funeral?

That's easy. The next to last movement of the "Cabrielle Suites" by Peter Warlock.

Do you have any advice for people entering this wonderful music industry?

[laughs] Stay in your car. Wear your protective clothing. Hmmm. On his box set, Tony Bennett thanked Frank Sinatra for giving him the best advice of his career. "Only sing the finest songs." I believe you should put yourself in situations where good things are going on, and work with people you enjoy and respect. If you have songs which you feel are great, play them proudly.

LA, 2002

BT

Smack It, Flip It, Rub It Down

I've heard that you invented trance music. What is it exactly?

Trance connotes something really different to me now than it did when we were making it and there wasn't a name for it. In the early '90s, the tracks that I did then—lots and lots and lots of tracks—people would listen to the stuff, and they didn't know what to call it. Non-linear house music that was influenced harmonically by film scores and classical music, and has huge swells and breakdowns and stuff. The name *trance* came up.

"The Fast and the Furious" soundtrack has, shall we call it, an orchestral score?

Yes, it is. I wrote a lot of music for an 80-piece.

How do you combine writing for an orchestra and getting a couple of your buddies to beat up a car with hammers?

It's all in the vein of contemporary composers that I really like—John Cage, Karlheinz Stockhausen, and other rebels. My heroes inspire me to do crazy things. I also love industrial music and musique concrete. I wanted to come up with something thematic that was subliminal. I wrote melodic themes—obviously you have to do that for a film like "The Fast and the Furious," but I wanted to come up with something subliminal that made the listener feel in motion, in movement, in flux. I thought it would be cool to use the noise derived from cars as percussion instruments.

What did you bang? The fenders? A carburetor?

Absolutely—we took two car chassis, a bunch of spare car parts, and dragged them into the studio. I wrote down and notated like you do for traditional percussion parts: orchestral bass drum, tympani, piatti, and all the rest. Then I sat down with my friends Curt and Allen, who are orchestral percussionists, with these car chassis. Orchestral bass drum part—let's see what we can do that will work. Improvising with car parts, we came up with the trunk. Dropping the trunk of this car sounded really good, like an 808 kick that was filtered. We used that for the bass drum. Instead of using a hand bell, we ended up using hubcaps. Instead of piattis we used brake drums. It was a process of substitution.

And how about processing those sounds?

I recorded everything individually so I could work on it very intensely. I just completely smacked it, flipped it, rubbed it down in Pro Tools, and completely freaked all those sounds.

Cornerstone Recording Studios, LA 2003

(L-R) Mastering engineer Bernie Grundman, Mick Fleetwood, Stevie Nicks, Lindsey Buckingham, engineer Mark Needham, Bernie Grundman Mastering Studios, LA 2003

Lindsey Buckingham

Go Your Own Way

What did you learn from your dad?

A sense of joy, enthusiasm, and compassion—not judging people, which I don't always adhere to, I admit. He was the greatest father you could imagine. I have two brothers, and he shared in all the activities, games—he was just always there. He wasn't caught up in business, maybe to the point of it being a fault. He wasn't the best businessman in the world, but that wasn't his priority. Many friends had fathers that were caught up in the business world and they suffered because of it.

Was he a musician?

No, that's weird—there isn't a musical bone in my family. For me, it all started when I was six and my brother, who is seven years older, brought home *Heartbreak Hotel*. It was a revelation compared with records by Patti Page and The Sons of the Pioneers, or *South Pacific*, for that matter. I was suddenly hit with that song, and the image of a guy with a guitar. A lot of kids must have run out and got guitars at that time. That was it, and I managed to collect a lot of 45s, a lot of the great '50s classics. I don't read music and never had any lessons. Just played through listening to records. I'm a real primitive—what can I say?

So, how do you like the music business?

[burst of laughter] What kind of a question is that? Well…I like it, but it's like any other business. You've got the same problems; you've got politics to deal with. The competition is fierce right now. When you think of the demographic for someone who has been around for a while like me, there's more of a challenge to make a dent in something like MTV, which in itself has changed a lot in the past year or two. The demographics seem to be being pushed down; they've made it into a lifestyle kind of channel. But that's just a slice of it. It's a challenge like anything else. There is more competition now than there was when Fleetwood Mac was doing their thing.

Any tips to avoid the pitfalls of the music business?

Don't do drugs, that's one. Luckily, that was never my scene so I never squandered any money on expensive drugs. Also, if you are going to make the kind of money where you warrant having a serious business manager/accountant, find someone good who will invest the money for you. Find someone who is conservative and pays your taxes—wisely. During the late '70s and early '80s, accountants were drawn into the whole Fleetwood Mac thing and thought that you could do no wrong and that we were impervious to any downfalls—an illusion which was very powerful at the time.

Photo of Jimmy Buffett by Jim Shea

At sea, circa 1986

Jimmy Buffett

Margaritavillager

1986

What is a Parrothead exactly?

A fanatical Jimmy Buffett fan, in a brief phrase. They're probably normal people most of the time, but when they come to the concerts, they put on their feathers and go crazy. They know every word to every song I ever wrote.

You sing about being the son of a son of a sailor. What was your grandfather like?

He was an old sailing ship captain and he spoke nine languages, and had been around the world god knows how many times in sailing ships and then in steam ships. He had an overall knowledge of just about everything. He'd seen everything, but he was never a wise ass. He'd listen to other people telling stories when he'd seen ten times as much, but he'd only interject when he had something funny or useful to say. He had a great sense of timing, a great amount of knowledge, and a wonderful sense of humor.

When you sail, can you navigate by the stars?

Oh yeah, I can do all that stuff. I'm gonna do a little sailing this weekend. After being in the studio, I need to get out on my boat and just noodle around. We call it "hydrotherapy."

Does being out in the ocean make you feel like a little fly speck?

Absolutely. It makes you feel like all the shit that you have to deal with in this business doesn't really amount to much when put in a bigger perspective. Sailing keeps me sane, because I believe that if it all fell through tomorrow, I could go back to fishin'. I'd miss this, but it wouldn't be the end of my life. I could have a hit record or I could go fishin'.

What is so special about island life—being able to see your whole world?

It is your world. You have to be a little crazy to live on an island—that helps. Living on an island is like living on a boat, or like living with a big family, because you know everybody. Sometimes you get island fever and have to get off, but I couldn't live any other way. I go to the big cities and travel around, but when I want my peace and quiet, I like to sit down on a little island. I just think it's the most beautiful way to live. There's not much tension or hassle, and it adds years to your life.

Well, an artist can choose that life...

That's right, and that's why I took this job. I love my job a lot.

What's the most important question you can ask yourself?

Am I still havin' fun? If the answer is yes, I keep going. If the answer is no, then I have to do something about it.

How would you like to be remembered in history?

My epitaph is going to read: "Now we can get some work done."

43

LA 2002

Vanessa Carlton

Ballerina Music   2002

XXXXXXXXXXXXXXXXXXXXXXXXXXXXXXXXXXXXXXXXXXXXXXXXXXXXXXXXXXXXXX

When did you start making music?
I started playing piano when I was two-and-a-half years old. My mom is a pianist and she taught me.

When did you leave home?
I left home when I was 14. I moved to New York City to study ballet, because I wanted to be a ballet dancer. I was accepted by The School of American Ballet, but by the time I was 15, I became very uncomfortable seeing myself only as a dancer. That's when I started writing songs. I still dance, though.

When was your first professional performance?
I played downtown NYC when I was 18 at The Bitter End. It was really scary. The first time I ever played for anyone— the first time I played one of my songs, was for two really close friends of mine. I made them face away from me and they weren't allowed to look at me. For me to play in front of a crowd was—interesting.

Are you used to it now?
I couldn't not do it—it's the most rewarding and meaningful thing to do.

How long does love last?
I think it lasts forever. It's complicated sometimes. I think love becomes very subconscious, and goes to the core of you. It's not a surface emotion. It consumes you and once it does, it never leaves, even if you lose touch with a person.

Where do you find your power?
I feel it in my gut. I feel powerful in the way that I control who I am, what I do, the music I make, and I'm proud of that. It's nice, not just being a female with power, but to be a human being in control of yourself, and aware of yourself.

What is beauty?
I think beauty is love. Anything can be beautiful, but only if you care for it.

Can you imagine being anything other than a singer/songwriter?
I am more than a singer/songwriter and performer. I am a dancer, and a student, and a sister, and a friend—many things. And all those things contribute to my career as a performing artist, but I am so much more than that.

(L-R) Cheech Marin and Tommy Chong, LA 1986

Cheech Marin, LA 1986

Cheech & Chong

The Last Interview   1986

Who were your early comedy heroes?
CHEECH: Amos 'n' Andy, Red Skelton, Jackie Gleason, Redd Foxx, Lenny Bruce…

CHONG: Richard Pryor was the biggest for me. He was struggling when we were struggling. I once went down and watched him at The Bitter End West when he was really doped out. I loved him—he was real honest. Then he got his shit together, and we did.

Cheech, did you lip sync the video for "Get Out of My Room"?
CHONG: How could you tell? Even his moustache couldn't hide that job.

Do you have serious dramatic aspirations?
CHONG: Cheech learned how to act during his divorce.

What is the difference between animals and humans?
CHEECH: Animals don't sue for alimony.

Can you recall any odd recording sessions?
CHONG: Looking for sound effects. To get a toilet flushing, we'd follow people into the bathroom and record their sounds. They'd come out looking sorta upset.

CHEECH: But you find that a recording of a toilet doesn't really sound like a toilet. You have to record something else…

CHONG: Like Cheech gargling. Another time we needed a gunshot so we asked the studio guard. It thrilled the shit out of him—he'd been working there for 15 years and had never fired his gun. He was afraid it was going to blow up in his face.

Are there any old sayings that you really dislike?
CHONG: "You better off!" or "Don't worry, it's only money."

CHEECH: "What are ya gonna go, take it with ya?" And also, "Don't worry, they'll never hear it in the final mix."

CHONG: One that really gets me is, "But he's your brother!"

This isn't the end of Cheech and Chong adventures, is it?
CHONG: Until they come up with enough money to get us together again.

CHEECH: This is our year of living dangerously. We're working on separate projects that we wanted to do for a long time. But if they offered a few million for a Cheech and Chong movie, I'd be right there.

CHONG: I wouldn't—I have my standards. Five million each or I wouldn't do it.

CHEECH: You lyin' Chinaman.

Brooklyn Recording Studio, LA 1994

(L-R) Don Was, Jane Oppenheimer, Ronnie Rivera, Ed Cherney, Brooklyn Recording Studio, 1995

Ed Cherney

Right Between the Ears

So how's it going with The Stones?
I had the great privilege to spend four weeks at Ocean Way recording rhythm tracks. Keith playing guitar, Charlie playing drums, and Mick. Sitting there for a month with the three of them in front of you is as cool as it gets.

Which came first, music or the musician?
The melody and rhythm flow through the musician. Without that there's no music.

If you could go back in time before recording, what would you like to hear?
I would like to hear the first bongos. Actually, I wouldn't mind going back in time to beat on some logs in Africa with the rest of the tribe.

Who got you started as an engineer?
Bruce Swedien helped me get my first job as an apprentice in Chicago, and I worked for him as an assistant on a buttload of great albums. If I'm any good now, it has a great deal to do with the time I got to sit behind him.

What are your most important recording tools?
Ultimately, songs and great musicians—I believe you can record a great performance through a tin cup with a piece of string and it'll still move you.

What old saying do you really like?
"Never resist the obvious." Or is it, "Always resist the obvious."

Who is the most amazing artist you've worked with?
I've been lucky to work with some really good ones, but just working with The Rolling Stones—Mick Jagger just kills me. He goes and sings a song, and it's sexy, it's on the money, he sells the emotion. When he gets in front of a microphone, strange magic certainly happens.

Who was the most difficult to record?
Ry Cooder is the personification of someone whose ideas and panoramas are so big that I'm not sure electronics can encompass the emotion and feeling that this guy can play with.

What's your philosophy as a producer?
Get out the way.

What is the biggest mistake of your life?
Not continuing with my piano lessons.

Any advice for those thinking about a life in the music business?
Think about it again.

Suzanne Ciani and Don Buchla, San Francisco, CA 1998

Capri, Italy 1994

Capri photo by Sylvie Jacquemin, courtesy of Suzanne Ciani.

Dr. Al Kooper and Suzanne Ciani, Anaheim, CA 2005

Suzanne Ciani

Synthesis of Sources

1992

How would you trace your New Age roots back in time?
When I was seven, my mother came home one day from a fire sale with a huge collection of records and that was my introduction to music. My roots are basically classical. I grew up with the music of Bach, forward through the late 19th century and the Romantic era.

Is it true that you were playing Bach before you actually knew the scales on the piano?
Yes, I taught myself to read music, which is really pretty rational. If you know where one note is and one line, you can figure out the rest. I discovered where middle C was—under the "S" in Steinway.

What did you learn from Don Buchla?
I must say that I was totally under his spell. He came into my life when I was really searching, and it was a wonderful coincidence of time and place. I had come to the West Coast and graduate school, looking for this thing called "synthesizer," this electronic music and new possibilities. His designs for instruments were extraordinary. This was a guy who brought the thought process of designing musical instruments right down to the origin of physical human nature and music. He's a real instrument designer. There is nobody like him, still.

What were your basic electronic tools for your first album?
Well, numero uno was The Buchla synthesizer. That was my first instrument. The first four pieces on that album only used a touch keyboard. Even though I had been a pianist, it was under Buchla's influence that I began to see the traditional keyboard as an unworthy interface for electronics. The Buchla was fretted, something like the neck of a guitar. You had areas where you could call it a note, but it was totally flexible. In a performance you could hit a key and have it do any number of things—play a note, start one sequencer, stop another one, transpose something else. You could give commands from this keyboard, and also use it to play melodies. You could put in portamento, or non-portamento. It was a wonderful keyboard, but it was tricky to play.

Do you have any words of wisdom—any keys to success?
I don't have any words of wisdom. In my life I have always been passionate in what I do and I'm happy that I have something that I love and care about. But when you love something, that is when you are most vulnerable, as well. From a distance, people think things are ideal and easy, but everybody's life is filled with whatever it is that it takes to survive. You just do what you do. Life is day to day. Get up in the morning and don't be lazy. And eat more pasta.

(L-R) Bob Clearmountain and Carloquinto Talamona, Capri Digital Studios, Italy 1994

Photo by Roberto Russo.

Bob Clearmountain

Magic in the Mix

Where does the name Clearmountain come from? Did you make it up?

No, I didn't make it up. The original name is Chiaramonte, which is Italian. Clearmountain is the literal translation.

How did you make the transition from engineer to producer?

I think it's a natural transition. Who spends more time in the studio recording and mixing and doing all the things that producers are involved in?

What will happen in digital during the next few years?

I think the next thing is recordable CDs. If the record companies thought that digital cassettes (DAT) were a threat, wait 'til they get a load of recordable CDs. Everybody already has CD players, so they can just go out and buy bootlegs from anyone and play them at home.

For aspiring engineers and producers, do you have any words to the wise?

Yeah, forget it [laughs]. First of all, you should have a bit of musical background. You don't have to be able to sight read, and you don't have to be a virtuoso on the violin, but you should have some background. You should know about time signatures, and keys, some basic stuff in music. Music is what you are dealing with, and that is more important than the technology.

The technology is easy. They really make it easy for you nowadays. It's just a matter of pushing buttons, and you turn the knobs until it sounds right. Don't get me wrong, it's good to know about the technology, but just going to an audio engineering school—I don't think it's enough. You should take some music classes as well.

Anything else you'd like to say to the public at large?

Yeah, sure. Don't get hung up on the technology. The most important thing is the music, the songs, and the performances. What you record it on, and what mics you use—they're just nowhere near as important as the music. Do what you can, establish your own style. *Don't do what I do.*

There is no wrong way to make records. I don't care what anybody says. If you use a mic that I wouldn't use for hammering nails and it works, then that's great. SSL isn't necessarily worse or better than Neve. It doesn't matter. Whatever you are comfortable with using is what's right. Music is the most important thing.

Leonard Cohen, LA 2002

Leonard Cohen and Mr. Bonzai, LA 2002

Leonard Cohen

Haute Dog

1988

XXXXXXXXXXXXXXXXXXXXXXXXXXXXXXXXXXXXXXXXXXXXXXXXXXXXXXXXXXXXXXXXXXXXXXXXXXXXXXXXX

Do you have a magical relationship with your musical tools?

I think it is the opposite of magical. Magical is the word we give to relationships that we can't understand. I'm not very interested in the occult, especially the sensibility that goes with it and the kinds of things that people who are interested in the occult ask to be forgiven for. I'm not interested in that pursuit, but I do know that inanimate objects, especially when they have working parts, and depend on things like sound and light, are susceptible to the influence of the people who are working with them.

If we could invite one person to join us here today, from anyplace in the world, any place in history, is there anybody you would like to meet and talk to?

I don't like to disturb people, or stir the dust of graves, or summon people from their ordinary days.

If you could choose the music for your own funeral, what would you like played?

Well, you know, I don't like music very much, like most musicians. So, maybe they could pass on that. By that time—which could be any time from now on—the musical saturation has become so thorough, that this might be one of the few spots where there is no music. I would appreciate that.

Is there any old proverb, any old saying that you dislike?

Dislike? There's one I *like* very much. I believe it's Chinese, and it goes like this: "Why do you hate me? I never helped you." I like that saying because it evokes the complexity of a relationship, a friendship. Whether it's accurate or not is really not important. It evokes the complexity that is the background of any relationship.

Do you think you've made any enemies through the years?

(pauses thoughtfully) Probably not enough.

On the music industry side of things, do you know any useful business advice that people entering the business might benefit from?

Well, I remember when I went down from Montreal to New York with the intention of establishing myself in the music business. I was not a boy. I was in my early 30s and my mother said to me, "Leonard, be careful—those people aren't like us." I was very resentful of my mother suggesting that she could tell me anything about things. But you know, she was right. They aren't like us. So, that's a good thing to remember. Whatever you think it's going to be, it's not going to be like that. However, how crooked you might have heard it is, it's going to be a lot more crooked than that.

How long does love last?

Well, it lasts just like all the songs say. It lasts forever.

55

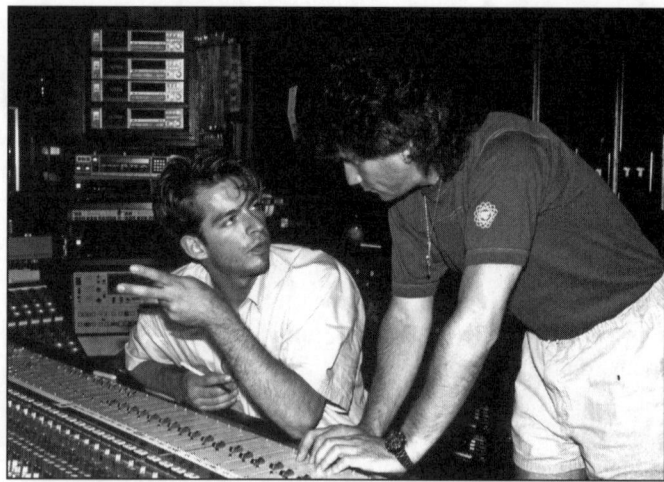

(L-R) Harry Connick, Jr. and engineer Joel Moss, Evergreen Studios, LA 1990

Harry Connick, Jr., Evergreen Studios, LA 1990

(L-R) Harry Connick, Jr. and engineer Joel Moss, Evergreen Studios, LA 1990

Harry Connick, Jr.

Nawlins Cat

When did you make your first records?

I made my first album when I was nine, and I've been performing since I was six, so I've been doing it for a while.

When you take an old standard, and are compared with many who have gone before you, how do you breathe new life into a song?

No one in the world looks like me; no one sings like I sing and no one plays like I play. There are better looking people, better singers, and worse. But there is only one me. Although I might sound similar to someone else, 'cause I'm young and impressionable, inevitably it will sound like no one else. Even if I imitated someone directly, I would still have my own flavor in it. The fact that I improvise and play songs in a new way means that it comes out like me, no matter what I do.

There's a word called "gumption." To me it means bold inspiration, or maybe balls, self-confidence. I imagine many folks ask, where does this kid come from, how does he pull this off. Where do you get your gumption?

Who knows? Both my parents were politicians, public speakers and could convince people of what they wanted. Maybe it rubbed off on me. Being lawyers, maybe that had something to do with it. Playing the kind of music that's not popular, but still wanting to be popular as a person—trying to find ways to make that music popular without changing it at all. Just having very set ways of how I do things. Some people might not agree, but I think it's the right way to do it.

I'm willing to argue about it. If people want to talk about my piano playing, then they can come up onstage and play. I'll play with anyone, I don't care who it is. Or if they don't like the way I sing and interpret a song, they can come up and try to do it better than me. If they can do it, I'll help 'em get a record contract.

This might sound cocky, but I'm the only person out here doing what I'm doing. If I'm not cocky, people are just going to pass me by and the record company will try to make me do things I don't want to do. You just have to be real strong. I won't have to be like this all my life, but I think it accompanies youth, or as you say, gumption.

Have you made any mistakes in your life so far?

Yeah, normal stuff. I don't think I've made any huge mistakes. Just normal, growin' up mistakes. I'm still makin' 'em, but what are you gonna do? Sometimes I talk too much, but as I get older, I'll cool out. I know I will, so I'll just let this energy run itself down. I'll become more mellow with time, I guess.

Stewart Copeland, LA 1990

Stewart Copeland

A Different Drummer   1990

You actually started The Police, didn't you?

Yes, but it's a technicality. I built the group, but the group didn't actually start to happen until Sting started to write those big songs. I put the pieces together in the first place, but it doesn't need to be emphasized too much.

What did you bring to your film scoring work from your years as a rock drummer?

A louder voice and a certain swagger. And in art, these things are actually significant. Every artist does what he has to do, and the quality is for other people to judge. But to actually get that opportunity takes a certain amount of swagger, so that you can realize what you want to do and follow through. It's easier for me than it is for a Juilliard graduate, who may be very talented and proficient. But those working with him may not know that, so he's not able or as free to follow through with his instincts. I'm someone who has the advantage of notoriety and previous success in other musical forms.

What was your most memorable moment on stage?

The night of our first show at Madison Square Garden. Our first arena gig. We were all a little bit nervous because of the distance between the stage and the audience. It felt a little cold up there and this was our big breakthrough gig. Right in the middle of this, my bass drum skin snaps. When you break a tom-tom skin, it's easy. Pull it off, turn it over. Snare drum skin—yank it off, throw in your spare. Anything can happen to the drums and it is replaceable quickly. But when your bass drum skin goes, you have to stop the show, pull off a forest of microphones, take away all the other drums to get to the bass drum beneath everything. It's like having to remove the engine from a car.

Did you panic?

No, as a matter of fact. The roadies did. Fifty roadies jumped out of the wings and leapt upon the task while the three of us were standing on the stage and telling jokes. We did a running commentary—"And now, Mr. Jeff Seitz is lifting the toms!" We made a big deal of it and actually it warmed the place up. When it was done and we went back and kicked in the first note, the place went ape crazy. New York belonged to us from that day forward.

I never have experienced stage fright since that day because I've had the worst thing that could possibly happen to me, at the worst possible time. Right there on the big stage. And it turned out to be a positive thing. The lesson is: Any adversity that strikes while you are on stage can be turned to your advantage. You can use it and turn it around. In fact, adversity can be opportunity.

Carmine Coppola, LA 1990

(L-R) Engineer Joel Moss and Carmine Coppola, LA 1990

Carmine Coppola

Godfatherly Music

How are things going with **Godfather III***?*
I hope I get it done! We haven't even spotted the film, marked all the music cues yet.

Is it typical that things are so rushed?
Well, I need some time to compose. It's not for five pieces—you should see the score papers, they're a mile high. It's a symphonic score and there's a lot of instruments on the page.

Is this continuing some of the themes that have been in the earlier films?
Francis would like to make this Wagnerian, in the sense that Wagner used leitmotifs. In *III* we're using some of the Rota themes and some of mine. There will be "Michael's Theme," for instance, which is a very dark, foreboding theme. There will be the "Love Theme," which the whole world knows.

Did you compose the "Love Theme"?
No, I didn't write that. That was Nino Rota. I wish I had.

Did you have a good relationship with him?
Oh, yes. Sometimes we worked together—he wrote four bars, I wrote four bars. Then he wrote his own pieces that Francie gave him to write, and I wrote what I had to write for certain scenes. I found him to be a very nice little man, very talented. A good composer—very simple. He never had anything on an orchestration page that wasn't necessary. He wrote very simplistically and to the point.

Before the first **Godfather** *came out, did you think that it would become such a huge success?*
No. I had no idea. In fact, it was a hard grind because Francie was having trouble with the studio, with the actors. They didn't want the actors he wanted. They didn't want Marlon Brando. Al Pacino was too short. Jimmy Caan—they said he's Jewish, this is an Italian movie. He said, "I either get the people I want or I won't do it."

I'm curious about your relationship with your son.
When I work with my son it is not as father and son. He is a director/producer and I am a composer. And that's how it goes. He wants certain things. He's very musical, he knows what he wants and he won't hesitate to tell you, "I want something else. I like it, I know you spent time on it, but…"

How important is a memorable theme to the success of a picture?
Well, the public would like to leave the movie humming a tune.

Marshall Crenshaw, LA 1989

Marshall Crenshaw

Honest Heart of Rock

Guitar was your first instrument?

Yes, but I can't even remember why. I just always wanted to have a guitar. My dad had one, but he couldn't play, and I was allowed to drag it around the yard and bang on it. It was one of my toys. When I was about six I got one of my own. I don't really remember deliberately choosing to play guitar. I just did it.

How did you come to an appearance in **La Bamba** *as Buddy Holly?*

That one came to me. They called me, and at first I thought, "Oh, no, a replay of Beatlemania." I was reluctant, and said no at first. But I read the script, and I had enjoyed being in *Peggy Sue Got Married*. I like the creative atmosphere of making films. It's a good hang. The story was good, and I was drawn into it because it's about '50s rock, something which I'm partial to. I knew if I didn't do it, they would get somebody else and I'd probably regret not being in the film. So I did it and it worked out great.

Can a pop record be a great work of art?

Certainly. Hell yes. But I'm not deliberately trying to produce great works of art. I don't think that's the way to proceed in this field. If you try to make a pop record that is a great work of art, you'll probably stink up the joint. People will listen and make their own decision about my music.

Have you met any people in this business who have really impressed you?

I really liked meeting Carl Perkins. He's a nice guy and he sets a good example for young guys like me in the rock-and-roll business. We were backstage at a show and there was another group onstage. All of us young guys were talking shit about them, and dishing on them. Carl wasn't willing to join in and steered the conversation to another tack. I thought that was good; it was honorable. Why talk nasty about fellow rock artisans? There's no point in it. I was struck by that. He's still good, too—one of the few. It's a pretty hard business, and a lot of people die, or go nuts. I can't think of a better encounter with a famous person. Meeting him was the most pleasant.

Do you know any good business tricks?

No, I don't know anything about business. I've had several tricks pulled on me, but I'd rather not describe the times that people have stolen from me, or taken advantage of my naiveté. It has happened though—it's a jungle out there. I don't know any business tricks, but there are some people I could refer you to…

(L-R) Engineer/producer Bill Dooley and Peter Criss, Brooklyn Recording Studio, LA 1993

Peter Criss

KISS Kat

1993

How did KISS come about?

Back in 1972 I put an ad in *Rolling Stone* stating that I was a drummer willing to do anything to make it. I got a lot of crazy phone calls from the ad, but one very mysterious call came in during a party at my house. This real mature voice says, "Hello, my name is Gene Simmons, and I'm calling about your ad. I have to ask you these questions. Number one, are you thin?" So, I called out to the folks at the party, "Am I skinny?" Somebody grabbed the phone and said, "If he was any skinnier you could squeeze him through a keyhole." Then Gene asks if I had long hair. I said, "Yeah, my hair is down past my tits, man." He invited me to audition and asked if we could meet in front of Electric Ladyland, Jimi Hendrix's studio down in The Village.

At the reception desk, I said I was there to meet Gene Simmons and Paul Stanley for an audition and was told that they were waiting for me outside. It was like magic—I auditioned and the three of us really clicked. We made a handshake deal and started rehearsing together. We put an ad in *The Village Voice* for a guitar player.

We interviewed about a hundred guys, but one night this guy named Ace walked in, blasted out of his mind, walked past a guy who was auditioning at the time, plugged his Les Paul in and blew the guy to kingdom come. Gene and Paul were pissed, but I thought he was great. He just said he hoped he passed the audition and left. We called him back and asked him to join us. We rehearsed eight hours a day, every day of the week, for months and months in this freezing New York loft. We were determined.

How did you cook up the image of KISS?

We needed an image—we needed characters. Gene worked on a demonic look. Paul was the star, and Ace was the space cadet. It took me a while to find my character—I had a big black tom cat and one night I was staring at him, and sketching a combination of my face and the cat. That became my look—for many, many years.

How long did it take to reach superstardom?

Two years. By 1975, we knew we were on top.

Were you the hottest selling band of the '70s?

We were picked two years in a row as the biggest band in the world by the Gallup Poll. We sold out concerts wherever we played, and I've got 52 Gold and Platinum records.

You were fairly visible onstage—didn't your drum kit rise up 40 feet?

Three stories high—what a view. I felt like I was on top of the world, like a god. It was scary—the power trip was unbelievable.

(L-R) Steve Cropper, Donald "Duck" Dunn, Booker T. Jones, House of Blues, LA 1994

Steve Cropper

Soul of the Guitar

How did "Sittin' on the Dock of the Bay" come about?

Well, Otis started it in Sausalito, an idea among several ideas. He always had more ideas than any writer I ever worked with. Most of the time we got together a day or two before recording and we'd write all night long in a hotel room. This time he came down to the studio that afternoon and was so excited—we probably finished it in less than an hour. He had an intro and that first little verse about watching the ships come in and watchin' 'em roll away again. He was humming a little melody and I sat there and finished the lyrics with him and wrote the bridge to it.

What was it like being in The Blues Brothers Band?

Who knew that it would be that big? It was kind of an experiment, and it was something that John and Danny had dreamed of doing. They played all the time, sitting in bands, had a little band up in Toronto. The nice marriage when Duck Dunne and I got involved was that I am always thinking commercial and these guys wanted to do this Blues project, which I thought was great. I said, "Guys, if you're going to make a record, can't we lift it up from the street level and bring it to the radio level?" They said, "What do you want to do?" I suggested something like "Soul Man" and it was the biggest hit we had.

How many guitars do you have in your working arsenal?

I have several guitars, and a lot of them I've used through the years, and sometimes you move on. Sort of like girl-friends, you know? You go with them for a while until they start getting serious and you go on to the next one. Every now and then you call 'em up and go to dinner. I've got a couple of guitars that were on well-known albums that I love pulling out once in a while to take along to a session. The engineer's eyes light up—"Yes, this is the one I played on 'Tonight's the Night' for Rod Stewart."

How would you compare the old days of writing with today?

You can't write one night and record the next. Booker T. and I could get excited by an idea, like we're talking now, write this thing tonight and go into the studio tomorrow and have William Bell or Otis Redding or Eddie Floyd say, "Hey, let's do this." By one in the afternoon we'd have it leadered and mixed and ready to go master. If we wanted to, we could have it out on the streets in a week. I miss that a lot, but as far as the physical writing, it's pretty much the same. We get in a room, get our instruments, and hash out ideas.

(L-R) David Crosby and Graham Nash, Center Staging, LA 2004

Engineer/co-producer Nathaniel Kunkel, Center Staging, LA 2004

James Raymond, Center Staging, LA 2004

David Crosby & Graham Nash

Harmonic Convergence 2004

XXXXXXXXXXXXXXXXXXXXXXXXXXXXXXXXXXXXXXXXXXXXXXXXXXXXXXXXXXXXXXXXXXXXXXXXXXX

I wanted to comment on how youthful David sounds, the classic angry young man. There is certainly a contrast when you look at a man who's been…
GRAHAM: Close to death's door many times?

Any explanation?
GRAHAM: Yes, I have a great explanation. Music.

How's it going with Russell Kunkel, your drummer and co-producer?
GRAHAM: I've known Russell since he was 19 years old. He was on every Crosby Nash record that we made, and he was the drummer in the 1974 stadium tour that CSNY did, so we go back a long way. Incredibly cognitive of where not to play—what's very important in a musician is the breathing space. Anyone can play all over things, anyone can be flash and look groovy. Russell plays the song.

David's son, James Raymond, plays piano on this album. Why is the last name different?
GRAHAM: Because he was adopted. Thirty odd years later, when David was in danger of dying with his liver transplant, he was on the cover of *People* magazine. James' adopted parents, who are wonderfully warm people and brought him up magnificently, knew who the father was. Because he was in danger of dying, they felt they owed it to James to tell him. And when they told him, he wanted to meet David. Now he is in David's band, CPR.

David, are you pleased with Nathaniel Kunkel's work here?
DAVID: Yes, and Nathaniel is old enough now that you can't call him a child prodigy, but coming from where he comes from, and having watched him since he was born, I'm astounded with how he turned out. But what he's done that has really set him apart from everybody is twofold. One, he was raised around music, so he is tremendously musical. He listens to a song not only as being sonically gorgeous, but does it out of content being content. And he understands that—very few technical guys understand it. Secondly, technically, Pro Tools is an interface and he has learned to work that interface more skillfully than anybody else I have ever seen. I think he is musically and artistically one of the most advanced engineers I have ever met in my life.

Don't you have anything nice to say about him?
DAVID: Well, he is a good guy, but he is opinionated as hell. He's got a very low bullshit acceptance quotient, so he could be very difficult for regular people to deal with. In this circumstance, which is kind of a no-slack zone in the first place, with his dad and me and Nash, he is just perfect.

(L-R) Neil Finn and Tim Finn, LA 1995

Crowded House

Where the Heart Is

So, the album Woodface *is done?*
NEIL FINN: Yes, as we speak it's just been finished.

What surprises are there on this new album?
NICK SEYMOUR: Paul is singing a song on this one…

PAUL HESTER: Yes, "Italian Plastic." And Tim takes lead vocal on one song, and sings throughout the album.

MITCHELL FROOM: [as he walks by the lounge] You guys are losers—sod off!!

Wasn't that your producer!?
PAUL: Yes, he's off to other projects now, one with an all-girl band, I believe. [shouting] Good luck with Julio! We love you!!

[Bruce Springsteen walks by]

Have you heard the new tracks?
SPRINGSTEEN: No, but I've heard the old stuff—love that last record, too. You guys have finished your record?

NEIL: Yes, right this minute with the sequencing. And you're nearly finished, too?

SPRINGSTEEN: Yeah, just about… I'm hustlin'.

NEIL: We'd like to get to some radio stations before they dive into your record…

PAUL: Maybe we could slip our record into your jacket cover…

SPRINGSTEEN: You know, one of my early records ended up in a Barbra Streisand album jacket. Before the actual release date, they went out and people were bringing them back, wondering, "What is this?"

NEIL: Barbra's voice has really changed.

SPRINGSTEEN: Hey, good luck with the record!

Well, with this new album, I would guess that after 20 odd years you're finally all going to be launched into super-megastardom.
[entire band cracks up]

NEIL: We'll go with that prediction.

(L-R) Scott Kirkland and Ken Jordan, LA 2004

The Crystal Method

Beats in the Bomb Shelter

What does The Crystal Method mean?

KEN JORDAN: The name just came by chance. We knew a girl named Crystal, and it came up in conversation. At the same time we realized the drug reference and we thought it was funny, so we put it on our demo tapes. Lo and behold, the name stuck.

SCOTT KIRKLAND: Don't look for any deep meaning in the name [laughs].

How do you break down the writing duties between the two of you?

KEN: Scott starts almost all of the songs, and then I am perhaps more of the engineer, producer—although he can do that as well.

SCOTT: We both do everything. When you have a studio for yourself, you don't have limits on time and the hourly concerns. We are able to spend as much time as we need crafting each track and we do everything here. While you are EQing, you are writing; when you're producing, you're mixing. When you are in the studio, you are doing it all at the same time. Sometimes we split up the responsibilities, but 85% is done here with us both working together. It's hard to say who did what on each track, because it's a collective effort.

For somebody from another planet, what is a DJ in 2004?

SCOTT: In my view, it's still what it has been since the mid-'70s—someone who plays music to small, medium, or even large crowds, and just controls the flow of the evening with music on vinyl, or nowadays on CDRs. There are some DJs using the MP3 format, but we will hopefully abolish the practice of using MP3s in the computer DJ format. We saw a show in Las Vegas and the DJ brought his computer and he just hooked it up to the mixing board.

KEN: We're not too fond of the computer DJs. Good DJ-ing is really an art form. There are many kinds of DJs—such as the ones who just play "Celebrate good times, c'mon c'mon," at a wedding reception…

SCOTT: And sometimes that can be done really well, and then again, it can be done really badly.

KEN: For the most part, we are talking about the DJ as an artist, who can craft a really great sounding set. A true DJ is an artist who has an identifiable sound. We think it should have "spinning," and that there should be some skill involved in the mixing of tracks from one to another.

How would you compare your DJ work with your concert work?

KEN: It's night and day. When we DJ, the mechanics are the same as others, and we have a distinctive style. When we play live, we have all of our instruments, a big light show, we play our own music, and it's more like a rock concert.

Do you use pre-recorded material?

KEN: Well, we have our computer out there and we do live sequencing, but there's nothing on tape.

(L-R) Bob Casale, Gerald Casale, Mark Mothersbaugh, LA 1983

(L-R) Gerald Casale, Mark Mothersbaugh, Bob Casale, LA 1983

(L-R) Gerald Casale, Mark Mothersbaugh, filming "Theme From Dr. Detroit," LA 1983

Devo

Whipped It

Does your music have a cold vision or would you describe it as a Zen breeze?
MARK: A Lysol breeze.

Do you consider yourselves alienated?
GERALD: No. Alienated is when you want to be part of the club and you're pissed off. In that sense, we have never been alienated. We gladly walked away from the club and didn't want part of it to begin with.

MARK: When those recombo DNA labs get it together, we're going to look for alternative life forms.

What will the planet be in the distant future?
MARK: We can think of the real or the ideal. It will probably be like *Planet of the Apes*, but that wouldn't be our choice.

What would your choice be?
MARK: We'd like to see a world where love and hate are things of the past.

What's your favorite love song?
MARK: I like the Bufferin commercial where the lady tells her husband "No," because she has a headache. Then she takes the Bufferin and the music all of a sudden goes "bloo-pud-a." It's a very good synthesizer piece. It's real short, lasts about five seconds, and repeats over and over again. Then they look at each other and smile. You can tell "tonight's the night."

What makes a good engineer?
GERALD: Engineer boots—that's really important. If an engineer's boots are worn out, you shouldn't use him. A good engineer never leaves his seat. His boots are shiny and the heels aren't worn.

On the subject of Devolution, and evolution—why do we have pubic hair?
MARK: Because early Homo sapiens used to ride around in those log cars where their legs went through the bottom. Mud would fly up from underneath and the pubic hair acted as protection for the genitalia.

GERALD: Now it's there to show people how to cut clothes. You've got to cut the fabric enough to cover it, so it determines the cut of clothing. Form follows function.

Do you have any predictions for our future?
GERALD: The world's gonna be a beautiful place. People will stop fighting, monorail systems will be built throughout America, cars will be eliminated, the air will clean up. You'll see beautiful vistas and horizons. Nuclear power plants will give way to solar energy.

MARK: We will experience hidden benefits from the nuclear ring of fire around our oceans.

Do you have any advice for extraterrestrials?
GERALD: Stay away. Go back.

If music were food, what dish would Devo be?
GERALD: Whipped potatoes.

Duane Eddy photo courtesy of Duane Eddy

(L-R) Steve Douglas, Duane Eddy, Joe Puma, 1958

Courtesy of Lana Jeanette Douglas Sartain.

(L-R) Darlene Love, Jack Nitzsche, Fanita James, Phil Spector, Steve Douglas, Gold Star Recording Studios, LA early 60s

Courtesy of Lana Jeanette Douglas Sartain.

Steve Douglas, Gold Star Recording Studios, early 60s

Steve Douglas

The Joy of Sax

What is the true secret of the saxophone?

Well, I got some really good training by playing along with old rhythm and blues records—trying to duplicate the nuances in the solos. I can name one record, *Honky Tonk, Parts 1 and 2* by Bill Dogget—Clifford Scott did the tenor sax solos, everything you need to do, and if you could master everything he did, you'd be on your way.

Did you go to high school with Phil Spector?

Yes, I was two years older than Phil. When I was in the twelfth grade he was in the tenth grade. We were acquaintances and had a music and orchestra class together. I got to know him better after I graduated because I had a band and Phil was in it. He's a very fine guitar player and a pretty good singer.

And then later, he was the boss—was that cool?

Oh, yeah—sure. You see, Phil went back to New York and did all that work there. He would fly me in to play on his records. When he came back to Los Angeles, he called me to put a studio band together. I had been working with some fantastic musicians, like Hal Blaine, Leon Russell, Glen Campbell. I knew who to call, and this is the band that became known as The Wall of Sound Band or The Wrecking Crew. The first session we did was "He's a Rebel" and that went to Number One. Everybody started asking for the same crew. We worked with The Beach Boys, Jan and Dean—just about all the top bands.

What about your historic work on "Peter Gunn" with Duane Eddy and the Rebels?

Well, I'm proud of that one especially, because we were doing an album and I suggested we do "Peter Gunn." Duane said, "Well, gee, what am I gonna do?" I said, you just go "Da, da-da, da da-da" and then I'll play. He begrudgingly did this and that record has been a hit twice and did a lot of good things for his career, and put some money in Henry Mancini's pocket, too. Great tune.

Who is the most amazing artist you've worked with?

Bob Dylan. He is the only guy I know who can play sloppy and out of tune, and have it be so charming that you can't *stand* it. Brian Wilson was another amazing guy I worked with. I worked on the *Pet Sounds* album. It was so hip, so interesting, and so challenging musically. Spector is another one—maybe the greatest record producer who ever lived. The thing that was great about those days and watching these people work was, first of all, we knew we were making hit records. It made the sessions particularly exciting and rewarding when we were working with Phil or Brian, because we knew we were making hit records. They just had an edge over everything else.

Dr. Demento, Westwood One Recording Studios, LA 1985

Dr. Demento

Curator of the Curious

1985

How did you get into this business?

I was a record collector first, and had been a record collector for many years before the *Dr. Demento Show* ever came into being. My first radio show just grew from my record collection.

Thinking back to your famous discovery, "Weird" Al Yankovic, did you envision that he would be catapulted to such heights?

I suppose if I had been told that day after I discovered him in 1976 that nine years later he would win a Grammy and become a household name, I might have been pleasantly surprised. But as it's happened, I've seen his career grow in a series of stages. He's gone from little triumphs to big triumphs. First there was one song that he sent me that was good enough to play on the air. His next songs started getting better, and then a song that was an across-the-board smash. We received a huge volume of calls for "My Bologna," his parody of "My Sharona." Then came the one that got such heavy requests on my show that it was lifted illegally by radio stations across the country and added to their playlists. "Another One Rides the Bus."

What kind of a guy was Spike Jones?

From all accounts, he had a complex personality. His first hit was "Der Fuhrer's Face" in 1942—that put him on the map. In '44 came "Cocktails for Two," his biggest hit, and another million seller was "All I Want for Christmas Is My Two Front Teeth." His biography and people who knew him give the impression that he was tremendously imaginative, yet no-nonsense, very businesslike in running his career. I can compare him to Frank Zappa today, who has a some-what goofy stage image. People assume he smokes five lids a day, but in fact, he is also no-nonsense, is totally against drug use, hires only the best musicians, and tolerates no mistakes on or off stage. I think Spike Jones was the same way—he formed a band that could do routines timed to the split second.

What are some of the worst records ever made?

Rhino Records recently released their album of the world's worst records, and I wrote the liner notes. But, in a way, I would not have picked any of the records they picked because they're all fun to listen to. The worst records are the ones that are boring. This collection includes things like "I Want My Baby Back" by Jimmy Cross, "Crusher" by The Novas, "Fluffy" by Gloria Balsam. Those are great—they strike people as being hilariously bad. They are in the same category as movies people love to hate, like *Plan Nine from Outer Space*. The worst records are the boring ones, and they come out every day by the thousands—or by the dozens, anyway. If you listen for half an hour you've wasted your time. That's bad.

Dr. John, Club Lingerie, LA 1989

Dr. John

Mos Desitively Boneroo

Is it true that you started out in show business as a model, and that your baby picture was on the Ivory Snow soap package?

Yes, but I really never saw whatever I did. I know about it from a lot of people and from my family. When my mother was modeling, she ran me out, too, as a little baby and that's why I had a social security card from when I was one-year old.

Did you switch to bass playing because you got shot in the finger?

Yes, in 1960, I was playin' in Jacksonville, Florida, with Ronnie Barron, who couldn't have been more than about 15 or 16 years old. I went to get him for a gig one night and walked in the room and a dude was pistol whippin' him. I went to try and get the gun out of the guy's hand and in the altercation that ensued, I thought my hand was over the handle, but it was over the barrel. When the gun went off it blew the tip of my finger off. They sewed it back on, but to this day I can't use it too well on the guitar, but I can use it to some degree on the piano. While I was recuperatin' I played bass with a Dixieland band on Bourbon Street at a nightclub called The Famous Door. I also played drums for a little while around the same time.

Any advice for people thinking about a career in music?

I think if they get into music 'cause they love to play it, they are doin' it for the right reason. I really discourage a lot of people from getting into this racket. I don't think it's something you should get into for the money—you should get into it because you just love to do it.

What's the biggest mistake of your life?

The biggest mistakes I ever made was when I turned down every big gig that was offered to me—like when they asked me to play at Woodstock and I turned it down to play another festival. I turned down gigs that didn't seem like much of anything and they turned out to be huge issues. But I've consistently done these kinds of things, so I guess it isn't such a big mistake in the long run, 'cause things have a way of straightening out anyway. Whatever mistakes I've made, and I've made a whole gang of 'em, have led to something pretty cool.

How do you feel about getting older?

I've always believed that age is a state of mind. We age ourselves only in the ways that our spirit is aged. The meat may decay, but the spirit never will. As long as we keep some focus on the spirit, we're doin' alright. The spiritual side makes it all immortal.

George Duke in his studio, LA 1996

George Duke in his studio, LA 1996

(L-R) Engineer Gary Ladinsky, George Duke, Smokey Robinson, LA 2001

George Duke

Brother of Invention

1996

Can we talk about the evolution of synthesizers from your perspective?

Well, in the beginning, I rebelled—I didn't want to play any electronic gear, because it was like going back to school. I started with the Fender Rhodes, the one with that gray top. It "plunked," but it had this vibrato that was interesting. I got into electronic music that way.

Eventually, Frank Zappa told me, "You should play synthesizers." I said, "What's that? That thing with all those knobs? No, no, I'm not interested." I said, "Look, I don't even know how to turn it on—not interested." So Frank says, "I'll buy you one. We'll put it on your Fender Rhodes. If you like it, fine."

I just loved the fact that you could bend notes. I had never been able to play piano and bend a note—and that was interesting to me. I wanted to play the blues on that synthesizer. I found that I could play it like a guitar, like a blues guitar—or even like a flute.

So you fit into the Zappa camp nicely with your new synthesizer?

Oh yeah, and Frank loved it. But the hardest thing about working with Frank was that we had no pre-sets. When he would assign you different timbres and things, between me and Ian Underwood it was very tough to make those patch changes during the space of time he allowed you to do it. And he would know if it was wrong.

He was a strict disciplinarian. If it was wrong, even in performance, he would make you do it again. I had it happen once—he stopped the band and said, "Stop. George made a mistake." I went, "Oh, Frank—" He said, "Do it again." It was embarrassing, and the crowd all laughed, but Frank was serious. I screwed up once and he let everybody know it. I said to myself I would never let that happen to me again.

Could you point out a few things that you learned from Frank?

I learned quite a bit from Frank. He was an incredible arranger, composer, and he knew stuff about the studio that I never realized musicians even cared about.

And I learned a lot from the way he rehearsed a band and what he required of his musicians. There was a world of Frank that was very intuitive and genius-like. Musically he was so broad—he was the one that really broadened my musical horizons, and that's why I'm so crazy now.

The reason I do so many different things musically is because of him. He was into rock, and he was into jazz. He would say he wasn't into jazz, but he lied—we played a lot of jazz; he just didn't call it that. And then there was the contemporary orchestral music—we used to do all that kind of stuff. He challenged the musicians.

Gallery I

(L-R) Pablo and Ray Manzarek, LA 1987

(L-R) Snoop Dogg, DJ Battlecat, engineer Chris Puram, Skip Saylor Recording Studios, LA 1999

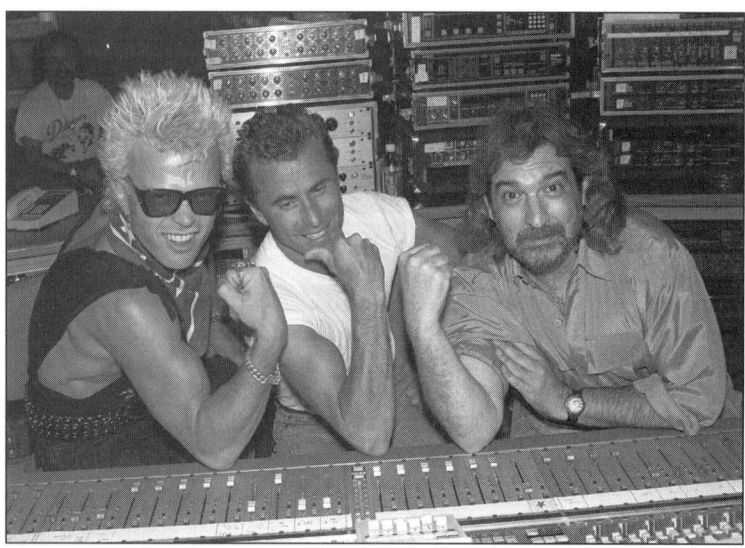

(L-R) Billy Idol, producer Keith Forsey, engineer Tommy Vicari, Record Plant Recording Studios, LA 1989

(L-R) Graham Nash and engineer Nathaniel Kunkel, Hawaii, 2000

(L-R) Director John McTiernan, engineer Tim Boyle, composer Basil Poledouris; scoring *The Hunt for Red October,* Record Plant Recording Studios, LA 1990

(L-R) Bob Seger and producer Don Was adjust the volume at Record Plant Recording Studios, LA 1991

(L-R) Dave Navarro and Chad Smith of the Chili Peppers, outside Brooklyn Recording Studio, LA 1997

(L-R) Tchad Blake, Bonnie Raitt, Mitchell Froom, Sound Factory, LA 1997

(L-R) Shawn Colvin, Paul Westerberg, producer Don Was, drummer Jim Keltner, engineer Al Sanderson, Ocean Way Recording Studios, LA 1997

(L-R) Engineer Greg Collins, producer/engineer Jack Perry, Barry White, Record One Recording Studios, LA 1998

Robbie Robertson, The Village, LA 1998

(L-R) Bassist Nathan East and Eric Clapton, Record One Recording Studios, 1999

(L-R) No Doubt's Tony Kanal, mix engineer Jack Joseph Puig, Gwen Stefani, producer Glen Ballard, Gabe McNair, (kneeling) Tom Dumont, Adrian Young, Ocean Way Recording Studios, LA 1999

Anouk, LA 1999

(L-R) Engineer/producer Jack Joseph Puig, Courtney Love, and Hole guitarist Eric Erlandson, Ocean Way Recording Studios, LA 1999

(L-R) Green Day's Mike Dirnt, mixer Jack Joseph Puig, Billie Joe Armstrong, Tre Cool, engineer Ken Allardyce, Ocean Way Recording Studios, LA 2000

Duane Eddy, LA 1996

(L-R) Duane Eddy and Hans Zimmer, LA 1996

Duane Eddy

Twang It

Are you still playing the same Gretsch custom-made Chet Atkins guitar that you got when you were a teenager?
Yes, but it's not custom-made. I just bought it at a store in Phoenix when I was 17, and I still use the same guitar. Guild made a Duane Eddy model in 1962, and I also use that onstage and in the studio. And I have a Danelectro, which is a bass string guitar, about an octave lower than a regular guitar. That's what I used on this *Broken Arrow* film. I had some very low notes to reach and that took care of it.

Did your signature sound just come at once, or did it develop?
Well, I experimented and I had done a few sessions when I was young. I learned that the bass strings were more powerful for recording than the high treble strings. To give it that real dark and powerful sound, you had to use the bass strings.

You can't make an instrumental record with only riffs—well, once in a great while you can—but generally you need some substance, so I combined the low strings with playing a melody. The first thing I did, "Movin' and Groovin'," was basically high and low strings combined, which paved the way for my sound.

Can you describe one memorable recording session?
One of my favorites was in 1960, for "Because They're Young." I came to California for the first time, with my producers, Lee Hazlewood and Lester Sill. We performed a scene for the Dick Clark movie of the same name, and it was the first time I had worked live with a string orchestra. We'd overdubbed on some of my earlier records, but I wasn't around for the string sessions. This was the first time live.

I walked into the studio and it was Howard Roberts playing rhythm guitar. I had met Howard a few times before and he said, "Come over here Duane, I want you to meet a friend of mine." He introduced me to another guitar player and it was Barney Kessel. I started to reach out my hand, then stopped. I said, "Barney Kessel? What are you doing here?" It stunned me. I loved what he'd done with jazz and was a big fan. On bass was Red Callender, and on drums was Shelly Manne. The studio was United B, which is now Ocean Way Studios. Everyone from The Beach Boys to Frank Sinatra were recording there at the time. I was once invited in when Sinatra was cutting "Strangers in the Night."

You have such a relaxed way about you. Do you sweat onstage?
Copiously. I get drenched onstage. I work out onstage, not running around, but I put everything I have into every note.

Have you ever made any mistakes?
On guitar or in my life? [laughs] Yes, I've made mistakes. But I've learned a few things, too.

E aka Mark Oliver Everett, Ocean Way Recording Studios, LA 2003

E and Lisa Germano, Ocean Way Recording Studios, LA 2003

Eels

I am a little confused. Are you the Eels?
Yes, I am.

So, you pick people to join you for each project?
Exactly.

What is the origin of the name Eels?
No origin, really. I put out a couple of records as E. But there were some logistical problems with having only one letter as my name. In the newspaper: "Appearing Tonight—E." People don't even see it. So, I thought I better add a couple of letters.

What music would you like played at your funeral?
One of my most prized possessions is a Jim Nabors album, where he actually sings the entire album in the voice of Gomer Pyle. The last song is "Gomer Says Hey." It's become my philosophy and I have a deal with a friend to play that song at my funeral. It's a lesson I am trying to teach myself every day. "When it's market day and the hens won't lay, just remember, Gomer says Hey!" These are wise words. Don't sweat the small stuff.

If you could go back in time before recording, what would you like to hear?
I would really like to hear Abraham Lincoln's voice. Someone wrote that his voice was high and girlish. I thought, wow, you would never guess that. I'm a Lincoln fan, and I would love to hear him. But that's impossible. Isn't that heartbreaking?

Do you know any interesting business tricks?
I've got some serious advice for the young budding artists. Be the best artist you can be, and always try to do things for the right reasons, i.e., if someone wants your songs for a commercial that you wrote about your dead sister, don't do it. You'll feel better about yourself, and in the end, it might even be a better business decision—you might be around longer. The challenge is that you must have a strong enough character to say "No" to all these people who are going to try and make you feel like shit for saying "No."

What makes a great producer?
There are a lot of different styles of producing. There are those who don't know what to do and just surround themselves with people who do. I admire that. There is a skill to that. And then there are the producers who do everything and put their stamp on it. It depends on what you're producing, what makes a good one. One master producer for one project would be terrible for another project. That's an unanswerable question, but thanks for asking.

Danny Elfman, LA 1987

94

Danny Elfman

Knight of the Oingo Boingo   1987

XXXXXXXXXXXXXXXXXXXXXXXXXXXXXXXXXXXXXXXXXXXXXXXXXXXXXXXXXXXXXXXXXXXXXXXXXXXXXXX

What did your parents contribute to your life and career?
They gave me a lot of support. Certainly they weren't pleased with my choice of careers…

Are they now?
Oh, yeah, but I think any parent would have been a little bit upset. They're both schoolteachers—and they saw their child take a non-academic road in life, one that seemed so totally without any possible means of security, which it really doesn't have. Starting a band, working in a theater group for years—that kind of stuff. They always said, "We know you love doing this, but how are you going to make a living?"

Who gave you instruction in music?
I'm self-taught completely.

Can you remember a first profound musical experience?
Well, I remember becoming aware of music in the prime of my sci-fi horror infatuation—the ages of 10 to 13. I went to the movies practically every weekend. I realized at one point that all my favorite science-fiction movies had the same film composer—Bernard Hermann. He also did many of the Hitchcock scores. He was a very big influence.

It was a dream of mine to be able to score films, but I had no musical talents or inclinations. I imagined that if I worked in film it would be as an editor or a cinematographer. Funny how it all wrapped around two decades later, and there I was a film composer.

Besides Bernard Hermann, did you have any other musical heroes?
Nino Rota was my big musical hero—that's probably why I got the job to score *Pee-wee's Big Adventure*. I was infatuated with Nino Rota, and they had toyed with the idea of a score that would touch on Nino Rota's influence. When I said that he was my main musical hero, along with Bernard Hermann, I think that really clicked. What got me the job certainly wasn't my musical influence.

If we could arrange a luncheon with anyone in the world, living or dead, who would you invite?
I'd love to have Ellington, Stravinsky, Gershwin, Django Reinhardt (with a French translator), John Coltrane, Bertolt Brecht, Kurt Weill (he was another big influence on me), Nino Rota, Bernard Hermann, Jean Cocteau…

What's the most important question that you can ask yourself?
The same question I ask myself all the time. Could I be doing better, could I be working harder?

Geoff Emerick, LA 1992

(L-R) Nellie McKay and Geoff Emerick, Capitol Recording Studios, LA 2003

Geoff Emerick, Capitol Recording Studios, LA 2003

Geoff Emerick

An incredible series of albums for you: **Revolver, Sgt. Pepper, Magical Mystery Tour, Yellow Submarine, The White Album, Abbey Road.** *It seems to me that it was* **Revolver** *where all the weirdness began.*

Revolver was the first album I'd engineered. It was, "Well, Geoff's the engineer. We don't want the piano to sound like a piano. We don't want the guitar to sound like a guitar, and we don't want the drums to sound like drums." This was mainly coming from Lennon.

If making a record is like building a house, what is the foundation?

The foundation is obviously the band. The cement and mortar would be the bass player and the drummer. When I left school and entered this business, I was taught by Norman Smith, who was the original Beatles engineer. He always said that the basic backbone is the bass and drums. If that tightness and feeling is there, then you can build anything.

With Ringo's drum sound, you were miking much closer than had ever been done before.

Yes, that's true. To get that sound, I'd first go down and listen to Ringo's drums. Put my ear next to the top skin, or to the bottom, looking for the resonance from the skins. We took the bottom skins off the tom-toms, and put the mic up inside. This gave us the slap of the top, with no resonance of the bottom skin—what a thought. In my opinion, *Revolver* was the album to change all sounds. Better than *Pepper* from a sound point of view.

Did you actually once have John suspended from the ceiling, swinging around for a vocal?

It was his idea, but it didn't really work out. He'd gone through a funny stage at that time. We'd put the voice through the Leslie and the speaker revolved around. I think he once asked George if he could just plug a voice feed from himself and swing around from the ceiling to get a similar effect. George explained that he would have to have an operation to put a voice box in his throat and have a jack plug attached to his neck.

Of all the sounds you came up with for The Beatles, is there any one that you are especially proud of?

I guess it would be "A Day in the Life." The gradual long fade, done manually, was monumental. To make that end crescendo loud—it wasn't written, the orchestra was told to go from A to E in 37 bars and do the best they could. I was playing the faders as the song progressed and realizing that what I wanted was another 6dB by the time I got to the end. I pulled the whole thing way up. I'm proud of doing that—how else could you have done it?

(L-R) Engineer Tal Herzberg and Ron Fair, Enterprise Recording Studios, LA 2001

Ron Fair, LA 2001

(L-R) Mixer Dave Pensado, Christina Aguilera, Ron Fair, Enterprise Recording Studios, LA 2001

Ron Fair

Creative Control

How did you get involved with recording?

My grandfather started a daily LA radio program that ran for 25 years called *The Jewish Hour*. He had a recording studio in the '50s, built into a garage and then converted to a broadcast studio that operated with the radio station through special FCC lines. I've been around recording, microphones, and broadcasting since I was two years old.

What was your first success as an engineer?

The original soundtrack to *Rocky*. I was one of two engineers, and I worked for Bill Conti, who was a mentor to me in those days. I had done a lot of engineering for him before he got his big break with *Rocky*.

How did you make the move to producer?

I was always playing piano and arranging music, and then producing, pulling my friends in after hours at the studio, making tapes and demos, knocking on doors of publishers and record companies, trying to break in. I used every means available to me, and my engineering was always connected with my playing ability. Back in those days, technology was a lot simpler and the process of recording was much more related to making music than it is today.

Now that you are the head of a record company, are you still on top of the technology?

Definitely not. Back in the days of analog recording, I was completely on top of it. I could walk into any studio, anywhere in the world, and record and mix a record on my own with no help whatsoever. Now, with all the digital media, with hundreds of formats, and the way that music syncs to film, and 5.1, and all the issues—it's so far beyond me that I can't focus on it anymore. I have to delegate, and focus on the major issues of the singer and the song.

Could you take me back to that moment when you signed Christina Aguilera?

I arranged a meeting—she was 16 years old, with no makeup, her hair in a ponytail. A petite, teenage girl. I asked her to sing for me, and she said, "Here?" I said yes. She did a song from *The Preacher's Wife*, a Whitney Houston song she had been listening to. She stood there, her feet firmly planted on the ground, her eyes went into sort of an icy stare—a total sense of self-possession and perfect intonation. She had the complete command of a seasoned performer in Carnegie Hall. No inhibition, no sense of containment. In that moment, you know you are in the room with greatness. The combination of spectacular pitch and stupendous tone, and that fearlessness—there were automatic bell ringers for me. If it happens one or two more times in my life, I'll consider myself very lucky.

Jerry Finn, Andora Recording Studios, LA 2001

Jerry Finn and Mark Hoppus of Blink-182, Bernie Grundman Mastering Studios, LA 2001

Jerry Finn, LA 2001

Jerry Finn

Hail Caesar

How would you describe your work with Green Day?
Life changing. Before them I was an assistant making eight bucks an hour. I was producing Gold records less than a year after them.

What the heck is this leopard skin covered box?
It's one of only two custom fuzz pedals made in Atlanta by Pancho and Lefty.

What is this Super Fuzz pedal good for?
Infinite sustain and a fuzz tone with more note than most pedals.

If you were a musical instrument, which would you be?
Theremin.

What's wrong with the music industry?
The labels are run by shareholders and not people who love music.

What music would you like played at your funeral?
Tenacious D.

What is your strangest characteristic as a human being?
I never know when to shut up.

Do you know any interesting business tricks?
I know enough to never get involved in the financial side of things. I'm the worst negotiator in the world.

What old saying do you hate the most?
"The early bird gets the worm." If the only incentive for waking up early is a worm, then I'll just keep sleeping in till noon.

Any advice for getting a good start in the music business?
Make goals for yourself, and keep raising the bar each time you reach one.

If you could go back in time before recording, what would you like to hear?
There was a time before recording?

What is the first music you remember hearing?
"Fiddler on the Roof."

What did you learn from Blink-182?
I learned the importance of thinking about the fans while making a record. Don't be selfish when you make an album, because that can be a slap in the face to your audience.

Tim Finn, Sound City Recording Studios, LA 1999

Tim Finn

It Started with Split Enz

"Protected" is almost a mystical song to me. What is the protection?

Well, Dharma, the Path, the Way. Maybe there is a way, maybe there is a path. You fall off it and then you get back on it. Just knowing it's there is a liberation in itself. And certainly this song comes from an experience. I went to the mountains outside Sydney and did a meditation retreat for ten days. I didn't speak to anybody and was silent for ten days. It was very hard—we had to get up at 4 o'clock every morning and meditated for ten hours every day. After that, I felt refreshed and songs began to just come through.

"Persuasion," which you wrote with Richard Thompson…

He had written this beautiful melody, this elegant tune for a film. I said, "Please, I'd like to make this into a song." And he had never thought of it as a song, because it has quite a wide sweep from highs to lows. It was just waiting to be written. There was a song inside it, and I didn't have to think about it much. The film was about a guy who could persuade people, con people and it seemed like a natural title. And then, "I'll always be a man who is open to persuasion." It just wrote itself.

"In Love with It All"—co-written with your brother, Neil.

Yes, that's one we wrote together before "Woodface."

You say "brothers come to blows" in the song. I get the feeling that the relationship with Neil is sometimes an emotional one…

Yes, it's very complex and like any brother or sister relationship it is multi-layered, and there is a lot of stuff that never gets said—and probably just as well. Neil sometimes says to me, we must talk and get drunk together and talk about everything. I say, well, I don't know if we should [laughs].

But isn't there a special kind of magic among siblings making harmony?

Yes, there is a closeness and a psychic harmony. There are definitely things that go on without words. And writing songs with Neil—in two weeks we wrote 14 songs for our album, which we never made because we began work on "Woodface." An amazing time. One day we will do a record together.

When are you happiest?

I love songwriting. When I am writing a song and it's coming through—it's like falling in love, being seduced by this sound. And you know it's good, all of a sudden you know something is there. That makes me happy. And on a different level, I like swimming. In Ireland when I used to go swimming—after the swim, the sun was shining. Walking and feeling happy. There are different levels of happiness.

(L-R) Phil Proctor and Peter Bergman, LA 1986

(L-R) Phil Austin, Phil Proctor, Peter Bergman, LA 1986

(L-R) Peter Bergman, Phil Proctor, Phil Austin, engineer Fred Jones, LA 1986

Firesign Theatre

A Firesign Chat 1986

PHIL PROCTOR: Nick Danger has really moved to the forefront of our work together. I guess it's because Phil Austin, who portrays Nick...

PHIL AUSTIN: I finally got old enough to play Nick...

PHIL P: And I have become so twisted through my nefarious work in the industry that I *am* Rocky Rococo...

PETER BERGMAN: And I'm dressing so sharp now that I can play Al Bradshaw or Nancy, depending on where my mind is at the time.

PHIL P: It's most extraordinary how the most dramatic music in the Nick Danger piece creates intense comedy out of the stuff we're doing, because everything is done with a tremendous feeling of reality.

If you could be women, who would you be?
PHIL A: Betsy Ross.

PETER: I'd like to be the Goddess Diana—the Huntress. That would be fun. I'm an outdoor type.

PHIL P: Dustin Hoffman.

Who is the Pablo Picasso of humor?
PETER: George Carlin—he can create more out of nothing...

PHIL P: He's a great observer. He understands the primitive origins of everything and that is what makes him so brilliantly funny.

Who is the Abraham Lincoln of humor?
PHIL P: Bob and Ray, the most honest observers of American culture to this day. We should also mention Ernie Kovaks, since we're talking about great comedians. He has had a great influence on our work. He had a wonderful sense of surrealism.

PETER: He's the Bacchus of comedy.

Who is your favorite homosexual?
PETER: Well, we have such a wide choice now with all these Congressmen coming out of the closet.

What causes lesbianism?
PETER: Men.

PHIL A: Women.

(L-R) Jim Keltner, Mick Fleetwood, Kenny Aronoff, Ocean Way Recording Studios, LA 1996

Mick Fleetwood

Drumming from the Heart   1993

XXXXXXXXXXXXXXXXXXXXXXXXXXXXXXXXXXXXXXXXXXXXXXXXXXXXXXXXXXXXXXXXXXXXXXXXXXXXX

Were you discovered playing drums in your garage when you were a youngster?

Yes, I was discovered by a gentleman named Peter Bardons, who lived near me when I was about 16 years old in London. I had a drum kit which my parents had bought for me and he heard me playing. He knocked on the door and offered me a gig because he was managing a little Ventures-style band. I had a brand new Rogers drum kit and it was probably more the drums than my playing that seemed valuable [laughs]. That was the beginning of us playing together. And then Peter went on to play with Van Morrison in Them, and a band called Camel.

What is the guiding glue of the entire history of Fleetwood Mac?

John McVie isn't a very public person, so I often get more of the credit than I deserve, but I have paid a lot of attention to keeping this band together. Sometimes John and I wonder what it is, but there is a real practical element—being a drummer and a bass player, we need a band to play with. I always need to reach out to other people to fulfill my desires. That has been a motivating reason for why this band has never broken up. If someone decided to leave, we just kept going on.

Fleetwood Mac has gone through many changes, and not many bands have retained an identity which the audience follows. We've been very lucky. The acid test is when you make an album and find out if you've got it right, or not. Bottom line is that John and I like to play, it's what I do, and we've never given up.

Lindsey Buckingham told me he felt that you were an intuitive drummer… a musician who would come up with parts and then you would have to learn them.

Absolutely true. I don't know what I'm doing, and it's become my style, I suppose. Lindsey is a fairly ordered jigsaw puzzle type of writer. He takes a lot of bits and crafts them together. He doesn't readily sit down and pour his guts out on a three-chord song. I've never seen him do that, and I wish he would try it—he's capable of it. He talks about doing that, but always retreats to the alchemist approach. I believe it was a bit of an eye-opener when he first met me. He said, "Why don't you play this and that, and this and that bit, do that." I was staring at him with this blank expression and said, "Let's forget about that, 'cause I don't even know to this day what a chorus is." I just play it. If you sing or mumble something that will help out, and nod your head when you want me to stop. And that's how it is, still. I've come up with some sort of style, which seems to be fairly identifiable, so I'm happy.

David Foster, LA 1988

David Foster

What It Takes

1988

Did anyone have a profound personal effect on your early training?
Absolutely—Oscar Peterson. When I was 13 I was fortunate enough to win a scholarship to the University of Washington for the summer music program where I was thrust into a situation with college kids. I went to Seattle for two summers in a row and the bandleader was a friend of Oscar Peterson's. He was playing there at a nightclub, but I couldn't go because I was only 13. Our bandleader said that he would get his autograph for me and afterwards he handed me a sheet of paper. "Dear David, keep working on your music. It's a worthwhile endeavor. Oscar Peterson." It was written in this beautiful handwriting and I kept it in my wallet for about 20 years. It was a small thing, but he had taken the time to write the note and it really made an impression on me.

I read somewhere that you played on tour in England when you were 16?
Yes, by age 16 I had quit school, much against my parents' wishes. But they knew I would do music for the rest of my life. They let me go to England, under the auspices of older guys in the band who were sworn to take care of me. We moved to England and toured with Chuck Berry and Bo Diddley. Now, the picture is complete. By age 16, I had been exposed to just about every musical influence—which is why I feel just as comfortable producing The Tubes as I do Kenny Rogers. It relates back to my early musical training. I would say to anybody starting out that it's great to be in a garage band and be an ass-kicking rock and roller, and it may get you through life, but it may not. Training is not such a bad idea.

What's the best advice you can give about the music business?
Quite honestly, you have to know how to politic. You have to be willing to be a nice guy, and be willing to try and put yourself in the right situations. Being a session player was the best thing for people like Jay Gradin, David Paitch, Richard Marx, and myself. You put yourself in the right place all the time. Just by the nature of doing sessions every day, you are with all the artists you want to be writing for, and producing. If you're on top of it, and you're talented, and good, and sharp, and don't do drugs, and show up on time, and are an all around go-getter, things will come your way. Broad strokes advice: If you are absolutely 100% convinced that you want to be a musician, or a songwriter, and are willing to devote your whole life to it, and not get sidetracked, and are prepared to work 16 hours a day, then you might make it. That's what it takes. Nothing less will do.

109

Mitchell Froom, Sound Factory, LA 1999

Mitchell Froom

Producer with the Keys

What's the concept of your first solo album, **Dopamine?**

I was trying to get at this raging party always going on in my brain. It keeps me up all night. I get stuck on one bar and it just keeps cycling all night. The album is like interior brain music, even though it's quite aggressive. What's your impression?

It's a Naked City, film noir jazzy groove and then the record explodes with Sheryl Crow's "Monkey Mind." How did that song come about?

I was explaining to her about the pounding in my head and she said that's called "monkey mind." And she has it, too. She drove to the studio, sat out in her car for about an hour, and when she came in she had it. She sang it once, put the harmony on and she was done.

Isn't this a rather breezy recording style?

If it is really good, you need the confidence to accept it and not work it further. When you hear something that is absolutely right, you don't say, "Maybe we could try it again, maybe it could be better."

Which came first, music or musicians?

Music, and then musicians came along and got in the way of it. If a person has the right attitude, music can develop, get more intense, but sometimes musicians come in and use the experience as a way to glorify themselves, or get in the way of the purity of where the music wants to go. If music is going to succeed, it requires that you come to it with a very generous spirit and a humble attitude. If you get in the way, it's destroyed.

Can you imagine a world before recorded music?

Being able to hear music at any moment has had an adverse effect on the way that music is made now. It has to grab you by the throat and entertain every second. People often don't leave any real space in music, thinking they have to fill it all up to keep you interested. The result is just numbing.

Any tips about the music business?

When I decide to work on a record, it is made very clear that I'm not looking for anybody's advice. If you make that clear, then everyone is happier. If you look for advice, you're getting yourself in trouble. I have never had a good musical suggestion from anybody in a record company.

Advice for getting a start as a musician?

Don't look to other recording artists, producers, or people in the record companies. Don't look to anyone to help you get started 'cause you just wait by the phone all the time. You're dealing with a lot of people who don't quite want to put you off, but don't quite want to do anything for you. You just waste a lot of time. People should go out and create their own buzz.

(L-R) Peter Gabriel and Mr. Bonzai, Museum of Contemporary Art, LA 1996

Peter Gabriel

Energy A to Z   1989

XXXXXXXXXXXXXXXXXXXXXXXXXXXXXXXXXXXXXXXXXXXXXXXXXXXXXXXXXXXXXXXXXXXXXXXXX

Has computerization in the studio helped you to realize your goals better?
Without question. I have a philosophy about these sorts of things. I think there are two ways in which we function as musicians. One is with what I call "Energy A," which is analytical, and for that the computer is wonderful. It allows you to pinpoint any small section of a piece, any sound, and have a very high level of control over it. However, that is quite slow and thoughtful, and produces a different type of music than "Energy Z," which is what happens when musicians are in the same room together and responding to what each person is doing. This is what happens when musicians see a red light go on and they know they must live on the spot. It's what happens during improvisation. You can have the same musician doing the exact same line in both ways and it will come out with very different feelings as a result.

For me, the ideal equipment in the studio is that which allows you to work in layers. At each stage of the process you allow for this spontaneous, adrenaline-pumping, red light of Energy Z to really milk the most out of a performance. Then you go back and pull out Energy A and go over it with a microscope and correct it and improve it and build on it.

Say you're working with a synthesizer. You do your first pass to establish melody. Red light on—improvise. Then switch over to the analytic energy to correct and improve, which is perhaps a standard procedure. In the second layer, you may have various sounds available, perhaps on a joystick. Put the red light on and you're off again. You are doing a performance, but this time you're working with the melody you've defined and you're mixing in new sounds. If you have an array of different sounds around this joystick, you can mix different quantities of each according to the position. You do it with the red light on with a definite performance vibe and then go back and analyze it. In level three you might play with the performance parameters—set your attacks, decays, and vibratos, put the red light on and improvise with those parameters. Then go back and correct and improve.

It's a way of trying, at each level, to allow both parts of our capacity to work for us. Improvising and being spontaneous, and the capacity to analyze and improve slowly and in detail.

The muse—the old idea that there is a guardian angel for the artist. Do you have any ideas in that direction?
Well, I don't think I've met my muse, but there are definitely times when you get the spine-tingling sensation and you know that something extraordinary is happening.

Albhy Galuten, LA 1995

Albhy Galuten

Birth of the Loop

When did you first pick up a musical instrument?

I played violin in the first grade, but it was just too painful—a violin is hard to listen to even if you're a mediocre musician, and it was just torture for me. I took up piano in the third grade.

Did you immediately have a sense that you were destined for musical greatness?

No, but I had an older brother and a sense that it would be hard to succeed in chess or basketball. Music was something I could do myself, work on alone and move ahead. In the first year with piano what drives you is that you can reproduce this melody twice in a row and have the teacher say it's okay. Once you get past that you have a place where you can go by yourself, a creative process which is rewarding whether other people like you or not.

What's the most important thing you learned from engineer Tom Dowd?

Tommy had a knack of not talking about the music at all. Instead he would tell a story that would create a state of mind. It might only be a thirty-second anecdote, but the singer would go back and be more comfortable, more connected, more in touch with the event. He was very impressive in his ability to understand the emotions of the artist, such as John Coltrane. Knowing how to advise people in the recording environment was quite an achievement.

I also believe he is the first person credited with splicing tape. He was on a Mitch Miller date and they had the early version of a breakdown where everyone would stop and clap their hands. There was one clap with a really bad flam and they planned to do it again. During the break, Tom started thinking about it. If he held a pair of scissors with his wrist cocked back all the way, it would always be at the same angle. He realized he could cut out that bad hand clap and splice it together. The group came back, listened, and nobody noticed. As far as I know, that was the birth of creative editing.

What are your big successes?

For me, the big successes were experiencing moments of great performance. Very few people are blessed with the chance to really touch greatness. Witnessing Aretha Franklin sing "Spanish Harlem" is one of those great moments. Being with Eric Clapton and Duane Allman working on "Layla" was incomparable. I played on some of those dates, and working on great records is a success in itself.

During the height of the Bee Gees period, Barry Gibb was incredibly talented, unbelievably on the money. He had amazing pitch, meter, and a true sense of what was touching people at the time. There were also incredible technological breakthroughs going on at that time. I believe "Stayin' Alive" was the first pop single that used a drum loop. It took ten years for drum loops to become a common element.

(L-R) No Doubt's Adrian Young, Tom Dumont, Tony Kanal, Gwen Stefani, and mastering engineer Brian "Big Bass" Gardner, Bernie Grundman Mastering, LA 2001

(L-R) Lloyd Banks, 50 Cent, and Brian Gardner, before the release of *Get Rich or Die Tryin'* 2003

(L-R) Brian Gardner; engineer Richard "Segal" Hureida; Dr. Dre's Director of Operations, Larry Chatman; Eminem; producer Dr. Dre; and co-producer Mark Bass, prior to the release of Eminem's debut, LA 1999

Brian "Big Bass" Gardner

Mastering Megahits

Where did you first encounter big projects?

At RCA, right near here on Sunset Blvd. My early clients were The Monkees, Jose Feliciano, Jefferson Airplane, The Jackson 5, Ike and Tina Turner, Harry Nilsson…

Did Harry come in when you were mastering?

Oh yeah, he was great. I remember talking to him the day after The Beatles were on Johnny Carson. Carson asked them who their favorite artist was and they said it was Harry. His career was going strong, but it really took off after that.

You got your nickname from Dr. Dre. Do you remember the actual occasion?

Yeah, I do. I had done *Straight Outta Compton*, and a few other projects around 1986, and one day I got a T-shirt that said "Big Bass Brian." I thought it had come from some other client, and then a few weeks later I found out who had sent it to me. Back in the day, talking to Dre, he told me that the records in the clubs sounded punchier and louder than everyone else's and he liked that.

Well, c'mon, how do you get that Big Bass?

I can't tell you [laughs]. Top secret. Actually, it's a combination of things—controlling the peaks, adding the right shape of EQ. Sometimes the material comes in here and it's too bassy, and you just have to work on it.

So, they come to you to get the Big Bass sound, and…

They may overshoot. It may have sounded great in their studio, but it can be out of proportion when we get it here and that's where we come in.

I remember photographing Dr. Dre with a new artist called Eminem. Can you describe that first meeting with Eminem?

He was pretty quiet, but seemed to know exactly what he wanted. He was right up at the console and if he wanted it brighter, he didn't hesitate to say so. I respected that. I heard murmurings that it would be a big record and I wasn't quite sure how big. But, sure enough, it came on strong right away.

Can you recall specifically what you did for his sound?

Pushed it to the max. Go as far as you can, without it distorting, so to speak.

And not too long ago, I met you and 50 Cent in here.

He was a cool guy. I had found out just prior to the session that he was pretty well known on the East Coast. He was kind of quiet but tuned in, even about the CD packaging. He seemed to be hands-on for the whole project. You could tell he had something that was going to be big.

(L-R) Audio supervisor Jeff Magid, Quincy Jones, mastering engineer Bernie Grundman, Bernie Grundman Mastering, LA 2001

(L-R) Outkast's Andre 3000 and Bernie Grundman, LA 2001

(L-R) engineer/mixer Robert Carranza, Jack Johnson, and Bernie Grundman, LA 2005

Bernie Grundman

Mastering Greatness

What makes a great master?

Success is not only due to a good job, but also a matter of taste. What goes into making a hit record is very elusive and you always try to make it a joint effort with the producer, artist, and engineer. The mastering engineer is really trying to help the original vision become realized. My feeling is that you could go to five different mastering engineers and get five different recordings. I just try to find that extra bit of improvement that the client responds to. Mastering is the final creative aspect in making the recording most effective. It's basically post-production for the recording industry— the final creative step before delivery to the manufacturer for mass production.

Why did you focus on mastering?

I just wanted to be in the industry and was fascinated by the equipment, especially the cutting lathes. It was magical to me, and it gave me the pleasure of listening to music that was well recorded.

I've always gotten along well with machinery, so it wasn't that difficult for me to get involved in something that was more equipment-oriented than mixing. I did some mixing, but I found that some of the music I worked on wasn't that interesting. The recording process was fun, but if it's music that you're not really passionate about, you can be stuck with it for months. Until you make a big name for yourself as a mixer, you can't pick and choose. But in mastering, most jobs are done in a three- or four-hour session. You can maintain your enthusiasm even if you aren't passionate about every project.

Do clients ask you to make the records sound louder on the radio?

Yes, that is one of the big factors in mastering. How can we make this record stand up against the rest? It's very competitive. We want our mastering to stand up with other product, but there are certain albums out there that are just loud. In fact, they are so loud that they have lost some of their musical values. I don't believe in going to the extreme where you sacrifice the musical values. It's impressive, but that's all it is and over time it just doesn't hold up.

Of all the artists you've worked with, could you name some of your personal favorites?

Well, it's always a thrill to master a record which gains international success. Some names that come to mind are Michael Jackson, Quincy Jones, Stevie Wonder, Van Halen, Prince, The Carpenters, Steely Dan, Herb Alpert, and Barbra Streisand.

Herbie Hancock, LA 1990

Herbie Hancock

Cool Fusion

In performance, have you ever gotten lost while improvising?
Sure, because I always challenge myself and push myself to my musical limits. I try things, and experiment. I get lost—a lot of people get lost—but the other guys in the group can tell if you're lost and one of them will establish something to let you know where you are. I've gotten lost with the time, turned the beat around so that where I thought beat four was actually beat one. The drummer can usually flip me back around by playing certain things, maybe a crash at the beginning of a phrase. If it's a matter of form, and if I can't remember exactly what bar I am on, the bass player can usually straighten me out by certain standard approaches to the chord structure and I'll hear it right away and know where I am. And I'll know where they are [laughs].

How have you managed to keep your cool, maintain composure, that openness in your life?
For one thing, I really love people. Even though I've had a lot of great fortune in my life and my career, and gained a degree of popularity, I think most people would say my personality hasn't changed that much. It's just basically the way I am.

The other thing—had I not started practicing Buddhism back in 1972, I would probably have become a lot more selfish. The more popular you get, the more frustrating it is when several people bombard you at the same time. If that happens a lot, it can really get on your nerves, 'cause you're just a human being. After a while, you don't want to be bothered with it. You need a little peace, and you might get snappy with people.

Buddhism has affected my perspective about the importance of human beings and everyone's life. It's made me automatically feel compelled to acknowledge another human being if someone taps me on the shoulder or stretches out his hand to shake my hand.

You must respect people, and I realize that my popularity came about because people bought my records. The least I can do is shake their hand. They paid for my house, and all the food, and all my synthesizers. They even brought you out. If it wasn't for them, you wouldn't be interviewing me. They pay all our salaries.

Gemma Hayes, Cello Studios, LA 2005

Gemma Hayes

Sweet Chaos from Ireland   2005

Did you know early on that music was your calling?

When I look back and think about it, I guess I did. It was the only thing that I really liked. It was the only thing where I actually felt that time passed really quickly. And everything else was very slow. Music was always easy and always a joy.

When did you discover your voice?

Well, I wanted to become a songwriter. I never saw myself as a singer, and for the first part of my life I never really sang. I had a kidlike voice and never really thought about it. Eventually, I was staying at my sister's house in Dublin, when I was 16. She had a party and I was too shy to go downstairs to the party, so I was up in her bedroom playing the guitar and singing.

A guy at the party sat outside the door and listened to me sing, and he happened to know about the songwriting shows in town. He invited me to come to one of the shows and get up and sing. Even at that stage I didn't think of myself as a singer, but I went to the club, got up onstage and I played the song and used the voice that I had without really thinking about it. I got a really amazing reaction from the audience, and I suddenly thought that there was something there. Slowly but surely I started to gain confidence in myself as a singer, which added to the confidence I had in myself as a writer.

Aren't you known as a particularly strong guitarist, too?

I think I am, but people may come to my shows and be surprised with my abilities as a guitar player. In the past, with female singer/songwriters, it was more about the voice and less emphasis on the guitar.

There is a fellow in Dublin named Dave Murphy, an older singer/songwriter, and he once told me that I should master the guitar separately from working with my voice and my music. He said I should work on my writing, and on my guitar, as two separate things. And only bring them together when capable with the both of them. This advice really did help, both with confidence and getting the song across strongly.

What advice would you give to people just starting out in the world of music?

Follow your gut, when you are writing music, when you are surrounding yourself with people. A lot of folks will tell you something different than what you feel or think. I would say follow your gut, and keep the music free in your head. It's got to be free, and you must be in love with music. When you stop being in love with music, you are not going to be able to convince anyone else of your worth.

(L-R) Brian and Edward Holland, LA 1988

Brian and Edward Holland

Brothers in Song

How did the team of Holland-Dozier-Holland form?

BRIAN: Well, I was at Motown as an engineer, and as a songwriter/producer. My brother was a recording artist at the time. Lamont then came to Motown and was signed as a songwriter/producer. Lamont and I first worked together on a song called "Forever," which we later recorded with Marvin Gaye and the Marvelettes. Anyway, I walked into the room where he was working and I said, "Hey, that sounds pretty good." We started working out some chords together and that was the beginning. The first Holland-Dozier-Holland song was "Come and Get These Memories," which was recorded by Martha & the Vandellas. Before that I had worked with other people, like Freddy Goreman, Georgia Dobbins and Robert Bateman—we wrote "Please Mr. Postman" together.

Was writing lyrics your main responsibility?

EDWARD: Yes, and also teaching the singer the song—taking them into the studio and making sure they had the right interpretation that we were looking for.

Did you make demos before taking it to the artist?

BRIAN: No, we rarely did demos. It's not like today, where you make a demo and send it to the artist. We wrote the song and could pretty much cut with the artist we wanted. Berry Gordy allowed us that freedom.

What about working with Stevie Wonder?

BRIAN: We wrote Stevie's first recorded song. Ronnie White of The Miracles brought Stevie to me for an audition. I thought he was great and I called Mr. Gordy and he came down and we signed him. We cut his first release, "Contract on Love," but it didn't do all that well.

What makes a great producer?

BRIAN: In my opinion, a great producer is one who studies the material and the artist, the instrumentation, and what is happening in the marketplace.

What were the magical ingredients of working at Motown?

EDWARD: Looking back, the Motown situation was a very strange phenomenon. It's unheard of to find that many creative people working that close together. Basically, we all lived in the same facility and worked for one organization. You often find many creative people in one company, but not creative people who had so many distinctive and unique talents.

I think the nucleus of Motown's early success was Berry Gordy's philosophy and overall leadership. It enabled people to develop in an environment with a lot of freedom to experiment. It was a place to learn the craft of making records in your own way and in your own time.

Paul Horn, LA 1985

Paul Horn

Blowin' in the Wind

How did you make the transition from jazz appeal to reaching such large audiences?
I did the solo flute album in the Taj Mahal in '68. It came out in '69 and became a big underground thing. It was different than anything that had been out there before—just solo flute and nothing else, and there were wonderful acoustics in the Taj Mahal, great echo and acoustics. A note could hang in the air for 28 seconds. It started a whole new trip for me.

How did you end up in India?
I was doing my own spiritual pilgrimage and spent time with Maharishi Mahesh Yogi.

Did you spend any time with The Beatles?
Yes, in 1968, when I did my album and The Beatles were there at the Maharishi's ashram. I played music with them quite a bit, with George especially. We would play a lot of flute and sitar things. Donovan was over there at that time, too, and as a result of meeting him I did two tours with him in '69 and '71.

What do you look for in new places to record?
I'm cautious about that because I don't want it to be gimmicky. It was eight years before I did another one, in The Great Pyramid. It's not just a sound I'm looking for, although that's certainly part of it. There is a quality of the sound from the structure, the echoes and reverberations. There is also a spirit and a mystery of a building that becomes part of the music.

Your China album is especially interesting, with the sounds of the temple...
We recorded two solo flute albums in The Temple of Heaven in Peking, now called Beijing, right outside of The Forbidden City. It's circular and all wooden and has its own special vibe and ambience. I had to record at 7:30 in the morning and the temperature was around 20 degrees. It was so freezing that it's a wonder anything happened, but you have to transcend the discomfort and forget about it.

What was it like playing for whales?
They would make sounds back to me when I played which were different each time. They pay attention and they are obviously interested in the music. Once a whale died and its mate was nearing death because of the loss. They claim that my flute playing brought the whale out of its depression.

Mark Hudson, Village Recording Studios, LA 2004

Mark Hudson

Brother in Arts

1987

Do you have a musical hero?

I had a hero—I still do. John Lennon. The day he was murdered, I was in a recording studio with Harry Nilsson. He got a bit hysterical and ran out of the building. My brothers and I had just finished an album for Elektra, and John was working on *Double Fantasy*. I had asked for special thanks to John on our album, because he had been such an inspiration to me. I even quote him regularly—"How can we go forward when we don't know which way we're facing?" He said things that still make a difference in people's lives.

I could never get over my awe of John, but we did have some interesting conversations. We were in a club one night and he was just coming up with wells of information. I asked him what was their worst song—which one do you hate? I had to know. He looked at me and said, "'Run for Your Life'—it was a piece of shit."

What did your folks give you?

They were emotional, musical Italians. You could come to my house and you would find people weeping, people dancing, somebody playing the piano or a bad accordion. My mom and my uncle had a dance act. I grew up with all this emotion around me and I couldn't change.

Can you remember the first song you wrote?

Yes—I wrote it with my brother Bill in the kitchen. It was called "All in a Day, Girl," and it was heavily Beatles influenced. I was 13, and John had already done some damage to me. It was so simple—"All in a day, girl/You'll be in my dreams / You're makin' me scream…" That was the beginning for me; we pulled it off.

Any business advice for musicians?

First of all, be as talented as you possibly can, but remember, the key to business is not the talent. The key is to be aware that it is a show *business*. The ego is the show part, but the bigger word is business. Never lose sight of the political side of the industry. I can say it, because I've got the skid marks on my ass. I've been thrown out of offices because I complained about the "image" that was being publicized. Another quote from Lennon—"If you want art, buy a painting."

Michael Hutchence, Amerycan Recording Studios, LA 1993

Michael Hutchence, outside the Greek Theatre, LA 1993

Michael Hutchence

Inside INXS   1993

XXXXXXXXXXXXXXXXXXXXXXXXXXXXXXXXXXXXXXXXXXXXXXXXXXXXXXXXXXXXXXXX

So, not a bad life—around the world making records?

Right, for this album we started off in a house in France for about three weeks, just rehearsing and fucking around as a band—which we hadn't done for a long time. From there we continued with that theme and attitude into Capri Digital Studios for over two months. We also worked in Paris, where I now live, doing vocals for a week and then went on to L.A. to mix. I did one vocal in London at Olympic with Chrissie Hynde, and another vocal here in Los Angeles with Mr. Ray Charles.

What was it like working with Ray Charles?

To hang with a legend and record a song was a real joy. Our roots are very much Motown, soul, and where he comes from, mixed with other stuff. It was quite a big reach to get to him, and the first track we sent him he didn't like because it was in the wrong key for him. I'd forgotten how deep his register is.

The second track was perfect, in D, called "Please, You Got That…" So, we went into his studio yesterday and mapped it out with him. He said, "You show me what to do—you've sung it, you know where it's at." This was a unique experience, because I didn't know how he worked. I could have walked in and he could have said, "This is the way it's gonna be." I think like most guys of his era, whether they play the blues, or whatever, they've been though the mill, they've been ripped off, and if you get burned for 40 years something happens. You could get very weary, and cautious, I guess.

Do you think you'll last as long as Mr. Charles?

I'd love to have as much fun as he does at 64 in the studio. I tell ya, it's inspirational. And humbling, actually. I'm really glad he loved the song and wanted to do it. The whole thing is kinda surreal. This is a great thing—not only an absolute privilege for us, and myself to sing with him. But I think it's great for him, because he's a hip cat—and it's a strange and wonderful thing for him to do. I'm really happy he's taken that jump, you know? I think they've been trying to get him to do things like this for years.

(L-R) engineer Chris Lord-Alge and Chris Isaak, Record One Recording Studios, LA 1998

Chris Isaak

True Blue

1995

Why do we human beings write songs?

Why do we make art? You've got something to say and you're trying to communicate on some level. It's funny to me— if you just take a look at artists, they're not necessarily the most communicative people in real life. Maybe it's people who have a hard time saying these things one on one, so they put it on a record or in a movie.

Did you break your nose boxing?

I used to box and it comes with it. I wish I could have grown up surfing, or if my parents had had some money they could have taught me how to golf or something. Unfortunately, it comes with being white trash in a small town. "Gee, what sport can we do?" "Hey, let's beat the hell out of each other!"

Does it hurt when you break your nose?

Not at all. I'll tell ya something—it just feels like somebody snapped your head back, and your nose feels a little bit numb. It's not a big deal, but it hurts about six hours later. You can't drink from a cup that day 'cause your nose swells up and the top edge of the cup will touch your nose and you go "Oh God!"

Has anybody said you look a little like Bob Hope?

I like that. I'll take it. I can work with that.

Do you have any business advice for musicians who are green?

Make sure the boss is real happy with your work and he won't fire you. And if you don't know who the boss is, take a look out from the stage. That's the boss. If you think you can cut corners, you're nuts. The boss is gonna check it out.

I do a ton of preparation so that I can have fun onstage. I work hard, we do rehearsals, and we'll do the two-hour sound check even when we're dead tired so that it sounds good when people get in there. You think you can have a rock-and-roll lifestyle, party all night and then skip sound check? That kind of attitude shows up and the audience catches it. Pretty soon they fire you. Sometimes they fire you a little at a time. You got a thousand people coming, then you've got 800, then 600, 400. Pretty soon you're playing on Tuesday night.

Mark Isham, LA 1991

Mark Isham

Film Composure

What drew you to the trumpet?

I love the classical music for the trumpet. That was my first attraction. My parents are both classical musicians, and my mother works professionally as a violinist in many orchestras. She would drag the kids along and we would sit in the back of the orchestra halls while she rehearsed. I had a genuine affinity for the brass, and the trumpet specifically. It was baroque music that got me—the music of Bach, Vivaldi, Telemann. At Christmas time we would listen to Bach's B-minor Mass, the Cantatas. I was in heaven. To play trumpet in a church with a great chamber orchestra is one of the most sublime experiences.

How do you combine acoustic instruments with synthesized music so well?

My background is originally as a classical musician, and then as a jazz musician. And I am a performer on a very traditional acoustic instrument. I know what that is; I am very firmly rooted in the tradition of acoustic music. Electronic music has advanced dramatically in the last twenty years, but I still don't think it really has the expressivity, the ability to emote as a single performer can. It takes a human being to get that emotional expression out of the traditional instruments that have evolved.

How do you subdue your solo instincts and fit your creativity to the film?

You have to realize what the assignment is. You can't think of the film as a vehicle for the composer, although it can happen. The first priority is that you are a vehicle for the film's success. You are a contributor to the overall success of the motion picture. The perfect balance is to have both working together. One successful action for me is to pick the right film. Don't pick a film where you will run into trouble.

What did you learn from Van Morrison?

The power of simplicity, that if you pick the right notes, it only takes a few of them. He's the master of that. The fundamental aspect of art is that it must communicate and Van exemplifies that more than anyone I've ever worked with. When he decides to communicate, he's just unbelievable. When he gets it right, it is *so perfect*.

Any words to the wise?

Persistence. When I look at my life and what has paid off for me, there are no secrets. The most dismal points in my life were when I chose to do musical things that weren't me—either for the money or some other reason. That got me in trouble. It all comes down to persistence and integrity.

Maurice Jarre, LA 1987

Maurice Jarre

The Master Scores

Did your work as a composer and conductor for theater help prepare you for film scoring?

Yes, it did in many ways. I worked in the French National Theater and wrote about 70 scores for plays by Shakespeare, Moliere, O'Neill, Chekhov, Brecht, Goldoni—a large spectrum. I was doing everything: writing the music, attending the rehearsals to know what the director wanted and also conducting at night.

What was it like working with Hitchcock?

It was a strange thing. *Topaz* was a departure for him, and I don't think he was comfortable with the story. I had a great relationship with Hitchcock, but it was a bit of a disappointment to work with him, because he didn't give me any indication of what he wanted. I said, "Hitch, I would like to play the theme for you." He said, "Okay, nice theme, that's good." I asked him what I should do next and he told me to do what I wanted. It scared me to death. I felt uncomfortable, because I wanted more feedback—but he was pleased with the results.

I think most filmgoers are not aware of the music—it's a subconscious effect.
The scenes are the building blocks and the music is the cement.

Exactly. You see, maybe because I was trained in the theater, I see the music as a part of the whole, part of a work of collaboration. You must understand that if you want to do music for film. Your music won't be up front—you have to be happy with the counterpoint. For me, the most fascinating thing about writing music for film is to meet so many different directors, like Hitchcock, Huston, Visconti, Weir, Schlondorff.

When you are composing, do you use the piano?

No, because I am not really a pianist. I started music very late—I was an engineer before. Actually, I started to study the notes of music when I was 16. It was too late to become a pianist. It was percussion that I studied seriously—tympani, xylophone, vibraphone—so I could make my living with the orchestra in Paris. For one year, I was the principal tympanist with the National Orchestra.

As for composing, I can write anywhere.

Without an instrument?

Yes, I don't need it, but I like the piano—it's very beautiful instrument. And it's convenient to write on top of it.

Any advice for aspiring film composers?

Actually, you have one chance in a hundred to make a living. There is a lot of luck, meeting the right people at the right moment—nothing to do with talent. Of course, if you don't have talent there is no way, but if you have talent, it doesn't necessarily mean you will succeed.

Booker T. Jones, LA 1984

Booker T. Jones

The Original Mr. T.   1984

Was there a point as a child when you knew for sure that you were going to be a musician?
My parents sang and my mother played the piano, and I was always asking for musical instruments. I got a clarinet when I was ten and then I got a real ukulele—a baritone ukulele. I thought that was the greatest instrument. You could get low tones that would actually rattle your belly. What resonance. It was a hobby, but I knew that I either wanted to be a musician or a physician. I just did much better in music than I did in chemistry.

How did Booker T. and the MGs come about—and what does MG stand for?
Memphis Group. I had another band in high school. We recorded "Green Onions" just before I entered Indiana University. I knew it was getting popular, but I didn't know it was going to be a big hit. I didn't know how I was going to pay for my education, and "Green Onions" paid for my first year of school. We had just recorded it; it was all part of making the 10 and 15 dollar gigs.

Who discovered you as far as making that record?
David Porter, the guy that used to write songs with Isaac Hayes, took me to Stax Records with my baritone sax. He had seen me at some gigs—I was in the 11th grade—and they let me play on a song and paid me for it.

Who produced that first record?
The members of the band and Jim Stewart. At that time they weren't putting producer's credits on the records. We were all at the studio for another session and the artist didn't turn up. We decided to use the time and recorded some songs that Steve Cropper and I had been working on. We did "Behave Yourself," a slow blues ballad. I played the organ like I did at the clubs. Jim Stewart was trying to start the record company and liked what we did. "Green Onions" was the B side. We took it down to the radio station in Memphis and the disk jockey, Dick (Cane) Cole, played the flip side and people started calling in. We were just having a good time. We thought at best we could make 10 or 15 bucks out of the session—that was good enough.

Is there a consistent musical identity in your life's work?
There has been something that I have strived for. I don't know if it was there in "Green Onions," which is a basic 12-bar blues. But what I have strived for over the years was to find things that were musically out of the ordinary—slightly more interesting than other things you might be hearing at the time. It might be a change of melody too soon, or sooner than expected—I've tried to inject things like that into my music.

(Foreground L-R) Rickie Lee Jones and co-producer Bruce Brody, (standing L-R) engineer Larry Alexander and assistant engineer Tom Sweeney, Record One Recording Studios, LA 2000

Rickie Lee Jones

Sugar and Spice

Do you have an affinity for the Beat Generation?

Yeah, but I didn't know anything about Beatniks. I was 14. My affinity must come naturally, not from reading about them. I just naturally lived a kind of life that they were famous for. I think my being related to them came through Tom Waits—me being connected to Tom, and Tom being connected to that.

Well, when I began, we were living together, and I talked about him a lot. I will forever be related to him.

Lowell George recorded your song "Easy Money" before you made your first record. What effect did that have?

It was Lowell who brought me to the attention of Warner Bros. That had a big effect, but his recording of my song didn't. My recording did, though. In another way, having a songwriter like Lowell record one of my songs was amazing, now that I look back in retrospect.

Did one instance move you from obscurity to prominence?

Yes, my performance on *Saturday Night Live* in 1979. That did it. You felt it. Electrifying.

You and Dr. John won a Grammy in 1990 for your "Making Whoopee" duet. How did that come about?

We go way back. I met Dr. John before I got signed. I was talking with three labels at the time and his producer, Tommy LiPuma, was running Portrait Records. He was thinking of signing me and he sent Dr. John to meet me—as his liaison. I'll never forget him walking down La Cienega Blvd. in all his Dr. John regalia, with his cane and his mojo, and the patchouli oil wafting down the street. And me in my beret. When we met it was an incredible moment. I put my arm in his and we became friends immediately. We walked down the street—it was like a little movie. Then he took me to a house and we played a couple of numbers together. We've been friends and played together ever since, but "Whoopee" was our first recording.

Any advice for newcomers to the music business?

Keep your publishing. Don't sell your publishing, because that's how you'll live when things aren't going well.

As I was listening to your albums last night, a name came to mind: Van Morrison.

He's my idol.

If I had to make a label for you, I would call you the female Van Morrison. The storytelling, the delivery, the anguish, the spirit…

Absolutely. That's perfect. If I had a soulmate, and wanted to be compared to anybody, that would be the highest compliment.

Led Ka'apana, LA 1998

Led Ka'apana

Shining Hawaiian Star

What was the first music you heard as a child?
My mom used to sing "Punaluu." It's about the black sands of Kau—Hawaiians write songs about special places with natural beauty.

Who was your first music teacher?
My dad, George, taught me how to play my first slack key guitar tune: "Maui Chimes." And I was influenced by my uncle, Fred Punahoa. He plays guitar, autoharp, piano, saxophone. He once told me that he had a dream when he was a boy—he was taught how to play the guitar in seven nights. He couldn't see the visitor's face, but he was dressed all in white with a red sash. When I was growing up, I just watched my uncle and learned from him.

Didn't slack key start when the Mexican cowboys left Hawaii in the early 19th century?
Yes, around 1830 the Hawaiians picked up the guitars left behind by the *paniolo* (cowboys) and created their own tunings. It's an open tuning and you can use one finger to press in notes while you play rhythm and bass together. Hawaiian steel guitar developed from slack key in the 1880s when they experimented with playing the guitar flat on the lap with fingerpicks.

How do you mic your ukulele?
I usually use a D.I. electric pickup, but I learned from Bob Brozman about the Neumann KM-84 condenser mike that's perfect for guitars and ukuleles—brings out the sound of the wooden body and you combine that with the electric sound.

Do you have any advice about the music business?
Accept what you are and love what you do, and do it because it comes from the heart and not just for the money. Be humble to everybody and move on.

Hawaiian music was such a worldwide phenomenon in the '20s, and then again in the '50s. Do you think we're due for another wave to sweep around the world?
Could be. In my touring around the world, as soon as I start to play the Hawaiian music, I feel and hear the great response of the audience. When I get home to Hawaii, and my friends ask me about my experiences, I tell them the audience is all *haoles* (foreigners) but the response to the music is greater than back home.

I've heard that when you were a child, you told your parents that you wanted to be a musician when you grew up…
Yes, and they told me I had to pick one or the other.

Paul Kantner, Record Plant Recording Studios, LA 1989

Paul Kantner

Plane Talk   1989

XXXXXXXXXXXXXXXXXXXXXXXXXXXXXXXXXXXXXXXXXXXXXXXXXXXXXXXXXXXXXXXXXXXXXXXXXX

Why was the Jefferson Airplane the first of the Bay Area bands to sign a major contract?
Random factors. A big accident. We just happened to be in the right place at the right time and we were pretty good.

What is the life of rock-and-roll?
A rock-and-roll musician lives on the edge of good and bad, positive and negative. You walk the gauntlet of total pleasure, happiness, completion—and excess, drug addiction or crashing in cars like James Dean, one of the first rock-and-rollers. You walk that fine line and are given access to anything, just because of the amount of money you make. If you are young enough, and have lack of control, you can go over the edge without anyone being able to stop you.

How is the youth culture doing today?
I have no idea. How would I know? We didn't know back when we were beginning. When Jefferson Airplane went out to play the "Human Be-In" [January 14, 1967], as they called it, we expected a couple of hundred people. All of a sudden there were 20,000, all looking weird. [laughs] It was a children's army—a strength in numbers.

Will we ever have another "Summer of Love"?
No, of course not. But there is something about it that is charming to remember. We like to go back to the places of our childhood—some of us do—to see what it was really like, and sit there for awhile and absorb. We haven't moved away from it, so we are still children—struggling mightily to remain adolescents as long as possible.

Any thoughts about preparing a young artist for the rigors of the business world?
You can't prepare for it. It's like a ritual that you have to go through. It's part of the weeding-out process. It's been said that true writers write because they have to. Whether anyone reads it or not is unimportant.

It's almost like rock-and-roll is becoming an establishment profession. Are you going to be a dentist, a doctor, or a rock-and-roll musician? Then you retire, move to Hawaii and do God-knows-what for the rest of your life. Some of us just do it, because it has to be done. And, some of us are in a position to be able to do it. We happen to be in a very lucky position.

Well, bon voyage…
Let the sparks fly—and take care.

Jim Keltner, LA 1985

Jim Keltner

The Sunny Side of the Beat 1985

When did you play your first professional gig?
It was at Jefferson Recreation Center in Pasadena—seven bucks for the night.

Can you remember the first session or gig where you really felt like you were on your way?
Well, I jumped quickly. Around '65 I joined up with Gary Lewis & The Playboys, and went directly from playing jazz on the Sunset Strip to playing pop-rock. I was with Gary for just a couple of months before we went into the studio. Hal Blaine had played drums on all his stuff prior to that, but they decided to give me a shot. I hadn't really been in a studio before, other than doing a few demos, and I didn't know exactly what to do. I watched Hal on a few sessions and he gave me a few pointers. By the way, did you know that the great drummer Earl Palmer helped Hal get started doing sessions? To tell the truth, I wanted to sound like Hal, and I didn't. To me, I sounded real clumsy and weird, too tight and a little too busy—like a little mouse. I had a jazz kit, and I didn't know at the time that tuning was so important. Hal gave me some important tips, and by the time we cut "Just My Style," I had it together enough to sound convincing. It was a hit. Blam, the first thing I did in the studios was a big hit record. It was a thrill to hear it on the radio, and I was really hooked.

Of all the people you've worked with, who are your favorites?
It's impossible to say, when you've worked with people like Lennon and Dylan, and Randy Newman—some of the great songwriters of all time. Hard to say, but I guess Dylan is my favorite. Everybody's got a story about Bob and a lot of them are about how cold he is. I've heard people say that they worked for Dylan for 12 hours and he never said a word. That always makes me laugh, because I've been in that situation, too—but I know the other side of him as well.

I loved working with John, too—I always felt like I was on a cloud when I was around him. Musically, the one thing that always stood out for me with John was that his songs played themselves. They were just so complete when he came to us with them. He would bring a little chord chart and there was hardly ever any reworking. I never had to search for a drum part. Generally, it all just fell into place. It always amazed me.

Where do the drums fit in the grand scheme of recording?
Well, in a great many records that are made by hit artists, the drums play a hugely important part in whether they become a hit or not—the way it feels when it comes over that little speaker. Generally, the first thing that a person feels is that heartbeat—the way the drummer has constructed the heartbeat of that song.

(L-R) Burt Bacharach, Elvis Costello, assistant engineer Al Sanderson, engineer Kevin Killen, Ocean Way Recording Studios, LA 1998

(L-R) Duncan Sheik, Kevin Killen, producer Patrick Leonard, Cello Recording Studios, LA 2002

Kevin Killen

Luck of the Irish   2002

Could you share any of your engineering tips?

One of my main techniques is the illusion of space, especially around vocals and the rhythmic elements. My wife describes my vocals as "moist." It's really something that I do by ear—work on it until I have a sound which is personal, emotional, and isn't trying too hard. Some of it is mic placement, and choice of mic, but you must get the singer relaxed in the studio so that they can deliver a good performance.

How did you capture Tony Levin's bass on Peter Gabriel's "Sledgehammer"?

People often think it's an elaborate setup, that it sounds like I did all these amazing things to the bass, but the reality was that the sound very much came from Tony's fingers. He'll come in, plug into a DI, and while he's learning the song, it sounds pretty good—but then as soon as he knows the part and he actually starts performing, there is this richness, and these overtones will come out of the bass just from his particular style of playing—which I have never heard from any other bass player. It's a unique sound.

How did you get the sound of The Edge?

Around the time that I was working with him he was using a few Vox AC-30 amplifiers, probably from the '60s or '70s. Obviously, he had been into using delay pedals, but at that time he was using an Echoplex tape-based delay unit. That's very much part of his sound—the sound of the guitar mixed through the Echoplex and into the amplifier. It came from the way he played the guitar and the choice of notes that he used, to get that signature sound. In the majority of instances, we never even ran the amplifier at a very highly distorted level. It was medium distortion, or less—just enough to get a little bit of grit in there, but not heavily amped.

What did you learn from working with Daniel Lanois about tracking and mixing?

From both Dan and Brian Eno, I learned not to be afraid to print effects. When you've got a particular sound that is inspiring the musicians, don't be afraid to take that effect and print it to the track, along with the performance. Up until that point, I was a little reticent about printing effects. People would tend to leave effects aside until the mix.

And then in mixing, what I learned from Dan and Brian, was not to be afraid—if you have a rough mix that has an incredible spirit to it, don't be afraid of using it. In fact, we ended up using a rough mix on *The Unforgettable Fire* for "A Sort of Homecoming," the opening cut of the record. Don't be so precious about mixing. If you don't like it, you can always come back and do another one.

(back row L-R) Jim Keltner (drums), Bill Payne (keyboards), Marty Stuart (guitar and vocals), Joette Phillips (project assistant), John Porter (producer), Tisha Fein (project coordinator), Mickey Raphael (harmonica), Bonnie Garner (Marty's manager); (front L-R) Tommy Eyre (keyboards), Randy Jacobs (guitar), B.B. King, Ocean Way Recording Studios, LA 1997

B.B. King

Shake My Hand

What is a secret of your guitar playing?

I invented the "trill" that a lot of people use. Some of the guitar makers have even made a long handle that shakes the whole bridge on the back to simulate what I do with my hand. I've always been crazy about the sound of bottleneck guitar and Hawaiian steel, and when I trill my hand it kinda fools my ears a bit to make it sound like that. It became a habit and I can hardly play a note now without shaking my hand.

Do you use computers when you're making records now?

Sure, the average studio now has computers. I have a computer at home and I have a laptop for the road that helps me put the music together for my arranger to write. Before the computer I never had an arranger do anything exactly like I wanted it. The better ones would get maybe 95-97%, but when I got a computer I could put the stuff down myself and let them hear it. I can't play on the guitar a lot of the things that I hear, but I can put it on the computer with the music program I have and the computer will play it.

Is the computer a good partner in creating blues music?

Why not? The same notes that play the blues play any other music. The computer is the thing of the future and nobody can visualize how far it will take us. I say to your readers that the computer is the best thing that's happened since electricity.

Do you have any advice for students of music?

If you want to be a musician, don't try to be a blues player, a rock-and-roll player, a country player, a jazz player, or any one particular category. Just try to be a good musician and find somebody to teach you. Don't try to go as I did because that's the long way around. You don't have to be like B.B. King or Clapton, or anybody else. You can be yourself and play what you like. And when people need a great musician you don't have to say you're a blues player or a jazz player. What I like to hear them say is "I'm a musician, so what do you want?"

Kitaro, Katsu Restaurant, LA 1987

Kitaro

Very Happy Man

What did your parents give you as a child?

My parents were farmers and I lived in a regular farmhouse. I don't have one particular image, but I lived close with nature every day. My parents watched after me gently, but I can't point to one particular gift.

Did they encourage your music?

Not at all. When I was a child I liked sports—I never thought about making music.

Can you remember the first music you heard?

The first music I heard was folk songs, traditional music. When I began to hear popular music, I became interested in the guitar and wanted to learn how to play. I thought The Beatles were great, R&B—my favorite was Otis Redding.

Kitaro means "very happy man"?

Yes. It was a nickname I was given in high school.

New Age music is a common label these days, but I've heard your music referred to as "New Science." What does that mean?

It means *shizen*—nature. There is big energy and we move in it. This is a principle that I try to understand and use in my work. It means more than science, though. It means spirit—a return to the spirit. It is science; it is spirit; it is religion—everything. Finally, these concepts become one. There is old energy that comes from somewhere, and passes through us. Creating music is using this energy to communicate with an audience. Like being a messenger. This is "New Science."

My idea of "New Age" music is that we should have a philosophy, and an appreciation of traditional ways, and we should also think of the future. If people think that our generation will be the end, there is no hope for the next generation. Most people, especially young musicians in Japan, don't think of the next generation for the world. Maybe they are so young that they aren't aware of their effect on the future. We should have freedom, and move beyond destruction. In past times, we have had many kinds of destruction. We should move on.

We should be aware of what we give to others. If someone listens to music, maybe their ideas will change. The responsibility comes to me. It relates to my feelings about Otis Redding, for instance. He is dead now, but there is still a big influence. So I can't do my work easily; I must act carefully.

Al Kooper, LA 1986

Al Kooper

Soul of a Man

How did you get involved with Bob Dylan?
Basically, I was invited by his producer to watch a session. At the time, I was making my living as a studio musician. I decided the night before that I couldn't go to a Dylan session and just watch. So, I got there an hour early and plugged in. When the other musicians came, they assumed I was there to play. It didn't look weird to them, because I might have worked with them the day before and the day after.

Then Dylan walked in with a guy who had a Telecaster over his shoulder—like Johnny Appleseed. No case, and it was covered with snow because it was the dead of winter. He just toweled it off and started playing. I was thrilled—I'd never heard anybody play like that. It was Mike Bloomfield. I thought I was a good player, but when I heard him, I packed up my guitar and went into the booth.

The producer hadn't noticed this little scene and about two or three hours into the session he moved the organ player over to the piano. I suggested that I sit in on the organ, but he just said, "Oh, man, you don't play organ." Then he got a phone call and while he was gone I walked out and sat down at the organ. They started taking this song—the only complete take of the day. I couldn't even hear the organ because the band was playing so loud. I just played by touch, knowing that if I played a C it would work with the F chord, and like that. During the playback, Dylan asked the producer to turn up the organ. He said, "Oh, man, that cat's not an organ player." Bob just told him to turn it up. That was "Like a Rolling Stone."

What's the difference between two groups you formed: The Blues Project and Blood, Sweat and Tears?
The Blues Project was very punky for their time, a very punky band at its best. B,S&T was a more polished pop music band, with a plethora of influences.

What was your role with Lynyrd Skynyrd?
I found them, signed them, and produced them. I just heard them play, and after three nights in a row it got to me. I thought they were fantastic.

If you could go back in time before the birth of recording, what would you like to hear?
The music they played at the Marquis de Sade's parties.

What old saying do you hate the most?
You have to learn the rules before you can break them.

Do you have a favorite old saying?
If I'd known I was going to live this long, I would have taken better care of myself.

Danny Korchmar, LA 1984

Danny "Kootch" Korchmar

A Fistful of Guitar

What can the guitar do that no other instrument can?

The guitar is really a combination of a lot of instruments. It can be a rhythm instrument; it can play soaring lines—it can provide so many elements and always have that human sensitivity. The electric guitar is the first heavily processed musical instrument—the first synthesizer. And it still responds to the touch and has a fluidity that no other electronic instrument has.

Of all your recordings, where has your identity come through the clearest?

It's difficult to say. There are parts of performances that demonstrate what the essence of my style is. For instance, my playing on Linda Ronstadt's "Hurt So Bad" is a good example of my playing. On Don Henley's "Dirty Laundry" I play a rhythm part that has my personal brand. I really liked what I did on Warren Zevon's "Ain't That Pretty?" Jackson Browne, James Taylor…

How did you get the nickname Kootch?

When I was about 13, people found it difficult to pronounce Korchmar. In summer camp, somebody called me Kootchmar, and then they called me Kootch, and it stuck.

Who is the Attila the Hun of the guitar?

Meaning somebody that's just the conqueror, the destroyer? Then I would say Steve Lukather. He's Mr. Everything. He will run you around; he can hurt you in so many ways—he's like a prize fighter. He's got so much going for him as a musician, along with a soul and an integrity and a real joy in his playing.

Why do people have pets?

Because you can train a pet to love you.

What do you appreciate in an engineer?

A good engineer is somebody that thinks like a musician as much as thinking like an engineer. Everything he does is designed to help the song and to help the total situation, which is the way musicians think when they're recording a tune. Another element would be speed, along with efficiency.

Why are you a survivor?

Because I never think about quitting. It just never occurs to me. I love music. I don't think of myself as being in the music industry. I think of myself as a rocker—somebody that just will always be a diehard rocker, that just loves the whole idea of the backbeat—turn up the amps and let's knock the shit out of it.

(L-R) Producer Steve Berlin and Leo Kottke, Brooklyn Recording Studio, LA 1991

Leo Kottke

Strings Attached   1991

▨▨▨

When you're composing or playing, do your hands have a mind of their own?
When things are going right, yeah. When things really work well, the reasoning-tracking part of my brain just parks itself and remains disconnected. It's the part that remembers or notices when something good happens, but it's the same part that screws everything up when I can't get it to relax. So, it waits—that's its job.

Maybe it's the deeper reptilian brain that's playing.
[laughs] Yes, it may have preceded me. I don't mean to be lofty about all this, but it's more for me a process of tuning in on that frequency and getting the transmissions that invent something. I like the idea of the reptilian brain—I know it's in there somewhere.

Does your clock run slower than most people's?
I think it does. I know I talk slower than a lot of people. And I inject long pauses at inappropriate times. As a kid, when I expected to live my life as a trombone player, I noticed that there were two tempos at which I could function. One was very frantic and the other one is the one which I chose, which is kind of glacial.

Ever thought about what music you'd like played at your funeral?
I have! Jeez, what a funny question. Yes, I have, a lot. And I've come down to no music.

That's what Leonard Cohen told me.
Is that right? Hmm. Yes, I'd rather have nothing. That's my funeral; I'm done. And I know if they played something of mine, I'd want to jump out of my grave and change the selection [laughs]. It's always the wrong tune.

How about some advice for the youngsters. Anything you could offer in the way of a survival tactic?
Absolutely, although it's not a tactic. I believe that if you pursue something that you have a passion for, you can't go wrong. You may starve, but you're satisfying something that is outside of yourself as much as it is a part of you. It doesn't depend on success. The only thing that needs to be nourished is this passion. I know that if you ignore that, and do something else in the name of sanity, let's say, or revenue, you suffer for it. I've seen musicians do it, switch to another kind of living so that they could either support their family or find a saner day-to-day existence and all of the people I think of wound up being unhappy. In some cases, profoundly unhappy.

If you're not playing because you have to have it every day, if it's not a matter of appetite but a matter of fascination, I think you would be in terrible trouble pursuing it. I know that if I fall flat on my face commercially, I can always play. I can *always* play. And no time I've spent trying to play will ever be wasted. It's good for you. It's like food.

Eddie Kramer, Brooklyn Recording Studio, LA 2000

Eddie Kramer

Engineering Greatness

What did you learn from Jimi Hendrix?

Stay open-minded and let the sounds take you on a journey. When we first met, he was very quiet, very soft-spoken, very shy. We hit it off because I was able to deliver some sounds that he hadn't heard before. He would come up with new sounds, crank up an amp, do things that left us breathless. That would inspire us to be different, take a chance, mic it in a different way, EQ in a new way, whatever was needed to take his ideas to another level.

Could you tell me about the Whole Lotta Love *sessions with Led Zeppelin?*

The entire album was mixed in two days at A&R Studios in New York. It's 8-Track and by the way, the console had only two pan pots! We put the tracks up and 7 and 8 were the vocals. Track 8 was the final vocal, and 7 was the one prior. For some reason 7 was breaking through the console and I couldn't turn it off, so you could hear it, "Wo-man. You need it," slightly out of time, so I just cranked up the reverb and Page heard it and said, "Great—Just leave it!"

David Bowie and John Lennon, "Fame."

Talk about a "high level" conference. Bowie walked into the studio and Carlos Alomar was playing this riff and Bowie said, "I love that." Built the song around it right on the spot. John Lennon was in the vocal booth playing rhythm guitar. He was the greatest rhythm guitar player I had ever heard—absolutely like a rock!

Joe Cocker?

What surprised me was that in the studio he didn't flail around like onstage. Just a great voice, and a very tight band—the Grease Band.

Rolling Stones?

The tracks for "Parachute Woman" and "Jumping Jack Flash" were cut with the band sitting around Jimmy Miller's Wollensak cassette deck, with the mic in the middle of the band. We played that back through a little Philips speaker and recorded it onto one track of a four track and that was the basic track.

The Beatles?

This was the only time I was scared shitless. Working with Jimi, The Stones, Traffic was great fun—but The Beatles, Oh Jeez! I was the senior engineer and I was understandably a bit nervous, but they were very sweet. I cut the basic track for "All You Need Is Love."

What makes a great producer?

Patience, tenacity, a degree in psychology.

What old saying do you hate the most?

Fix it in the mix.

Kris Kristofferson, LA 1994

(Standing L-R) Kris Kristofferson and producer Don Was, (seated) engineer Ed Cherney, Brooklyn Recording Studio, LA 1994

Kris Kristofferson

Road Scholar   1994

XXXXXXXXXXXXXXXXXXXXXXXXXXXXXXXXXXXXXXXXXXXXXXXXXXXXXXXXXXXXXXXXXXXXXXX

What do you primarily think of yourself as?
Songwriter. I think that I can interpret my own material honestly and effectively, but I wouldn't be doing it if I didn't write it, because I haven't got the tools—for my ears—to sing something I didn't write.

Could you tell me about your first job in Nashville?
The job title was "studio setup man," but I kept the studios cleaned up and supplied the engineers with all the stuff they needed. It could feed my wife and child, and kept me in touch with the music part, not the business part, where I didn't have to use my brain. I got to hear Bob Dylan the first week I was there, the only songwriter in town that could be in the studio. They had police around—he was working on *Blonde On Blonde*. And Simon and Garfunkel, and then I got to know Johnny Cash.

Was performing with The Highwayman a high point of your performing experience?
It was definitely one of them. When I look back on my life for some kind of perspective, it seems like something you would fantasize—seeing myself with Barbra Streisand, and looking next to myself onstage and seeing people who were my absolute heroes. When I went to be a songwriter, I did it for the love and not for the money. I loved everything about it and admired the people who were good at it, and Johnny Cash and Willie Nelson were right up there at the top. And Waylon Jennings is the closest to a hero.

To be up there with them and singing along on these songs that are such a part of your soul because you grew up with them—it's a wonderful thing. I'm sure it drives 'em crazy sometimes when I'm harmonizing [laughs]. One time John said, "I don't think there's another person in the world who would have the nerve to sing harmony with me on "Folsom Prison." And I didn't know how to take that! [laughs] So, I didn't do it for the next show, and then I guess he got to feeling bad about it and told me to start singing harmony again.

(L-R) Nathaniel and Russell Kunkel, Conway Recording Studios, LA 1996

Nathaniel Kunkel, LA 2002

Nathaniel Kunkel, LA 2002

Nathaniel Kunkel

Born to the Craft

What was life around the Kunkel household as a kid?

I remember being in the basement of our house when Russ had a 4-track studio set up. He and Danny Korchmar were working there. I also remember crawling underneath the console in the main room at Record One and sleeping. These are some of my first memories.

Did you feel that you had a musical calling as a kid?

Musical, yes. I play drums as well and have since I was about four. It wasn't until around 1985 that I got really into audio though. In grade school I was very interested in technology and lighting and when I would go on the road with my dad, I was really interested in the lighting board. It wasn't until I met George Massenburg at The Complex when Russ was working with Bill Payne on some films that I really got into it. I remember George typing SMPTE numbers into a synchronizer—seemed big as a washing machine. I liked that. I thought to myself, this is cool, this is hip stuff.

The summer of 1985, I was just out of 8th grade when I met George. The very next summer, just before I got out of school for the year, I was speaking with Greg Ladanyi on the phone. At that time, Greg and George owned The Complex. Greg offered me a job—running basically, but I didn't have a driver's license. I was just there, and would do things like clean the snakes when they came in off the road, clean the connectors, solder patch bays. There was a great technical staff and I learned how to wire and all that.

What was cool, was that George was doing so much R&D. At the end of the day he would go, "Great, you go in there and mix because I have to watch the logic analyzer hooked up to the automation computer while it's working. He'd put a mix up and say, "Don't touch any of the EQ—go for it." I would mix and mix and mix.

What was your first solo gig?

The first record I did solo was Lyle Lovett's *I Love Everybody*.

Could you point out a few engineers who inspire you?

I am consistently in awe of mixes by Ed Cherney and George Massenburg. I hear things that George does that just blow my mind and the same with Ed. There's a warmth and a texture that Ed gets.

What was the most valuable thing your dad gave you?

To find that I would look back at the conversations I've had with my dad, the ones that stick in my mind as being important. It has to do with diligence, staying with something, committing yourself and following through until the end. It means completing what you said you would do, in terms of records. When it's done, all that will be remembered is how the record sounds.

(L-R) Russell and Nathaniel Kunkel, Conway Recording Studios, LA 1996

Russell Kunkel, Conway Recording Studios, LA 1999

Russell Kunkel, Conway Recording Studios, LA 1999

Russell Kunkel

Drum of the Times

><><><><><><><><><><><><><><><><><><><><><><><><><><><><><><><><><><><><><><><><><

Why do you think you were drawn to the drums?
I guess it was because I had a jump on it, and I had a brother who was a drummer, and there were drums around. My first summer job was at a gas station, and after that experience I made a decision that I would never work a normal job again. I decided to become a musician. Getting that first $50 for playing one night—that was for me.

When did you first feel that it was becoming a reality?
I played in a lot of bands in high school and one of them made it to Hollywood. We played the Whisky-a-Go-Go for a few weeks in a row. That was a pretty big deal. The band was called Things To Come, about 1967, and we opened up for Cream.

Beyond that, the biggest thing that happened to launch my career was being hired by Peter Asher to play on James Taylor's first album, *Sweet Baby James*. There was a domino effect after that.

From that period, what work are you most proud of?
Early '70s? Well, the first album with James. When I listen to that, I still like it for its rawness, and acoustics. And Carole King's *Tapestry*, which I played on a good portion of. And Jackson Browne's first album, *Saturate Before Using*. Those albums stick out for me—pinnacle albums for those artists and I was fortunate enough to play on them.

Did you have any heroes in the drum world?
Ringo for sure. What I heard on those records was great, groundbreaking stuff. And, of course, I think every drummer has respect for the jazz greats: Elvin Jones, Buddy Rich, Roy Haines, and down the line. At that time I was in awe of the session drummers in Los Angeles: Hal Blaine, Jim Gordon. I met Jim Keltner at that time when we were both just getting started.

When did you first feel you had succeeded as a producer?
Before I started to work with Jimmy Buffett, I had co-produced a few projects. Two or three films scores with George Massenburg and Bill Payne, an album for Carly Simon, an album with Jimmy Buffett and Mike Utley called *Hot Water*, a song with Bonnie Raitt, and I co-produced *Exiles* with Dan Fogelberg.

I don't think it was until I produced Jimmy's *Fruitcakes* that I really felt like I knew what I was doing. He hadn't had an album out in six years and that one went straight to platinum. It was a turning of the corner for him, and he let me know that I was part of the reason why. That was the moment for me.

Greg Ladanyi, O'Henry Recording Studios, LA 1994

Greg Ladanyi

Building the Perfect Record

Who was the first major artist that you were responsible for?

I started with Jackson Browne on *The Pretender*. He was working with Val Garay, but Val had to leave for some reason and I was there. I said I would really like to have a shot, and Jackson let me do it. It was just being in the right place at the right time and I was lucky. I mixed the record, and then we did *Running On Empty*, *Hold Out*, and *Lawyers In Love*.

How did you get Mick Fleetwood's drum sound?

Mick is so great, because he has such an animal sound in the way he plays. For some reason I wasn't getting that and I didn't know why. I went to Hawaii and I saw him play live onstage, and I got up there near him so I could hear what he was doing. In the studio, when I put monitors around him, he started really playing the drums and I got the sound. He needed to feel the drum sound, the bottom end of his drum kit. His whole groove is about locking into it because he feels it.

When you're recording, do you use much EQ?

I used to do more EQ than I am now. This is my 17th year of doing this and I'm learning to stay away from it as much as possible. If I want something brighter, I'll go to the guitar player and ask him to either make his guitar or the amp brighter. There are ways to make things brighter or darker, by asking the musicians to help you, instead of sitting here and not saying anything and messing around with the EQ.

How did you make the transition to producer?

I was working during a time in the record industry where artists became more involved. Engineers became more and more valuable and I was lucky to be around. We became valuable because we could sit with the artist and help them as co-producers. That led me into co-producing, and later to producing because I got better at it, better at listening and capturing performances. And I learned about arranging songs from people like Jackson Browne and Don Henley.

What advice would you give to the aspiring young engineers/producers?

Be around music as much as you can. Understand it from the live aspect, as well as the studio. Live it, don't just dabble with it. I don't think that the lucky breaks will ever stop—that's part of this business. If you're sincere about it, and good at it, and somebody notices, you might get that shot. You can't go to school to learn all this stuff, although it can't hurt you. You'll get your shots, they'll come—it's just a matter of can you wait? Be persistent, don't give up, and knock on any door you want to. All they can do is say no.

k.d. lang, Chateau Marmont, LA 1995

k.d. lang

You Don't Have a Choice

Was Patsy Cline an influence on you?

Yes, because I loved her voice, the emotion and pathos and humor and power. She was a very progressive woman who was trying to make it in this business. I guess I related to her in a sense—the woman struggling against the odds.

When did you first discover your voice?

I was pretty young. I competed for the first time when I was five, and won. That seemed to give me a boost. It was never a discovery, though, it was just sort of there and understood.

When did you realize it was your calling?

I knew it all along. I also went through stages where I wanted to be a cinematographer and involved in sports, but I knew it was music all along.

What's most important to you, love or a recording career?

Number one, they're inseparable, because I don't think I'm capable of either one without the other. Number two, I think it's shifted a bit. For the first ten years of my career there's no question that was it, but as I get older and more comfortable, I've gotten more "over" show business. I'll never be over music, but maybe a little tired of show business, and I think love will ultimately be king. But it's inseparable. I'm a singer. I can't dissect myself that way.

How do you deal with phonies?

I try not to; I try to eliminate them from my life. But I don't want to answer the question simply. I can't judge, because I'm sure that people who meet me in certain instances say, "She's phony." I just try to adhere to my own value system, as it pertains to my music and my life. You just try to live really clearly with your own instincts and morals, and react to situations staying true to those instincts, that's all.

Any advice for those just getting started in the music business, something that might help them avoid pitfalls?

I'd avoid it in general [laughs]. It's a conduit. I don't think true musicians, actors, artists, have any choice. You don't have a choice.

Timothy Leary, LA 1983

Timothy and Zach Leary, LA 1983

LA 1983

172

Timothy Leary

The Doctor Is In
1983

What role has music played in your life?
Well, it's well known that the music you listen to when you're an adolescent, when you're losing your virginity, always stays with you as the automatic access code to that big circuit of your brain. That's why gray-haired people go to Las Vegas and cream over Frank Sinatra, because that was the message.

I have followed a life pattern of rejuvenilization, so that I have gone through adolescence many times, and I owe a tremendous debt of gratitude to musicians at each stage of the game. The music is always the key to your adolescent sexuality. It's many other things, too, but that's why the powerful access code is there.

So you have a number of these access codes?
And I could write the autobiography of my life in terms of the sounds I was listening to at the various stages.

When we started running those early (LSD) sessions we got into Ray Charles, rhythm and blues, the basic down stuff like that. Then we were influenced by the folk music—chants. If you were taking big drug trips it was comforting to have the African and Indian chants. And Coltrane was very important. The rock-and-roll wave came—we all remember where we were the first time we heard "Sgt. Pepper's." So do The Bee Gees.

I can't finish the musical part without mentioning that David Bowie is our standard of musical accomplishment. We have all his records, we listen to him a lot particularly when we are taking strong drugs. His ability to change and grow and take risks and to keep moving and evolving is at a tremendous level of what anyone can do in any field. I have great admiration for him.

You spent some time with The Beatles, didn't you…
Yes, but I really spent more time with them after they broke up—mainly with John and Ringo. I'm still close with Ringo—he's a fun lover. I always felt that The Beatles were irreverent, but it wasn't a down irreverence as in Dylan. I feel that juvenile irreverence and disrespect for adult authority is the key to individual evolution and species evolution. You've got to laugh at the adults, but you've got to do it in a way that's not destructive, that's not self-destructive.

173

Gallery II Devo–20 Years of Devolution

Mark Mothersbaugh prepares his costume for "The Theme From Dr. Detroit" music video, LA 1983.

Mark struggles with the tricky rubber outfit.

The outfit is inflated and Mark is ready to go.

A touch of make-up on the set. Bob #2 Casale in the rear.

Laraine Newman of *Saturday Night Live* and Mark.

Mark and Gerald Casale discuss the progress.

It's a wrap. Mark powders and folds his rubber suit for later use.

Mark and Gerald plan the music video for "RU Experienced?" LA 1984

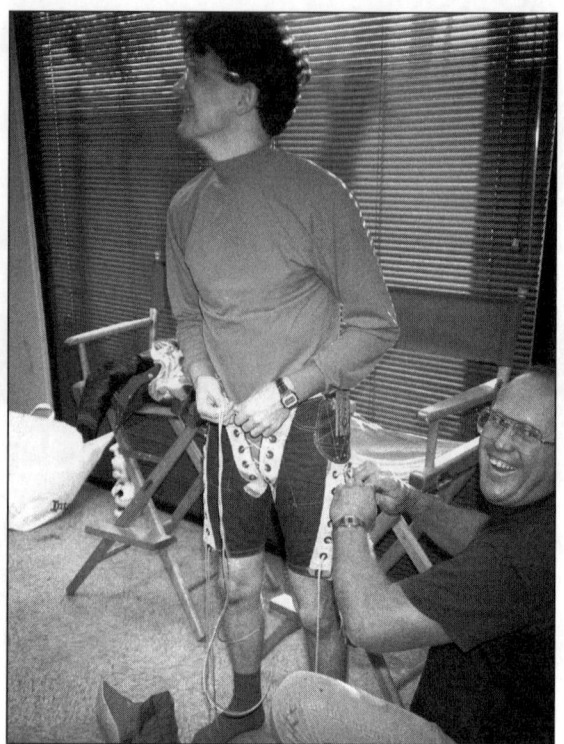

Mark is cinched into his flying harness.

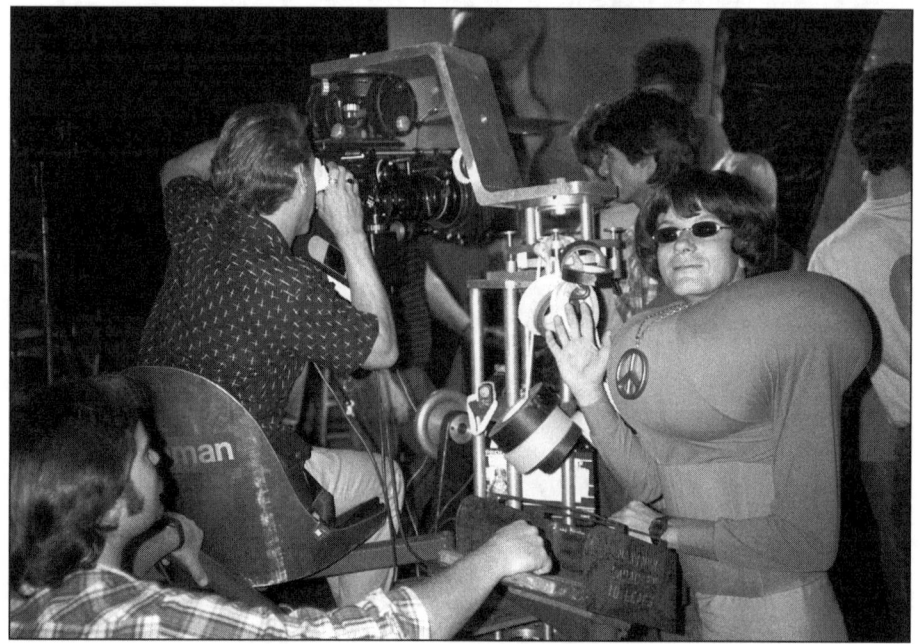

Mark is ready to fly.

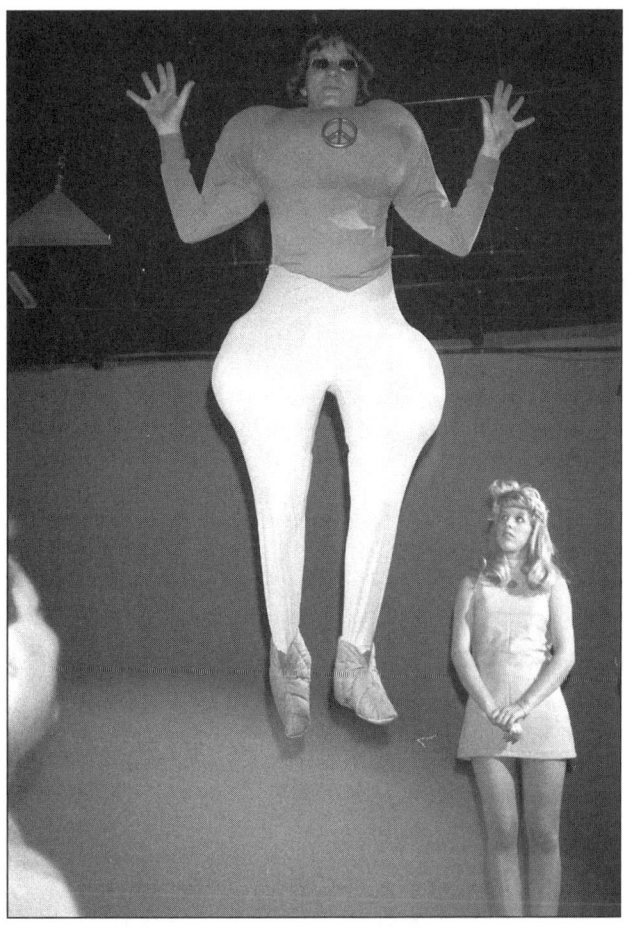

Mark is airborne.

(L-R) Bob Casale, Bob Mothersbaugh, Mark Mothersbaugh. Devo reunion for Lollapalooza festival, LA 1996

(L-R) Mark and Gerald, LA 1996

Bob #1 and Mark in rehearsal, LA 1999

Mark and two of his Booji Boy alter egos, LA 1999

Devo reunited, (L-R) Gerald, Mark, Bob #2, Bob #1, LA 2003

David Lindley, LA 1990

David Lindley

Tuggin' at the Artstrings

Any words of caution for those kids whose hearts are in the music?
There is a tradition in the music industry that is perpetuated by certain people who say, "You just play the music, and we'll take care of everything else." And they try to convince musicians that if you go into the business area, and publishing, it will take away from your music. It does *not* take away from your music—it makes it better, because it stretches your mind in an area that is musical, too. They say, "Leave all that to us. Concentrate on the playing and have fun." [Jamaican voice] "No, mon, don't believe it. That's Babylon talkin', mon."

Have you ever really pissed anyone off?
Oh, yeah. Because they were wrong and I was right. We won't name names, but these people—*ooooh*. They were officious people abusing their position.

They weren't record company people were they?
Of course, where else do you find people like that?

What does your family think of your career?
They like it. All my brothers like it very much. My sister and her kids are all for it. My dad is, but in the beginning he was hesitant, because it's a rough life and a lot of the musicians he knew had a terrible time. He was worried for me, which is natural. After he heard what I was playing, he said, "Yeah, you got something there. Just keep doing it. " Both my mom and dad were very encouraging.

Do you have anything to say about Les Paul?
I met him in New York and got to talk to him for a while and watched him play onstage. Seeing him do what he does—the stuff that he does doesn't die. Les Paul is the proof of life after death. The ideas and the music he makes will always be there. It was quite a moment when I looked him in the eye and saw how he loved doing what he does. He's got an appetite, he chews on it. That's what I find common among some musicians—you can tell if they have that kind of madness. They eat it up. Anybody who's really serious—they're mad. A great kind of madness, and he really has it. Not only a great player and a great mind, but multitrack recording—that's Les Paul, right there.

What music would you like played at your funeral?
Turkish Mevlevi music.

Is there any guitarist that can bring a tear to your eye?
Django Reinhart. It's not bad tears—it's good tears.

I understand. I was listening to your music last night and I got a few shivers.
Good! [Evangelist voice] That's what I *want* to do! I *need* that.

photo credit: Cesar Rosas and Mondo Tavares.

(L-R) Louis Perez, Steve Berlin, Cesar Rosas, Conrad Lozana, David Hidalgo, LA 2005

Los Lobos

The Wolves of East L.A.

XXXXXXXXXXXXXXXXXXXXXXXXXXXXXXXXXXXXXXXXXXXXXXXXXXXXXXXXXXXXXXXXXXXX

Why the name "Los Lobos"?

LOUIS PEREZ: When we started in 1974, we were more or less moonlighting from the other rock bands we were in at the time. We got together to play Mexican music and have some fun. There are many bands called "Los" this and that. One band was called "Los Lobos Del Norte," which means The Wolves of the North. Joking, we called ourselves "Los Lobos del Este," The Wolves of the East, because we lived in East L.A. Over the years, we dropped the "del Este" and stayed with Los Lobos. After a while, it became a symbol for us. The Wolf—a mysterious animal.

How did you get involved in the film La Bamba?

DAVID HIDALGO: Well, we've been playing Richie Valens music live for years, and the screenwriter Luis Valdez is an old friend of ours. It came together very naturally.

STEVE BERLIN: And we were playing in Santa Cruz, where Richie's family still lives, a few years before the film was made. They told us that someone had bought the rights to the story and requested that we do the music.

How has that affected your career? Did it open doors, or did it typecast you?

DAVID: It has both opened doors and typecast us at the same time. It worked for a while, helped enlarge the audience and attracted younger people. But it just came and went. It's back to reality now, picking up where we left off before it happened.

How did you re-discover the Mexican music you heard as kids?

DAVID: We were pretty much like any other eleven- or twelve-year-old kids. We were listening to The Rolling Stones and the same music like other kids. The Mexican music was our parents' music. It was old-fashioned, around the house all the time, so we took it for granted. It wasn't until later that we became interested, when we were in high school and the cultural awareness thing happened in the Mexican-American communities throughout the Southwest. Farm workers were trying to organize, and equal opportunity movements began. We started taking interest in our own culture, through literature, history, and the arts. Being musicians, we took on the musical aspect of our culture— something that no one our age had done anything with.

We tried to play this music, almost as a joke to begin with, just for the hell of it and to do something interesting. Then we got hooked, and found out that there was much more there than we had realized.

Lyle Lovett, Conway Recording Studios, LA 1991

Lyle Lovett, LA 1991

(L-R) Producer/engineer George Massenburg and Lyle Lovett, LA 1991

Lyle Lovett

Large Country

Who taught you how to sing so well?

Gosh—I'm untrained, for sure. I did sing when I was growing up. I went to parochial school and sang in the choir. Here's how you found out if you were in the choir or not: They would line us all up in class and we'd sing a hymn. The choir director would walk by and put his ear in front of each of us. You were either in or out.

Can you imagine what kind of songs you'll be writing when you're 80?

I hope I can still make something up. I find writing difficult and I hope I can still think of something.

Do you have any business tips?

You've got to constantly try to figure things out, because things are never the same. This is my fourth album, but it's different than any other album I've done. You can never completely rely on experience.

On this pinnacle you've created for yourself—do you ever feel lonely?

Oh, sure. I'm very lonely.

Does this loneliness boost creativity?

No, I don't think so. Sometimes. I think creativity is having a good idea, or just figuring out a way to get to a good idea.

Do you believe in luck?

Sometimes good things happen for no reason at all. I don't know if it's luck. And then sometimes bad things happen for no reason at all. That's luck.

Who does your hair? No, forget it, that's a stupid question.

That's okay. The same person has been cutting my hair for several years at home, but when I stay out here—well, it takes a few times to get it right.

Well, the cappuccino is almost gone. Do you have a final thought? Can we leave the folks with something inspirational? What looks good to you about the world these days?

The good things about the world are the great people. There are lots of good people, but somehow good things are losing out.

We're not going to give up, are we?

No, you can't give up, but I think it's possible for good things to lose out to the bad.

Does your music bend things in the right direction?

I don't think my music makes any difference in the big picture. I just hope that my music is appreciated by some people as a good thing, whether it makes any real difference or not.

Put 'er there, Mr. Lovett.

Steve Lukather, outside Dupar's Restaurant, LA 1987

Steve Lukather

Attila the Hun of Guitar

xxxxxxxxxxxxxxxxxxxxxxxxxxxxxxxxxxxxxxxxxxxxxxxxxxxxxxxxxxxxxxxxxxxxxxxxxxxxxx

How was scoring Dune *with you and your Toto bandmates?*

[laughs] Well, the best thing about doing that film was working with David Lynch. I'm a big fan of his, and he a crazy mother. He looks real normal and straight-ahead, but what goes on in his mind—it was a bizarre experience. It's a tough business, and it's unusual to have five guys sitting around writing film cues.

Can you remember the first music you made?

I must have been around nine years old. I had a band and we used to play Grand Funk Railroad and Beatles tunes. We'd set up at this apartment building down by the pool and just blast. My father bought me the *Meet the Beatles* album when I was about seven years old, and I was sold. Then he bought me a guitar and people showed me a couple of chords and it's something I never grew out of. I was always playing in bands of some kind or another.

Who's the angriest guitarist in the world?

That's hard to say, these days. I'd have to say Hendrix was probably the angriest guitar player. He had a tremendous influence on me.

Why is he so important?

He was doing stuff before synths and sampling. He was making his guitar talk. I don't mean wah-wah pedal stuff, and all the bogus albums that have come out since his death. I'm talking about the records where he had creative control. The first four studio albums had something. There was a magic, an aura that hasn't been matched. There are guys who can play fast, but he had a soulfulness.

Who is the Picasso of guitar?

I could weld four or five players together and there would be Picasso. But Hendrix comes closest. He was painting pictures with sound and he wasn't copying anybody.

Do you know any interesting business tricks?

Yeah, my old accountant pulled one—stole all my money. I made the mistake of giving him power of attorney and the money just disappeared. My advice is to sign all your own checks and don't trust anybody.

What music would you like played at your funeral?

God, what a morbid question. Let's see—"I Gotta Be Me." And I'd like to have some whoopee cushions so when they sat down after the eulogy, there'd be a chorus of raspberries.

David Lynch, Asymmetrical Studios, LA 1998

David Lynch, LA 1998

(L-R) John Neff and David Lynch as "Blue Bob," LA 1999

David Lynch

No Coloring Books Allowed

✕✕

You played trumpet—for how long?

Four years. And then they made me join a marching band and I quit. You know, when you read music, there is a part of your brain that shuts down. It's like coloring within the lines—you don't take off. My mother refused to give me coloring books as a child. She probably saved me, 'cause when you think about what a coloring book does is completely kill creativity. In a way, I really feel bad that I learned the trumpet.

Diet. People know that you have some peculiar eating habits, like you had a Bob's Big Boy milkshake every afternoon at 2:30 for seven years.

Yes, I go for a long time on one thing [laughs]. Now, I have a choice of two different things for breakfast: a sausage patty, four strips of bacon and scrambled eggs, or a banana with peanut butter. At lunch, I have a salad of tomatoes, goat cheese, half a can of tuna fish and olive oil, a little bit of vinegar and some salt. And then at dinner I have cashew nuts and parmesan cheese, and sometimes little strips of chicken.

And that's it?

That's it.

Did you ever lose anything?

That reminds me of a story. I was in London, working on *The Elephant Man*. It was a five-day-a-week shoot. So I would be home on the weekends. This was a Sunday, and my wife, at the time, was going into town on the train. I was home alone. Somewhere in the morning I get a call from her and she's gotten off the train. She's sobbing. She's lost her ring and I said, "Well, I know where it is." I walked upstairs, went into the bedroom, put my hand between the mattress and box springs. Went in up to my shoulder, got the ring, came back down and said, "I've got it right here." And that's a true story.

Do you get a lot of your ideas from your dreams?

No. Hardly ever. Couple of times.

Do you have any interesting business tips for people in the music business?

Keep your eye on the donut and not on the hole.

Do you believe in magic?

Sure.

Do you believe in rock-and-roll?

Yeah!

Henry Mancini, LA 1988

Henry Mancini

Score Points

Those sessions for "Peter Gunn"—did that music catapult you into new fame?

That was it. The turning point.

Did you have any idea that the "Peter Gunn" theme would kick off like it did?

No idea at all.

And the music lives on with every high school marching band…

Oh, yeah. It's an anthem. We all like to write anthems, and I've had a couple. Just take the bass figure. You've got six or seven notes there and it never changes during the whole piece. Any kid playing guitar can pick that out. He can play and look real good if he plays bass with the band. And the melody is very simple and there is only one chord in the whole piece. What more could you give the world?

And it came back recently with **The Art of Noise…**

Yes, there are a lot of recordings. We've had more infringements—more people have tried to rip that off than anything I've every written. That and *The Pink Panther.* There are continual lawsuits. People think they can use it because they know it so well.

Like it's public domain…

No, no…it's not public domain yet, not for a while [laughs].

Did you ever have premonitions that your themes would become so universally classic?

No, even "Moon River"—nice song, great lyric. But no idea. In reverse, I've had some things which I felt had everything going for them and nothing happened. You really never know.

Do you have any gripes with the scoring industry—anything you would like eliminated?

Well [laughs], first you shoot most of the directors and producers. That's a sweeping statement, and there are some that are sweethearts, that are a big asset, and then there are those that are afraid. You are messing with their baby and you better not put the wrong clothes on it.

Is that a crushing experience when you come up with something that you feel is lovely, and perfect, and you get shot down?

Yeah, but then there's the next case, judge. I don't take it personally and I consider where it's coming from. Many times when you get shot down, it's the right decision. Sometimes you get shot down by your friends, too, you know. A composer isn't the end all and the final judge of what is right for the picture. Sometimes the people who make the picture have an instinct. I always leave the door open.

Rose Mann-Cherney, Record Plant Recording Studios, LA 1984

(L-R) Composer Harold Faltermeyer, Rose Mann-Cherney, Herbie Hancock, Record Plant Recording Studios, LA 1989

Rose Mann-Cherney

Rose of the Record Plant   1984

What was the first session you booked?

Oh, God… The Eagles' *Hotel California*. This studio brings in a lot of business by itself, so the trick is to keep them in and take care of them. That's why our overhead is so high.

What do you do when you have a scheduling problem and have to dump somebody?

You mean like when my boss made a double booking with Neil Diamond and Rod Stewart last year? I buy the time back. I just tell them I'm in trouble and one of them gives in and I give them their day. If I mess up, I have to pay, but most of the people that record here work it out amongst themselves.

What was the worst disaster at the studio?

The fire we had in 1978. Studio C went down in 40 minutes. That's when you know that you have friends. It was in the days when we had a lot of velvet and cushy stuff in the studio. Some sparks flew and it just went "poof." The first thing we did was to pull tapes from the library. Three artists had just finished their projects that weekend and there were masters everywhere. It was terrible. Steve Stills was there—in fact, he was the first person to work in Studio C when it opened and he was the last. He got all his guitars out, but Russ Kunkel's drums melted. We lost thousands of dollars in Telefunkens. It was like a night train and everybody just pulled for 24 hours. A few weeks later, the owner Chris Stone called a meeting and said he couldn't afford to pay anybody. We all worked together for three or four weeks without paychecks.

The first time I visited the Record Plant, Stevie Wonder was working here.

You know, when I first went to work here, I thought Stevie Wonder was lying about being blind.

Why, because he knew how to get around the studio so well?

Yes, that's true, but he was playing air hockey.

He could play by the sound?

Yeah, he could. That damned air hockey game—this was in '76. That's when I used to come to the studio at eight in the morning. It drove me nuts, because I'd walk in and the place would be going like it was five in the afternoon. We had a lot of good sessions, a lot of good times. We still have them. You go through generations of people about every three or four years, and every generation says it's not like it used to be.

Ray Manzarek, LA 1997

Ray Manzarek

What is the major difference between recording in the '60s and now?

More tracks. Nothing has really changed in the creation of music since that first guy started beating on a log and that woman found a reed with holes and blew in it and got a whistling sound. The art of making music has always been exactly the same. You immerse yourself in the energy of the universe and pluck your note. How you actually physically record it—who cares?

Why has the music of The Doors endured?

The Doors represent a kind of freedom, an alternative to today's restricted world that we live in. After the explosion of consciousness in the '60s, in which we were able to bring our consciousness up and see things outside of ourselves, we're now locked up inside ourselves again as individuals and as a society. The Doors were free and The Doors hint that you can be free.

What's the most important thing you learned form Jim Morrison?

Table manners. Not to lift up your slice of bread and butter it. Leave your bread on the bread plate. And don't use your coffee spoon to take the sugar out of the sugar bowl. That's why you have a separate spoon.

Business advice?

Business is very, very easy. Give everybody their fair share and don't drive yourself crazy over nickel and dime stuff in your contracts. Get your percentage, get some front money, recording costs, and you're outta there. You could try to do what The Doors did. We made a four-way split. Morrison, God bless him, said, "There's only four guys in the band. We all do something but then we put it into The Doors mind and out come Doors songs. Let's just make it a four-way split." And it's been easy ever since.

Can you recall one ridiculous studio anecdote?

Well, it's not ridiculous, but Jim hosed down the studio after we recorded "Light My Fire." We were just smoking and burning, and afterwards he hadn't had enough. He came back to the studio and it was closed. I think he had ingested a certain hallucinogenic substance that was legal at the time, LSD. He climbed the fence, sneaked into the studio, there wasn't a soul in the place, and a red work light was on. In Jim's hallucination, that red light made the place look like it was on fire. He saw flames and went right to the hose and hosed down the recording studio. He put the fire out, turned the water off, and left in peace. He had done his job.

Ziggy Marley, LA 2003

(L-R) Ziggy Marley, producer/engineer Ross Hogarth, David Lindley, Glenwood Place Recording Studios, LA 2003

196

Ziggy Marley

Spirit in Balance   2003

◇◇◇

How do you keep balanced in a business that disrupts so many people's lives, trying to keep their balance in a world of money and greed?

I keep myself balanced by not troubling myself with things, not worrying. There's more important things—like my spirituality and my faith in God, which is more important than anything else. I'm just an easygoing type of person, and I'm not worried about problems, like if the record is taking some time to make. I just want to make music. That's just my personality—I'm just cool and I don't let shit trouble me. I can look on both sides of the picture, from the outside looking in on what's going on, and I can look from the inside out. That's just my personality, I think. There is no technique in how I keep balanced.

Do you think some of your balance comes from Jamaica?

I really don't know. In astrological signs I am a Libra, which is the scales, which is balance. I've found that to be my personality, but I don't know what brings this balance.

It seems to me that there is a thread connecting you to your father's great spirituality and music—is it something with that as well?

Definitely, because his spirit is still in touch with me. And his inspiration is still ongoing, so definitely his spirit helps me keep that balance, too. 'Cause his life was a great example, and his music is a great example for me—just who he was, you know?

If you were a musical instrument, which would you be?

I think I would be like some drum, an African drum. The vibration would come from the drum, and I'm kinda like the vibration—like some midrange that goes to your middle, your solar plexus—those kind of drums. I'm like the drums—the drums have a very strong spirit.

Your real name is David, but I heard you got your nickname Ziggy because you liked David Bowie when you were a kid?

Oh, no, no—somebody said that a long time ago, but that was not true. In Jamaica, everybody has a name that is not the name on a piece of paper. Ziggy comes from football, from soccer—we zig, when we move, we're zigging around, like a zigzag.

How would you like to be remembered in history?

I don't really care. For me, the memory of me is not important. The important thing is to love each other. I don't care about people remembering me, 'cause when I'm gone I really don't care about that.

The Mars Volta with engineer Dave Schiffman, LA 2003

(L-R) Jon Theodore, Cedric Bixler Zavala, Omar Rodriguez-Lopez, Jeremy Michael Ward, LA 2003

The Mars Volta

Not at the Drive-in

How long has Mars Volta been together?
OMAR RODRIGUEZ-LOPEZ: A little over a year.

But Cedric and you have known each other for a long time?
OMAR: Almost 11 years.

You had a band before Mars Volta?
OMAR: Maybe.

What is the difference with Mars Volta?
OMAR: This one is fun! Just kidding. This is a lot looser, a lot more interesting for us, and there are a lot of different areas we are going into now.

When did you start playing guitar?
OMAR: When I was 15, but I started with bass when I was 12. At 15 I realized I needed more strings.

And Cedric the singer—do you play any instruments?
CEDRIC BIXLER ZAVALA: I play drums, and sometimes bass and guitar.

Who is your main inspiration as a rock vocalist?
CEDRIC: Bjork.

Omar, who is your main juice from the past?
OMAR: Larry Harlow, a piano player for a salsa orchestra.

But he doesn't play guitar.
OMAR: No, but he's the reason I play guitar.

What is it like recording in this haunted house?
CEDRIC: We really don't go up to that certain room at the top where the bell tower is. That one has a weird feeling to it. Every time I go up there to show somebody, there are certain doors that are open, leading to this attic. I keep closing them, and they are always open when I go back up there. Weird. And we did find the catacombs the other day in back of the house that lead to Houdini's old mansion nearby.

Are you scared?
OMAR: I think the first couple of nights we were, but now we're comfortable—except when you're all alone, it's strange.

Is this the first time you have recorded like this in a house?
OMAR: For Cedric and myself, it's the second time. We recorded once in a canyon in Malibu. For us, it's better than a studio, the only way to go. Studios are so stale. And an environment like this is much up our alley.

George Martin, LA 1988

photo by Hideo Oida

George Martin

The Fifth Man

Early in your career you produced hundreds of comedy records…

Yes, and I did a lot of spoken word records, a lot of musicals. I did children's records, and all of the Peter Sellers records, and worked with *Beyond the Fringe*—Jonathon Miller, Dudley Moore, Allen Bennet. I also produced the team of Flanders and Swann, which was a mixture of speech and music. In those days, this was pre-Beatles, I became known as the comedian's producer, as a producer of funny records.

Did those early comedy sessions influence your later work?

It was bound to, I suppose. You do what you do and you do it in the way which you think is right. So you build up a technique over the years and I suppose a lot of that rubbed off in things like *Sergeant Pepper* and *Yellow Submarine*.

*You were the first producer I ever met, Abbey Road was the first studio I saw, and my first session was the night Ringo was tuning in the BBC for a track on "I am the Walrus." Later on in Scotland, I was studying **King Lear** and realized the song has lines from Act IV of the play. That night, John seemed to be running the show. Ringo was reading a comic book and tuning the radio and John had his hands on those big gear shift faders. The next year, 1968, I was invited back for "Revolution 9." George was raiding the EMI tape vaults, John was with Yoko by this time, I learned about splicing, and there was a flurry of activity with huge tape loops running across the room. Was there a period of change, of participation, for you as a producer?*

Yes, the accent changed, but both occasions you mention were when John was experimenting. John liked playing around, but he was not a very good technician. He couldn't handle equipment all that well, but he was always trying to get new and different effects. Now the *King Lear* thing you're talking about—we used some of that on the record.

Yes, tuned right in off the radio and mixed in.

"I am the Walrus" was at the mixing stage when you were there. It had already been recorded with cellos and horns and so on. "Revolution 9" was a ménage of sounds. John was moving the faders around during "Walrus" because someone had to do something at random.

After The Beatles ended, John went on to do even wilder things. He didn't have the great toyshop at Abbey Road, but he used to bring me cassettes. "George, can we make a record out of this?" It would be Yoko screaming in a bag, and you know, that was the kind of thing you were seeing in those sessions. In fact, it was in its infancy there.

George Massenburg, The Complex recording studios, LA 1985

George Massenburg

Solid Transparency   1985

❮XXXXXXXXXXXXXXXXXXXXXXXXXXXXXXXXXXXXXXXXXXXXXXXXXXXXXXXXXXXXXXXXXXXXXXXXXXXXXXXXXXX❯

What are you now? An engineer, a producer, an electronics designer, a visionary?
Visionary? I'm not so sure, because my ideas are evolutionary rather than revolutionary. But I am most of these other things every day.

What are you most proud of—your equalizer?
Not necessarily proud. I didn't really design the parametric equalizer—I built it. It was an idea that was waiting to happen, waiting for the right kind of amplifier and the right application. What I'm proudest of is the fact that it survived when people said you couldn't make an equalizer without steps. When I first started showing it in 1968, they said it couldn't work—it didn't have detents. I'm proud of the fact that technology prevailed.

A major contribution...
Not at all. It was evolutionary—a circuit that was waiting for the right kind of op-amp. Francis Darwin said that the person who is recognized isn't the inventor but the person who convinces the rest of the world. My first console had parametrics, and a free group switching system. You could press an input and an output and do assigning. People thought it was a terrible idea at the time, but now, it's common. We did the *Feets Don't Fail Me Now* album on that console with Little Feat.

What is the quality of greatness in recording?
What I listen for is transparency, where the idea moves from its inception to the listener with the least amount of forces impeding it.

As if you were really there?
But it's all an illusion. The whole idea is creating an illusion, taking the idea—the spark—and making it come alive for a listener sitting at home in Davenport, Iowa.

Do you have any idiosyncrasies?
I'm perverse—if there is an easy way to do something, I will choose it last.

How can all this technology truly improve the human condition?
In the same way that the arts do. It's a mechanism that allows us to observe ourselves, a reflection of our politics, our daily lives. It helps show us at our best and our worst, and pushes us to develop ourselves. Music has such power to make the best of life. The future lies in dealing with each other through knowledge and wisdom.

Steve Miller

photo by Kim Smith Miller

Steve Miller

Soar Like a Joker   1984

XXXXXXXXXXXXXXXXXXXXXXXXXXXXXXXXXXXXXXXXXXXXXXXXXXXXXXXXXXXXXXXXXXXXXXXXXXXXXXX

What is it about Les Paul that sets him apart from other musicians?
He's a designer, an electrician, a brilliant mind.

You met him when you were quite young, weren't you?
I was around five years old. I remember Les, and Mary Ford very well. It's well known that he was in the forefront of electric guitar and recording. I learned about multitracking in 1948—I knew that Mary Ford could sing with herself three times and I understood how it was done.

He used to play at a club my dad used to go to. We used to go down with my dad's tape recorder and they became friends. My dad made him a Plexiglas pickguard for his guitar. I saw it as show biz, but Les was my first taste of something that was really fun. It was always exciting when we could go to see him play. He was a great comedian, too.

How did you land your first record deal?
My first record deal was the only record deal I ever made—with Capitol. I was in the right place at the right time—San Francisco—and I had a good band.

Why do you think you became one of the handful of musical heroes of the psychedelic generation?
It took a lot of people to make that movement happen—people like promoters Chet Helms and Bill Graham, bands like The Jefferson Airplane, Quicksilver Messenger Service, Big Brother & the Holding Company, The Steve Miller Band. It was a social phenomenon and I was able to take part, and add to it by having a good musical organization. The music was the vehicle for the social phenomenon.

Who's the most amazing talent you've ever worked with?
Chuck Berry—he was like a gazelle; he was that delicate playing onstage.

When you think music in your mind, do you hear it played on a certain instrument?
Usually my voice. I hear things in three-, four-, five-part harmonies.

What instrument do you compose on?
Guitar and piano—and voice.

If you could be any woman, who would it be?
Somebody who is really happy—Ella Fitzgerald.

Are you as successful as you would like to be?
I'm more successful in some ways than I ever thought I would be, and I'm not as successful as I would like to be in the overall picture of my life [laughs]. I can see room for a lot of improvement.

Robert Moog, Anaheim, CA 1997

Robert Moog

Still Synthesizing After All These Years 1984

How did it all start?

I built theremins all through college and in 1963 I was exhibiting them at a music teacher's convention. I met Herb Deutsch, a professor at Hofstra University, and he asked me if I knew anything about electronic music. He invited me to attend one of his concerts—my first real exposure to this type of music. Early in 1964 we got together for a few weeks of experimentation—I built things and he tried them out. Out of those few weeks came the basic idea for the electronic music synthesizer.

What did electronic instruments consist of when you came on the scene?

Anything that people could get their hands on: tape recorders, laboratory oscillators—anything electronic that could make a sound.

Did you put these elements together into one instrument?

That was part of it, to rationalize the components and then to introduce the concept of voltage control—the use of an electrical voltage to change some part of the sound. If you used a keyboard, it produced the voltage that could change the pitch, the loudness, the tone color, or half a dozen other things. These were the building blocks. You had one module—one circuit that made a waveform, another circuit that filtered it, a third that shaped the loudness, and then you had a keyboard with maybe a ribbon controller and you could interconnect these things. The voltage from one controlled the other and you built on that to make a complex sound.

When did the instrument bearing your name make its first appearance?

The first public showing of the prototype modules was at the AES Convention in New York in 1964. I was just a graduate student and didn't know what the hell I was doing. I guess it was a company—we took a few orders. We had modules in handmade boxes that cost about $200 apiece.

What is the basic contribution you have made to electronic music?

I don't think there's anything basic. I was one of the first to put it all in a box so that everything worked together. I explored and exploited the use of voltage control. I guess the single thing that accounts for the success is that I pointed the development toward the use of keyboards and the making of sounds that turned out to be popular. The Mini-Moog was just a distillation of the early modular synthesizers, with convenience and a sound that became a standard.

Synthesis is an appropriate term for what you did…

We started using the word "synthesizer" three years after we began in 1967. We picked the word because synthesis means to create something from component parts. That's how you think of sound when you use a modular synthesizer. Each module corresponds to a part of the sound that you control individually.

(L-R) Bob Mothersbaugh, Bob Casale, Mark Mothersbaugh, Mutato Muzika Studios, LA 2000

Bob Mothersbaugh, LA 2000

Bob Mothersbaugh, LA 2000

Bob Mothersbaugh

Devolving Guitar

×××

What did you learn from your brother Mark?

Hard to say. I'm sure I've learned a lot from my older brother, but there are things I wouldn't tell ya about what he taught me as a kid. He can look at you with a straight face and you don't know if he's telling the truth, or lying, or being funny, or making fun of you. I can't do that stuff very well. I remember we used to go down to the basement where all the dirty clothes were piled up. We had a little 45 rpm record player and we'd lay on the pile of clothes and he'd make me listen to The Kinks.

Do you know any interesting business tricks?

Nope.

You mean you just keep getting screwed over and over again?

Well, I seem to be a very lucky guy. Most of the time I come out on top, and I don't know how or why. I'm an honest person— which is kinda bad in business. Just lucky, I guess.

What was your most ridiculous experience on tour?

Actually, one happened before we were touring. We were playing at The Crypt in Akron, back in 1976. Somebody in the band found these giant safety pins, like the kind girls wore on their plaid skirts. We thought we could use 'em with towels and look like we were wearing diapers onstage. We went out and played two songs and the novelty wore off and we had to stand up there with these stupid diapers on for another hour and a half in front of all 30 of our friends.

And later, we played the Nebforth Festival in England, 1978, and we didn't have any roadies. We set up our equipment, ran backstage and changed into our yellow suits, and came out and played—but the power we plugged into was 110 volts and we had 220 volt equipment, so all the amps sounded like transistor radios. That's as loud as they would get. We had to play in front of a couple of hundred thousand people and all you could hear was the vocals and the drums. There was no stopping to fix things [laughs]. We were sandwiched in between Molly Hatchett and The Atlantic Rhythm Section, so it was the wrong crowd to begin with. They hated us. Luckily we were on a stage about 75 feet high so the stuff that people threw at us couldn't hit us.

Any advice for getting a good start in the music business?

[laughs] Have an uncle or a dad that owns a record company. Save up a lot of money for a good lawyer. And—maybe learn how to play an instrument?

Mark Mothersbaugh, Mutato Muzika Studios, LA 1997

Mark Mothersbaugh

Mutato Muzika   1997

What's the first record you bought?

The first single I bought was "Itsy-Bitsy, Teeny-Weenie, Yellow Polka-Dot Bikini," and in retrospect it doesn't really hold up all that well. At the age of 12, I bought my first album at Woolworth's after seeing The Beatles on Ed Sullivan. The album I found was a cheaper knock-off by The Buggs. I got it home and I didn't recognize any Beatles songs. One track pissed me off so much it eventually inspired the nasty Devo song "You Got Me Bugged."

Who were your heroes when you were a lad?

Without a doubt, The Beatles and The Rolling Stones. Music had just been a tool of torture and control in my life up until I was 12. I was watching *The Ed Sullivan Show* and when I saw The Beatles, music became something that was really great. I practiced Beatles songs and for a long time I fantasized that I was the fifth Beatle. When each one needed to take a break while onstage, they would just nod at me and I would jump up and fill in without missing a beat.

The Beatles also caused a depression when my friend Ronnie Wyzinski and I bought their sheet music. He played accordion, I played a little Spinet organ, and we worked on "Hard Days Night" for about a week, but somehow it just didn't sound right. I felt that I had spent six years learning how to play an instrument that was useless and sounded stupid, corny, and square. Then I saw John Lennon on TV playing a Vox Continental portable organ. It was totally cool—he even used his elbow to play. I just went wild. The Beatles were the ones who really turned me on to music.

What instruments did you move on to?

Around 1969, I met these ex-football playin' acid munchin' Vietnam vets and they wanted to start a band, so I joined and we drove to Chicago from Akron and they bought me a souped up B-3. My second piece of gear was one of the first Mini-Moogs. We actually drove to Buffalo because we didn't know you could order them. I met Dr. Moog at the factory and the rest is Devolution.

Could you continue your creative work without computers?

Absolutely. I really got into computers with hesitation. Having no computers would greatly affect what I do now. My music might sound better, but there would be a lot less of it.

Advice to teenagers wishing for a career in music?

Do one thing really, really good.

Graham Nash and Stanley Johnston, Record Plant
Recording Studios, LA 1991

Graham Nash

Were you musically inclined as a child?

Yes, I was. Allan Clarke and I met when I was five years old and we started to sing together immediately. I don't know why, but we were singing school prayers, and harmonized in school choirs, minstrel shows. Then in the late Fifties, Skiffle music came to England via Lonnie Donegan from America. Skiffle was a simple form of folk music, basically three chords. And it was fast, and easy, and it was fun. We got into Skiffle in a big way.

Then with the coming into our lives of The Everly Brothers, Elvis Presley, Jerry Lee Lewis, Buddy Holly, Fats Domino and The Platters, Gene Vincent, etc., we began to really realize that, A—we needed drums and bass, B—that this two-part singing which we had been doing for many years was coming of age. So we found ourselves in the early '60s forming a band called The Hollies, with basically Allan and myself singing lead, occasionally three-part with Tony Hicks. We cut our first hit record in 1963 and I haven't looked back since.

By 1968, The Hollies were behind you and Crosby, Stills & Nash was ahead of you. Singles had been the style of the record business and your forming CSN was around the time of album domination, FM radio.

Well, *Sergeant Pepper* had helped change that a lot. But it began to be obvious that the art form of albums was much more interesting than singles. The singles were like ads for the albums. I knew when I sang with David and Stephen what it was I wanted to do. We also knew we had tremendous song potential because we were three reasonably strong writers, young—naive maybe—but interesting.

Our first record was brought out in a time of pre-heavy metal, stacks of Marshalls. We came out with this acoustic feeling album and it threaded right the way through everything and made its mark. We knew when we left the studio with that two-track master that we had a hit record.

*You've also had solo success, such as **Songs for Beginners**, which still sounds so fresh and alive.*

I was very pleased with that record. I think I'm most pleased over its longevity. I get kind comments from people all the time about it being one of their favorite albums. I've tried to think what it was about that album that was so attractive and I can't really figure it out. I think it was very simple, very straightforward, and it had a very live feeling. There are some good songs, but I've never been really able to pin what it was about that album. I'm kinda glad, because I certainly don't want to repeat it. But I do wonder what it was that made it so attractive.

John Neff, LA 2003

John Neff, Asymmetrical Studios, LA 2001

David Lynch and John Neff as "Blue Bob," Asymmetrical Studios, LA 2002

John Neff

Arts and Science

What did you learn from your experiences with Walter Becker?
Walter wanted everything available at all times, as does any studio owner, but the engineer is to disappear into the woodwork. I produced and engineered many albums on my own there, but on his and Donald Fagen's CDs, creative input was frowned upon. We did some experimenting in the beginning. I think the most fun was the after-session late night "jams" in the studio. On the technical side, working with those guys, and with Roger Nichols, was "graduate school." As Walter put it, "Donald slices a finer hair."

Can you recall the first time you burned a CD?
Yes. People sent us an amazing number of tapes and CDs. Dropped them in the mailbox, threw them over the fence, slid them under the door. Walter wouldn't usually listen to them, but once in a while we'd toss them in the microwave and turn it on. That's a good show.

Do you know any interesting business tricks?
Yes, Walter taught me the Pretzel Logic—Lose money on every deal and make up for it in volume.

Who is the most amazing artist you've worked with?
David Lynch. He is a true Renaissance Man. There isn't a moment he isn't thinking. We go down some twisted roads, not everything works out, but man, do we find some interesting sounds! For instance, on "Blue Bob," he had me sing through his director's megaphone, into a beautiful tube U-47, with only multiple delays coming back into the headphones. No dry signal at all. You try that sometime…

What makes a great producer?
Hmmm… I have this thing about producers. Some shouldn't be let out of their cages. But, as a producer, listening to the material is the most important thing. The song or piece will speak to you. It will tell you what it wants to be. Your job is to carefully shape that, with the tools you have at hand.

How would you like to be remembered in history?
As someone who tried it all. It's funny—I was never huge at anything, but my education has never ended. Curiosity is a good thing.

Any advice for getting a good start in the music business?
Do what you love. Love what you do. Don't take no for an answer (except from me). Work your craft. Hone your skills. Make people need your efforts and enthusiasm.

Willie Nelson, Saratoga, CA 1991

photo by Susana Millman ©1991

Willie Nelson

Deep in the Heart   1992

You used to be in the Air Force—what was your job?
I went to military school to study radar, but I got out of there before I had a chance to become famous as a radar mechanic.

Was working as a radio announcer your inroad to the entertainment world?
It was just sort of a way to make a living until I could get back out there playing the guitar.

Did you start playing the guitar as a kid?
Yes, that was the first thing I picked up. My grandparents were music teachers, and my older sister knew music real well. She played the piano and I played the guitar, so I learned a lot from just the two of us playing together.

You've been compared with Sinatra, even called "The Sinatra of Country." In your mind, why is that?
I think it has a lot to do with the phrasing. I always admired his phrasing ability.

Is it true that you once rushed into a burning ranch house in Tennessee to save your favorite guitar, "Trigger"?
Actually, I went in there to get my stash that I had left. I think I made up the story about the guitar.

Who is the most amazing artist that you have worked with in your lifetime?
Leon Russell.

What is the biggest mistake of your life?
Oh, I don't know… I really don't know. I hope that I've already made it [laughs]. I couldn't tell you what it was at the moment, but the list is long.

What advice would you give to a youngster who wanted to follow in your footsteps?
Just play every chance you get, for anyone who will listen. Keep doing that until you get done with what you want to get done.

Have you had any lucky breaks in your life?
If you believe in luck, I am the luckiest guy alive. I have a saying that I'll take credit for: "Fortunately, we are not in control." That's really the truth. We sit around and think what we would like to happen, but if we have to make it happen—it's impossible. You just have to believe that it is going to happen—fortunately, we are not in control. If you get out of the way and let it happen, most of time it will. We get in our own way more than anybody else does.

Rupert Neve, Record Plant Recording Studios, LA 1986

Rupert Neve

Sound and Vision

Looking back on all your years in the industry, what do you think your most significant contribution has been?
Well, it's hard to say that there's any one contribution. I think I fell into the professional field in the early '60s at a time of opportunity which has never existed since. It was just when the idea of stereo was taking root. In the late '50s, the record companies began recording everything 2-track stereo in case stereo really caught on. The studios were finding this to be a very expensive thing to do, and very impractical. They were looking for some better ways of doing it. Big companies were producing audio consoles in a very stylized format. There was Siemens of Austria, and Neumann, and one or two other German firms. There was PYE and EMI in England, and one or two firms over here in America. The time was ripe for someone to come in who was willing to be flexible. If the customer said, "We want to do it this way—is it possible to do this, that, and the other?"—there was mutual stimulation. I would get excited by what was wanted and would add, "Yes, and we can also do some other interesting things." Customers became excited. The big companies couldn't operate like this. I think that was the beginning—it opened up a new area in the audio industry. This doesn't answer your question directly, but I found that there was a new market and I, if you like, was able to stimulate that market—and the market stimulated me.

Although you've been involved with such products as speakers and recorders, it's consoles that people know you for...
Yes, we started more or less willy-nilly, and we made a console. The first one was for Recorded Sound, Ltd. in London, 1961. It was a valve [vacuum tube] console and I think it took me six weeks to build this 10 into 2, with equalization on each channel, which was unheard of in those days. And we went on from there. People were asking, "These transistors—will they ever be as good as valves?" I just didn't know. I was an old valve man—well, a young valve man then. Transistors in those days were noisy, unreliable, and inclined to get into thermal runaway. With great trepidation, I started trying to use these transistors. After some months of messing around, we found that we could actually get good performance from some of them.

Can you describe that "eureka" moment when you were struggling with some sort of design and the solution appeared miraculously?
No, solutions don't appear miraculously. They are the result of a lot of hard work, a lot of burning the midnight oil, and a lot of intense frustration from doing it the wrong way until you find the right way.

Harry Nilsson, LA 1983

Harry Nilsson

The Beatles' Favorite Artist

How did you make that leap from being a bank teller to a singer/songwriter?

I wasn't a teller; I was in charge of a computer center for seven years at a bank. I dropped out of school in the ninth grade and became a theater user and then assistant manager of a theater. They closed the theater and I figured since I knew how to count money, I would get a job in a bank. I lied about my education on the application, but I did a super good job and ended up being in charge.

I also started hanging out with people on the fringe of the music business. I once saw an ad in the paper for turning songs into demos. I walked in and they asked what songs I had and I told them I thought they wanted someone to sing on demos. So they gave me a job at five dollars a demo and I got to meet people and have coffee with them. One day, a guy rushed into the office and he needed someone to sing a song real quick. I think the artist had died. The boss pointed at me, shrugged, and said "him." It was for Mercury Records and I wrote the B side. They never put out the record, but I was under contract for a year.

I used to work nights at the bank and I made a deal with someone who had an office who let me use it at night in return for washing the windows. I'd get off work from the bank at one in the morning, go to a bar and get tanked up, and then write a song a night in the office. One of the first songs I published was written there: "Without Her." "I spend the night in a chair thinking she'll be there, but she never comes…" that started my writing and I knew then that I would never write a bad song.

Who recorded your first song?

The New Christy Minstrels did "Travellin' Man," which I wrote with Scott Turner. That was the first time I got a royalty advance—five dollars.

I'm sure everyone is curious about the times you spent with John Lennon—how do you look back on those days?

Well, we were roommates here and there—a month and a half in New York, and about a month out here at the beach house while we were recording "Pussy Cats." We had the wildest assemblage of that part of history in that house—it makes the round table look like a toadstool.

You don't perform much these days, do you?

I've never performed professionally. I figure that people who are interested in the recording business have a right to make a living making records.

Jack Nitzsche, LA 1987

Jack Nitzsche

Scoring Success

What was it like working with Phil Spector?

I think Phil is the best record producer—no, I mean he is the *only* artist/record producer. He was firstly an artist. He knew what he wanted from me every time, and gave me lots of input for the arrangements. We had a way of working together that was easy and fun, because we were friends on top of everything.

Is there one record that established the famous "Wall of Sound"?

I think it happened gradually, and I can't remember when Phil started using that term. The sound just kept getting bigger and bigger. "Zip-a-dee-do-dah" was bigger than the one before, and "Then He Kissed Me" was bigger still. There was one record I remember with The Crystals, "Little Girl." When it was recorded, Phil used more echo than usual. Sonny Bono and others said that it had too much echo—it wouldn't get played on the radio. Phil said, "What's too much echo? What does that mean?" When does it become distasteful or offensive? I've always felt the same way myself. It hadn't been done before and people in the promotional side of the record industry felt that it was too different. But echo is like garlic. You can't get too much.

How did you make the transition from records to film scoring?

It really started with *Performance*, Nicholas Roeg's film starring Mick Jagger. I had been doing some work with The Rolling Stones for a few years before *Performance* was made. I played piano for The Stones and all sorts of things.

Mick flew me to London to see *Performance* and suggested we work together on the soundtrack. I asked him, "What do I need you for?" and he said, "Right." He took care of everything and made sure that I had the freedom to score the film. I was afraid that there might be trouble and I might not get paid, but Mick and the director made sure that all went smoothly.

How did you meet Neil Young?

Through Charlie Green and Brian Stone, who managed The Buffalo Springfield. They played me Neil's songs and I loved his work. Neil and I became friends and he would always play me his new songs. He wanted to leave The Springfield, because they didn't let him sing enough. So I helped him make a record called "Expecting to Fly." I did some arrangements for his first album, and also some producing. Then I came to a Crazy Horse rehearsal, played piano, went on the road with the band, and did some recording. I ended up moving to Northern California and lived on a ranch next door to Neil. This was around the time of the *Harvest* album and the tour of '73.

Do you have any advice for musicians?

Musicians shouldn't be playing on records if there isn't the energy and enthusiasm that you feel when you first start out. Be honest, you know?

Danny O'Keefe and artist Keiko Kasai, LA 1986

Danny O'Keefe

Good Time 1986

What does the average guy know about Danny O'Keefe?

If I mention "Good Time Charlie" to someone from the broad cross-section, he'll buy me a cup of coffee. It's good for something—a lot of tickets on a roll.

The song brought a sudden leap into the limelight?

They liked me. It's just that I haven't had anything else that was quite like that, something that people sat down and got. Maybe I've had some potential hits, but they've been so far apart. Everybody knows that particular song, but not so many know me. There's a club audience, but the song has an anonymity factor—it may have something to do with why the record still plays so well.

What is it that you find interesting in people?

A sense of confidence in who they are, whether it's a bricklayer, a sculptor—the title doesn't matter, it's that sense of self, which is an acquisition. That's the thing I value most in people.

Who has sung your songs?

Jackson Browne, Leon Russell, Elvis Presley, Cab Calloway, God bless his soul…

So you've touched some of the heroes of music.

Heroes that touched me, which is the great reward of being a song. "Good Time Charlie"—to a certain degree I am a one trick pony in the commercial world.

Is it a burden to live with?

No, it's a true joy, in uppercase, that someone like Cab Calloway, who lives in the mind like Blind Lemon Jefferson, Louis Armstrong, John Hurt—one of the pantheon of music's grandfathers—to have one of them be contemporary enough and think that my song was appropriate to their way of thinking. Lovely, lovely, lovely. And to have Elvis think that it was right for him…

What did you gain from your parents?

A whole DNA/RNA structure that is time coded, a time-based piece of hardware. One must always deal with that, as one deals with the gifts. My father's gift was a knowledge and a feeling for the world of flies and trout. He was a master at making split cane rods. To be able to make a fly that looks more interesting to the trout than the real thing, and to be able to case in a certain way—that skillful touch is the same, whether playing guitar or painting a picture.

You're a fighter, aren't you?

Yeah, but not necessarily a good one. Fighting, in the long run, is a matter of resilience—at least in the music business. It's how well you endure.

(L-R) Eddy Offord, Tony Kaye, Billy Sherwood, Chris Squire, Cherokee Recording Studios, LA 1991

Eddy Offord

Yes Man

You're most associated with Yes…
Along with Emerson, Lake and Palmer, I would say so.

Do you like that identification?
Yes, because that kind of music was very acclaimed for its sound—the clarity. That kind of music really lends itself to exploration for an engineer. Basically, there were a lot of different factions in Yes and they had contrary tastes and feelings about the music. I would try and channel all this high energy of wanting to do everything and act as a mediator, a referee, trying to figure out what ideas were good and which were bad.

When you heard Chris Squire's bass, it was the first time anyone had heard bass with high end on it. Before then, bass was more of a thumping thing. It wasn't the lead instrument that Chris Squire makes it.

What was it like working with John Lennon?
I recorded "Jealous Guy," "I Don't Want to Be a Soldier Mama," for the *Imagine* album. What happened is that I started the album out and it was going really well. It was a very magical experience for me, but I was so into the progressive rock thing at the time that I told John and Yoko that I couldn't continue on with the album because I had prior commitments. I started the album and then had to withdraw from the project.

Had you known John back in the early days?
I'd met him briefly at parties, but you never really get to know anyone that way. I didn't really get to know him until I started to work with him in the studio.

What was it like?
It was really great—he had a sixth sense and an awareness about him that you could feel. Although he hadn't gone to great schools or studied, and wasn't extremely sophisticated in terms of some things, he had this soul that just shone through everything. Yoko was really the intelligent one in the family—a smart lady, and a nice lady. I liked her, although I hated it when she sang.

Would you like me to leave that out?
No, not really. When we would have a break in the studio, John would say "Well, let's do some stuff with Yoko." She would go and scream into this mic while the band was playing. To me, it sounded pretty bad, you know? I'm sure she wouldn't mind me saying that, and I respect her as a person. I think John and Yoko were just made for each other. It worked extremely well. I know that some blame Yoko for The Beatles breaking up, but I don't really believe it. I think it was already over by then anyway.

Hugh Padgham, Brooklyn Recording Studios, LA 1990

Hugh Padgham

Engineering Life   1990

◈◈

Did you start off looking for a career in music?

Yes, I left school at 18 and always knew that I wanted to work in a studio. I come from quite a musical family and when I was at school I read science subjects and was also very interested in music. The amalgamation of the two equaled the recording studio. When I first saw a copy of *Studio Sound* and the consoles with all the knobs I thought, "That's the life for me." I also thought I wouldn't have to get up early in the morning, which I was never very good at.

When you're working on a project, recording and mixing, do you visualize the music?

Oh yeah, very much so. It's not so much I think of it in visual terms; I just get a concept when I hear a song. Almost immediately, I have a feeling of where I am going to put delays, or reverb—I just get a vibe and keep fiddling around until it equals what I'm thinking in my head.

Are there any exceptional artists you've worked with and felt they were overlooked?

Yes, I think a lot of projects are like that, because not everything you do becomes a hit. I'm very proud to work with Phil Collins, with Sting, and Peter Gabriel. I couldn't choose better people to work with, but I think that groups like XTC deserved greater recognition. Split Enz, to me, were one of the best bands ever.

The Police were really a breakthrough—a simple trio translated so well musically, so powerfully. In your mind, why did it have such a big impact?

Well, I don't think while you're in the studio you ever realize that you are doing something that might end up so special. I am just trying to relate the music to the recording medium. I think it was partly because I was the new boy on the scene, and Sting was writing songs that were somewhat more serious in terms of music and lyrics. Where I fit in was being able to understand what Sting was doing musically and it all worked out well.

Was it for you a new mature point in your engineering and producing career?

I think it was when I look back on it, but at the time, I was just trying to do the best job that I could. And usually I'm "shitting myself," you know? Especially when you're confronted with songs like "Every Breath You Take." You know it's a hit before you even start moving a fader up. On the other hand, I've made hit records which I didn't realize at all, at the time of recording.

For me, every day in the studio is a new day and I am going to learn something new. I think that's what keeps me going in this business—the fact that I don't know everything.

Andy Paley, LA 1995

Andy Paley

One Man Band Apart

1995

◇◇

Did you ever record with Phil Spector at the helm?

Yes, around 1976 I went to Goldstar, which is no longer there, and did a session with Hal Blaine, Ray Pohlman—you wouldn't believe it. I was playing upright tack piano. Barry Goldberg was playing a grand piano, and we had a third piano going. There was Ray Pohlman on electric bass. Jim Keltner and Hal Blaine—*two* sets of drums. We had a standup bass. Steve Douglas on horns. It was the guys, the Wrecking Crew, and I believe it was their last date together. It had the same beat as "The Doo-Ron-Ron," a rockin' song called "Baby Let's Stick Together." I think Dion did a slow version but ours was really kickin'. It never came out, but who knows, maybe it will some day.

Is it true that you wrote your first song when you were eight years old and it was actually recorded?

Yes, by a guy named Tom Glaser, who had a hit with "On Top of Spaghetti." Remember [Andy starts singing]—"On top of spaghetti, all covered with cheese. I lost my poor meatball when somebody sneezed." I did a little song called "The Little Porcupine" and asked my parents to send it in to him. I wrote down the chords and the lyrics and he cut it. It was really funny, because the liner notes said it was sung by Tom Glaser and the Porcupine, which was actually his voice speeded up. He's a folksinger, and used to be in a band with Pete Seeger called the Almanac Singers. I think he's still touring, doing concerts for kids.

Were you getting royalty checks as an eight-year-old?

No, this was a pretty small time thing. It wasn't a hit.

How did you learn to compose and write at such an early age?

Well, we had a piano in the house, and we're not talking about writing a symphony here [laughs].

Do you have any advice for musicians?

Yeah, don't be afraid to knock on doors. And go where the action is. Don't stay in the middle of nowhere and expect to be discovered, because it's not going to happen. Anybody can sit around and be a tortured artist in a garret someplace but that's not going to get you anywhere. You should go out and knock on doors, show people what you can do and go where the business is—New York, Nashville, London, L.A. I've met quite a few people who said, "I'm great and the world doesn't know it." Well, so what? Where's that gonna get you?

What's the biggest mistake of your life?

Sittin' around like one of those guys, thinking that I was great and that nobody cared about me, feeling sorry for myself. I used to do that—but I got over the hump and got to work.

(L-R) Richard Hill Parks, III and Van Dyke Parks, LA 1984

Van Dyke Parks, LA 1984

Van Dyke Parks and Stephen Stills, Record Plant Recording Studios, LA 1990

Van Dyke Parks

A Southern Gentleman in Hollywood   1982

What is your strongest characteristic as a human being?
That I am a musician, and I've taken the line of greatest resistance to health and happiness. I am not a mathematician, but I realize that music is the highest math and I would like to learn the language. My strongest characteristic is the application of what has been called virtue in playing the role. In the words of the bard, "The play's the thing."

What was the first piece of music you wrote?
I wrote down my first piece of music when I was seven, and it was called "March." There were two sections to the march, one was like a lion and one was like a lamb.

Ah, you were dealing with big themes.
I never told anybody about that, so that's a piece of news.

Who is the Van Gogh of music?
Van Halen.

Who is the Norman Rockwell?
I think I am.

Why do people think you're a bit of a crackpot or a genius?
Salvador Dali said in bringing to focus the imaginary line between insanity and genius, "The difference between myself and a madman is that I am not mad."

Do you have a fantasy lover?
Absolutely. I'm in love with the muse.

Do different musical instruments have different personalities?
Every instrument has a character. Instruments have in their invention the nature of a character and it is usually a national character. I use them very circumspectly, trying to observe the values that are in instruments. This is perhaps a very important question, because instruments have been very good to me.

Everybody is aware of the posture that the spirit provided in the invention of instrumentation, whether it be something that is born of a caste system, as you find with the steel drum—the way joy was triumphed—or whether it is instruments born of rustic masculine character that you find in the horns of chase—French horns for instance. Instruments sound masculine or feminine, or neuter. The flute has always been a great eunuch, but you find that it takes on new character with the language it employs. It is an elastic instrument. It's interesting to me how instruments take on a character representative of the collective personalities that gave birth to them.

Alan Parsons, Ocean Way Recording Studios, LA 2000

Alan Parsons

Dark Side of the Board   1995

×××

Who was your mentor at Abbey Road?

Geoff Emerick—not only was he The Beatles engineer, but he engineered for a large number of other acts and consistently got a great sound. I learned a lot from him.

Can you recall any specific pointers he gave you?

I especially remember his ability to set up a board before a session, before anybody had arrived, and then to push up the faders on the downbeat and everything would be there. That was a remarkable ability. I always feel that to be a true pro engineer, you should be able to achieve that, to anticipate and know what levels to expect out of what mics and how to record them and what EQ they are going to need. He used to do all the EQ in advance and just push the faders up and off we went. Amazing.

Any stories about your first session with The Beatles?

Well, it was literally just thrown at me. They were making their *Let It Be* film in their own studios at Apple and I tape-oped for the album, including the rooftop session. I couldn't believe it—there I was. One day I was making tea at Abbey Road and the next day I was working with The Beatles at their studio.

What was the next big leap in your career?

Well, I started to get work as an engineer, but the only big act I had was The Hollies. The next big step was getting the Pink Floyd gig. I mixed the *Atom Heart Mother* album, and that paved the way for *Dark Side of the Moon* and the first big name rock artist album project I got involved with. It was quite a good way to start, really. It wasn't an intensive recording period. We were out on the road as well during the recording. That was good experience, too. A lot of people don't realize I was their live sound engineer for the early days of *Dark Side of the Moon.*

What's your secret for a great mix?

One thing I do is perhaps a little unusual. Most people start with the bass and drums and I always leave that until last. I always balance up all the rhythm instruments to start with, apart from bass and drums. Then I will consider the drums separately and make sure that they sound good on their own. Then I will add those drums EQ'd and balanced to the mix I have of the other instruments. I think you can fool yourself into thinking that a track sounds great because everything in rock-and-roll is based on drums. If you take the drums away and it's still rocking, then you know you have something that is pretty reasonable.

(L-R) Les Paul and Mr. Bonzai

Photo with Mr. Bonzai by David Schwartz.

Les Paul, New Jersey, 1985

Les Paul

The Godfather of Modern Music

Was the harmonica your first instrument?
Yeah…

And didn't you build yourself a little brace?
Yes, I can show it to you. It's the original. I never changed it from the second I built it. It's made from a coathanger—never patented it and it's still one of the best harmonica racks around. You see, you can mount two harmonicas and change from one to the other without moving your hand, by turning them over with your chin. With two harmonicas you can play in four keys.

Can you remember those moments of invention, that "eureka"?
It was all accidental. You never can tell when it will happen. It just flashes in your mind. It goes all the way back to my first harmonica rack and my mother's piano rolls. As a kid I would punch new holes in the piano rolls and if I made a clam, I would put tape over the hole and move it over.

Did you ever think how similar that was to digital audio?
Not at the time, of course, but the thing that impressed me was that no matter how slow or fast you set the roll to go, the key remained the same. Analog changes pitch with the speed. It was in 1928 or '29, when I was about 12, that I invented my first recording machine. I built an electrical recording lathe and, to my amazement, I learned years later that the electrical application was patented by Bell Labs… in 1928, I believe. I was playing with the same thing and I thought that everybody was doing it. I was using a crank phonograph. I didn't have an electrical motor on there. I'm to this day very bad at patenting things.

Bing Crosby got me my first tape machine and immediately a light went on in my head to put a fourth head on it and make it do sound-on-sound. In '53, I devised this gem over here, which was my first multitrack recorder with tape loop echo and everything else I wanted.

Which of your inventions paid off the most?
The Les Paul guitar—but it took years to get it really going. Mr. Berlin, who was the head of Gibson, and I were having dinner shortly before his death and he asked me, "When you came to me with that broomstick with the pickup in 1941, did you ever believe in your wildest dreams that it was actually hockable?" Of course I did. I was the only one who believed it at the time, but I never got discouraged.

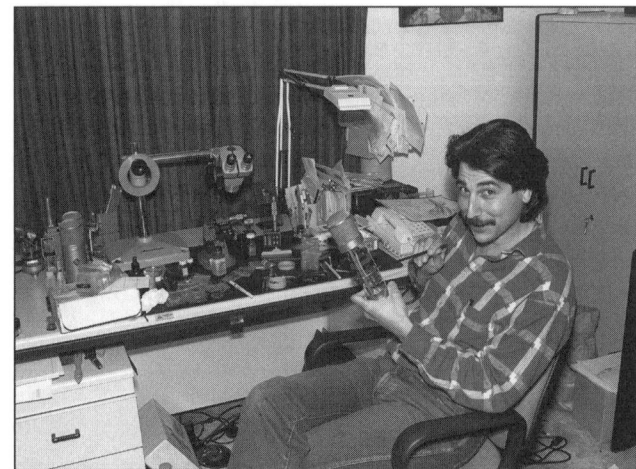

Stephen Paul, LA 1985

Stephen Paul

Dr. Microphone   1987

XXXXXXXXXXXXXXXXXXXXXXXXXXXXXXXXXXXXXXXXXXXXXXXXXXXXXXXXXXXXXXXXXXXXXXXXXX

Artists still hanker for that old sound of the great microphones…
Isn't that amazing? People are working with digital multitracks and computerized consoles loaded with all the latest high speed tricks, and what do they plug into this incredible state-of-the-art starship? They plug in a 30-year-old microphone. I love it.

The Neumann U-47 is really one of the legendary mics, isn't it?
Yep, it's a depth bomb. If you get one where the capsule is properly tensioned and in good condition, the bass response of that capsule is pretty awesome.

What does "condenser" mean in microphones?
It means capacitor. It means two parallel plates which aren't touching, and have so many coulombs of charge on them. There follows the well-known effect of surface area vs. spacing of the plates creating a capacitance, or the ability to hold a charge—if you then vary one of those parameters (the spacing, in the case of microphones), you will create a voltage drop in the circuit around it, which can be amplified and delivered to the outside world as sound.

You are a mic rebuilder, but also a modifier?
Yes. I am not so much a restorer as I am like the Carroll Shelby of microphones.

Who are some of the artists using your microphones?
Linda Ronstadt and Dolly Parton have used a very special U-67 I did for George Massenburg. Bryan Ferry is using one of my M-49s… Madonna… Elvis Costello has used a Telefunken AKG 251 of mine. Lindsey Buckingham, Ed Van Halen, Steve Perry, Jackson Browne—in fact, I did an AKG 414 for Dave Lindley and he told me that after the sessions at Jackson's house he wouldn't give the mic back to him.

How would you like to be remembered in history?
As an artist who cared for his work and tried to achieve perfection.

Do you believe in magic?
Oh, yes. We live in a vibratory universe. Our complete sensory experience is a vibration-based one. From the ditherings of quanta-packets which compose substance to the touch, to the force of the atmosphere—which, although invisible, is capable of lifting 600 tons of airplane off the ground, the phenomena of acoustics is so complex that no math can truly do it justice.

There is magic—produced by those who have learned to focus the will so completely that physical changes can be produced. This is the secret of great art, and I feel that microphones fall into this category.

Bill Payne, The Complex recording studios, LA 1988

Bill Payne

A Big Hand for Little Feat

1988

How did you get started in this business?

I've been playing in bands since I was about 15. I did my first recording session around '67—some psychedelic record. I joined Little Feat in 1969, and my first paying session was with a group called The Fraternity of Man. From there, Lowell George aided me in getting a couple of other recording gigs with groups like the GTOs [Girls Together Outrageously], which Frank Zappa produced. I guess the first major group I recorded with was The Doobie Brothers, who were not at the time a major act. I played piano on "China Grove."

What was the key to Lowell George and Little Feat's hold on their audience?

Well, I think with any group that has enigmatic qualities within the aspects of "cult" status, there is a feeling in the audience—"Hey, I know something that the rest of the world is not hip to."

Could you name some of the albums that you look back on fondly?

The Little Feat records, the Doobie Brothers albums, and certainly Bonnie Raitt—all of her records. There's Emmylou Harris, Nicolette Larson, Bob Seger, Jackson Browne, Linda Ronstadt. I enjoyed playing on an Art Garfunkel album called *Breakaway*, and working with Steve Cropper on *The Blues Brothers*.

What was your most exciting musical experience?

Performing in Amsterdam in 1974. The Rolling Stones, for the first time in a long time, came to see a group play. I couldn't believe that those guys would do that for us and that I was in the middle of it.

Did it boost your performance level?

Yeah, it did. There was a feeling of having arrived.

What music would you like played at your funeral?

"The Sounds of Silence," with a KABC talk show in the background.

Any advice for those aspiring to a career in music?

Judging from MTV, I would definitely suggest an acting course immediately. Forget the music—that's secondary. Deal strictly with perception—how you are perceived. If you're perceived as a musician, then indeed you are. That may not hold true for the '90s, so as a hedge you might take a few music lessons.

What would you do if you lost your hands?

Use my feet.

(L-R) Phil Ramone and Al Schmitt, Frank Sinatra *Duets* session, Capitol Recording Studios, LA 1993

(L-R) Broadcast audio supervisor Hank Neuberger, Phil Ramone, mixer John Harris, Effanel Music remote recording truck, Grammys®, LA 2000

Phil Ramone

Life in the Hit Zone

When was the first time you felt passionate about music?

I was three years old and a violinist in a restaurant just drove me crazy. It was gypsy music and I wanted to play.

How do you mic a tuba?

Carefully [laughs]. I mic it upstairs, at least three feet above the bell, using the ceiling as a reflector. I like an old AKG ribbon mic because it's not so sensitive to the "splat" and captures the warmth. The secret to making great music in the studio is to understand the instruments by studying them in natural settings.

What was your first hit as a producer?

I believe it was "Everybody's Talkin'" with Harry Nilsson for *Midnight Cowboy*.

How do you produce a hit?

It's about the song and the artist. Be true to the song. If everything is honest, there's a chance it will work. The "hit" comes after the fact.

What is the biggest mistake of your life?

Not continuing my studies in arranging, playing the keyboard, and practicing.

Could you give me one of your recording secrets?

If you are in trouble with a singer who is extremely sibilant and very soft, it might help to use a condenser mic with a ribbon or dynamic mic underneath. Mix the two for both depth and the cancellation of the sibilance. I tend to record many vocals with an omnidirectional mic, because it gives you scope in a nice little room and the cardioid pattern gives the artist more space to move around in.

Do you have any business tips?

No matter what you do, you must have a piece of paper. Even a letter of intent, which is witnessed and legal. When somebody loves you and thinks you are great, they will hand you all sorts of things in a verbal agreement. If things go wrong, your deal will change. I am very trustful of people, but it's important to be clear. It's perfectly okay to say, "Before we go to work on Monday, we need a proper piece of paper."

Any advice for surviving in the music business?

Don't lose your passion. Be faithful to your dream.

How does it feel being the Pope of Pop?

[laughs] It's okay, because whatever it refers to is flattering. I guess it has to do with my sensibilities in music, and if the works becomes popular, so be it. The moniker was intended to be humorous and it keeps me from taking myself too seriously.

(L-R) Anthony Kiedis, John Frusciante, Rick Rubin, "Spike," Flea, LA 1991

(L-R) John Frusciante, Flea, Anthony Kiedis, LA 1991

Red Hot Chili Peppers

The Blood Sugar Sex Magik House   1991

How has recording in this old haunted house affected the creative process?
ANTHONY: This has been the greatest recording experience of our lives. There is no comparison between a studio and making a record in this house. With studios we associate a sterile environment—impersonal, the anal-retentive, tight-ass quality that studios have. Here we have the most soulful house, living here and working here, never having to leave except to go out and pick up some girls for the night. We have a chef who comes and cooks her brains out all day long. It's the greatest—I feel like I'm living with my brothers. We all have our own bedrooms, and we get up for breakfast together—fruit, grits, fakin' bacon. We'll read the paper, have a chat, and then get down to making music.

By the time we start recording, we're happy, relaxed, and surrounded by all this beauty around the house. We can express ourselves without the inhibitions of a negative environment affecting the way we perform.

FLEA: Being able to hang out, be casual, wake up and roll tape is so beautiful. In the studio, you've got this feeling of "Okay, now we're rolling—this is it!" Working here just feels good—stimulating for our creativity. It's something we'll appreciate for the rest of our lives.

JOHN: Because the outside world isn't interfering with our work it's infinitely helpful. The outside world is always trying to fuck with creative people in one way or another. It might come out of a clock, or a garbage can, or a toilet seat, or a billboard—but it's there. We're reminded of *Willy Wonka and the Chocolate Factory*, living in a world of pure imagination.

When the songs are being written, do you all work together?
CHAD: Yeah, and there's no one formula of songwriting. Flea might bring in a bass line, John brings a riff to rehearsal. We jam on it and come up with parts. Anthony will start doing something over the top of that. Everybody has input and everyone is involved.

Most people have a bad boy image of you guys, but this is so homey.
FLEA: We love each other no matter what the fuck happens. Living here together has been enlightening for all of us. Working on this piece of art together. It's a commune with money, and a recording studio and guys who care.

Are you all jacked up to take this show on the road?
CHAD: When people come to see the Chili Peppers, they should be ready to have their faces peeled off by the hardest, bone-crunching, psychedelic sex-funk music that they've ever heard in their lives. Bigger and better and huger than ever!

Dave Reitzas, The Enterprise recording studios, LA 1999

(L-R) Lionel Richie, David Foster, Dave Reitzas, The Village, LA 1998

Dave Reitzas

Mix a Big One

Your education included music, harmony, percussion. How important is that training for an engineer?
It's very important—our job is to capture music and for me having a musical background is a necessity. We're called engineers but there is really a musical aspect, as well as the functional and the sonic aspects. Sound is so subjective, so it's very important to be musical—where you punch in, where you punch out. It's so helpful when you can subdivide for punching or timing, and you can tell when something is in tune, or you can talk in the right language. If the artist says, "Get me in on the G," you don't have to look at your numbers to know where the G is.

What happens when you go into the mix mode?
I try to discover the vision of the artist. Then I study what is on tape. I start out by learning the song and where the dynamics are in the recording. I'm trying to build on the things I don't need to change.

I used to have a tendency to listen to kick drum and try to make it better. Then I'd listen to the bass and I'd have to make the bass better to match the kick. And then everything else had to get changed because of the kick and the bass. You'd end up with a mix that sounded completely different from the way that it was recorded. Now I try to let the tracks speak for themselves, and then make adjustments as necessary.

Your rough mixes, such as the one for Whitney Houston's "I Will Always Love You" and Madonna's "You'll See," ended up as the final mixes. How did that happen?
It's because they came from the heart and there was very little brain activity involved. It's an emotional, unanalytical attempt to work with what you are immediately feeling from the song. As soon as you start adding automation and going section by section, it starts to become a thought-out process. Nothing wrong with that, but the rough mixes are uninhibited, spontaneous. It's almost like a live performance—something magical going on.

How would you summarize your job?
My job is to create an environment to capture musical moments and convert them to a listenable product. I am trying to figure out what the artist is looking for, what the producer is looking for, and trying to facilitate that. To reach that goal, I will use whatever equipment or tricks that I know. But it's not so much what gear I use, it's more a matter of finding out what the artist is looking for and then using the gear that is appropriate.

Gaetano Ria, Capri Digital Studios, Italy 1991

Gaetano Ria

Italian Style

How long have you been in this business?

Thirty years last June. I started with RCA, 1961, in Rome. After two years as a technician, I became an assistant engineer. A year later, the chief engineer asked if I could work on a Sunday session. I said, "Okay, I'll try."

The opportunity to work at RCA was very important because I became involved with every type of music. I started with pop music, but later recorded classical music, big orchestras, jazz, and rock. I worked with Ennio Morricone and learned the sound of the orchestra. We recorded many records together. He wrote the arrangements, but he asked me to let him hear the records with the current grooves of guitars and percussions.

You also worked with Henry Mancini.

Yes, a very beautiful experience for me. If you ask me what it means to be an engineer, the best feeling is when I worked with Henry Mancini. I had the opportunity to record a 120-member orchestra and 100-person chorus for the Vittoria DeSica film, *I Girasoli* with Marcello Mastroanni and Sophia Loren. When I open the faders and listen to the sound that comes from the microphone I have goosebumps. My most beautiful memory in the studio.

As a young engineer you worked with Rubinstein, didn't you?

Yes, I worked for four months recording the sonatas of Chopin for RCA Victor. Afterwards, we worked for six months editing. This was in the end of the '60s and we didn't use a razor blade and a block, we used a pair of scissors. We would make a mark with a white pencil, then pull out the tape and cut with the scissors.

How did you learn how to edit?

I started out in maintenance, but when I decided I wanted to be an assistant engineer, the chief engineer at RCA said, "Come with me Gaetano. This is your room for the next month. This is an editing room; this is the tape. When you are ready, come out of this room." I worked alone in the room, eight hours a day. I edited everything possible. On the drum it is very easy, or on the percussion sound. But the strings, on the cellos, and the orchestra is very difficult.

What is the secret of mixing?

The secret for me is what you have in your mind, and your heart, and the transmission to your hand. That's it.

Robbie Robertson, The Village, LA 1986

Robbie Robertson

One of The Band   1986

XXXXXXXXXXXXXXXXXXXXXXXXXXXXXXXXXXXXXXXXXXXXXXXXXXXXXXXXXXXXXXXXXXXXXXXXXXXX

Can you recall some early musical experiences that gave direction to your life?

I remember from a very early age the music that my mother was particularly interested in—something that came just after the big band era. She liked boogie-woogie. It sounds silly now, but at one time it was like outrageous pop music. One of the first things that affected me was the feel of boogie-woogie. It caught my attention.

I think my first direct contact with instruments and music came from my mother's Indian relatives. They all played something, and when the uncles and cousins visited, one guy played a mandolin and another played guitar, et cetera. They could all do something—it had a country, folk music kind of flavor. When I saw them, I wanted to be able to do it too. What's the trick, I thought.

Then rock-and-roll came along and pushed another button. I learned to play a bit of guitar, and rock-and-roll became a fever. It wasn't a matter of choice anymore; it was, "This is all I know and this is all I understand. I don't know where I'm going, I don't know about jobs, I don't know how to go to school." I became obsessed.

Did you have a particular teacher?

There were various people around—I took a little bit from one guy, a little bit from another. I went on a personal mission to get good. I started writing songs, playing and stealing as much as I could from everything in reach. By the time I was 15, I wrote some songs that were recorded, and by 16, I was on the road professionally with Ronnie Hawkins and the Hawks, doing Alan Freed tours and playing at clubs all over the country, and at colleges, hanging out with Carl Perkins and Bo Diddley.

Sounds like you grew up fast…

Yes, I guess I missed a segment of normal childhood. When I was about 20, I woke up one day and said, "Gee, I didn't get to do all the things that normal kids do." And then I became obsessed with reading. I had a thirst for education. From the age of 16, I had been on the road, going to bed at dawn. Things built up into kind of a volcanic frustration, and then I couldn't stop reading.

Do you ever get tired of being a hero?

I'm not a hero [laughs]. I don't think I've ever been a hero. I'm suspicious of heroes, to be really truthful, because I think that when someone becomes aware that they are a hero, in most cases in human nature, it makes them behave in a way of a responsibility to who they are supposed to be. Anybody who's a real hero is not going to be fooled by that.

251

Cesar Rosas, LA 1999

Cesar Rosas

One of the Wolves

How would you describe your role in Los Lobos?
Well, I'm one of the vocalists, guitarists, and one of the writers. That's what I bring to the party.

How long has Los Lobos been a band?
We're celebrating our 25th anniversary, and lovin' it. We've gone through everything together.

Mitchell Froom told me that you guys are so nice to each other that if anything gets uptight, you all get worried.
Well, Mitchell didn't witness the really ugly years [laughs]. Actually, we've always gotten along. If we had any disagreements, each of us is man enough to step forward and straighten things out.

When did you start playing?
I must have been nine years old when I picked up the guitar. It was just an awesome feeling to play, from the beginning. It went right through my body—electrifying.

When did your professional career begin?
Before Los Lobos, I was playing nightclubs for three years. Los Lobos came from different bands around the neighborhood, and we were already established rock-and-roll musicians. I was doing gigs for Art Laboe, and Huggy Boy, and backing up Big Joe Turner and all these R&B groups at the ballrooms in East L.A. I was making some money, but I was still at Mom's. That's the best time—you're still at Mom's, and you have no worries. You've got some spending cash. I graduated from high school in '72, and we formed Los Lobos in '73.

Any business tips for those who will face the music?
Never turn your back… [laughs] Advice for a young artist? It's a rough business—always be aware, and get advice from a good businessman and a good lawyer. It doesn't hurt, and nowadays with the big record companies, you have to be prepared. Be aware, and don't turn away from the business. If you have the talent, and you believe in yourself, you will do well. But pay attention to the business angle, because it can destroy you. And it has destroyed many people. You don't want to end up being another rock tragedy, and bitter.

Are you and Los Lobos heroes in the Hispanic world?
Yes, I think so. We're looked upon that way, and it feels good. If I can influence a kid to get into music, in a positive way, that's good for all of us. Whatever Los Lobos has achieved, we didn't take any shortcuts. We did it the good ol' fashioned way, and we tried to do it right, and sincere.

Todd Rundgren, Hawaii 2000

Todd Rundgren

Utopia Out of Hell

2000

In your entire career, which are the albums you are most proud of?

Well, I consider pride a sin, so I don't catalogue the albums like that. There are albums for which I set certain goals, and got very close to the goals—in some cases, certain aspects of the projects exceeded the goals. Albums by XTC come to mind, and any of the albums where my influence had more than a custodial effect on making the record.

It's hard to avoid mentioning an album like *Bat Out of Hell*, not for the fact that it was so hysterically successful, but because I did it for completely other reasons and it seemed to have achieved those goals in the process. I did it because it didn't seem like any other producer would do it with any enthusiasm. I approached the whole album as being a spoof on Bruce Springsteen. That's what it seemed like to me, and that was the principle influence. Bruce Springsteen was on the cover of *Time* magazine and had all this other visibility, and it was all being taken so seriously—no reflection on the quality of his music, but I thought it was a great opportunity to do something in the pop cultural realm, rather than simply making a record. I had no expectations that it would be so commercially successful. The songs were so freakin' long, but that was what sold it in the end—those shaggy dog jokes. Long songs with goofy punch lines at the end.

Chris Stone, founder of the Record Plant, once told me that you used to come in to the studio every day and blow up the speakers.

Well, I was one of the first clients in there, but with Hendrix working there as well, the speakers were probably gone on a nightly basis. Prior to that, most of the studios didn't have anything approaching what most bands were producing onstage. When you saw those stacks of amps, you had to have them and then suddenly you go into the studio and everything sounds puny, because they were used to doing R&B records on little Altec 12" speakers with little tweeters.

What's the biggest mistake of your life?

[laughs] Well, as I consider pride a sin, self-importance is not an indulgence I care to get into. There is no moment in my past that sticks out: "Gee, I wish I had that to do all over again, with all the karmic repercussions that would entail." I'm at a point where I feel I have a pretty good handle on how life works—for me. You can only say "for me." The most important thing to me has always been to satisfy myself and therefore, you can't really have a lot of regrets. I'm going to satisfy myself, and know when I'm satisfied, and I can't have any complaints later.

255

John Rzeznik, Ocean Way Recording Studios, LA 2003

John Rzeznik

Goo Goo Dude   2003

XXXXXXXXXXXXXXXXXXXXXXXXXXXXXXXXXXXXXXXXXXXXXXXXXXXXXXXXXXXXXXXXXXXXXX

How did the name Goo Goo Dolls come about?
Oh, we got that out of an old *True Detective* magazine. There was an ad for a toy, a doll's head—you put your fingers inside it and you could make all these funny faces.

You're from Buffalo, New York—is there something special about that city in preparing a person for the real world?
I think that the greatest asset of being from Buffalo is that you always know where you stand. You are always sure of who your true friends are. It's a very honest place, and it establishes a strong work ethic. That's something that I try to carry with me wherever I go. In a way, it's a lot to live up to. Sometimes you feel like people from everywhere else are lazy, just because they don't want to work 12 hours a day, 7 days a week.

What is the story with your tattoo of the person with the question marks?
I got it from *Art in America* magazine, by an illustrator named Saul Steinberg. It was from an article about what makes a great art museum and I liked it, sort of a variation on Rodin's "The Thinker."

What about the modern art tattoo on your right arm?
That's Picasso, "The Dream." I saw the painting and fell in love with it, and I waited a long time to get it done, because I had to find the right tattoo artist.

I understand you once had an argument with a record company…
Well, in my opinion, I didn't feel that our first record deal was fair. I didn't feel that selling almost two million records and not making any money was fair. I discussed it with my lawyers and in their opinion we didn't have a good record deal, but we needed a lot of money to prove our point.

We had been touring a lot, and were coming off a hit, so we were able to go out and play State Fairs, which pay really well. I still play the Fairs because they are fun and they pay well. So, we needed money and we created a "war chest" and we won—we got our record back and signed a new record deal. It's been pretty okay ever since. It was a lot of work, but we felt united in the cause to get back something that we had dedicated our lives to. We did all right.

Danny Saber, Record Plant Recording Studios, LA 1998

Danny Saber

Mr. Fixer

What is your main recording tool?
The Laminator.

Is that a new processor?
No—You laminate with it, you know? Fake IDs, backstage passes…

What is your job?
My main gig lately is the "fixer." I'm doing remixes, but even when I'm producing, I usually get some sort of demo or multitrack. Sometimes I just write and record the song from scratch. I record everything directly into the Logic and Pro Tools, then chop it all up and arrange the song. Get all the programming, the beats and the loops and all the keyboards happening. Get the skeleton of the song. Then I dump it onto multitrack and take it to a big room for the real overdub live drums, guitar, bass. Sometimes I'll go all the way in the project room and just take it out and mix it. Depends.

Stones, Bowie, Jesus Lizard, Marilyn Manson… When you slice and dice a song, what if the artist doesn't like it?
Tough shit—they don't have to use it. Naw, it's not that extreme. The greatest thing about all this work is that you get to develop relationships and get to know people. I know what the band wants and I have a feeling for what will fly. At the same time, I'm not afraid to go for it. That's what you gotta do sometimes—be unpredictable. It's improvisational.

Did you get your skull ring from Keith Richards?
No, but I showed it to him and told him I was ripping him off. He goes, "Alright, baby" and slammed his skull ring right into mine. Bam!

Do you know any good business tricks?
Lying, cheating, and stealing—those are good business tricks [laughs].

How would you like to be remembered in history?
Just to be remembered at all would be nice.

What's your advice for a good start in the music business?
Lubrication. It won't hurt as much when you get reamed. No, honestly—I've been pretty lucky. My nose isn't too brown.

Can you share some recording secrets?
This whole secret technique thing is a load of crap. It's all hard work; go with your instincts and have the balls to stand behind what you believe in. All the technical things will work themselves out. That comes with time in the studio. Get around some experienced people and steal—uh—learn from them.

(L-R) Gregg Rolie, Carlos Santana, Michael Shrieve, LA 1988

Carlos Santana

Inside the Note

✕✕✕

Carlos, I was curious about the time when you lived alone in Tijuana. How old were you?
12, 13.

And you were playing?
I was playing, yeah. That's why I went back. My family had moved from Mexico to San Francisco and I had the choice of going back to Tijuana and hanging out with black blues players and strippers or going to junior high school and hanging out with a bunch of squares. There was no choice. My mother was furious, but she gave me a one-way ticket to Tijuana and 20 dollars.

When I got there it was Halloween night and everybody was dressed up like skeletons. It suddenly dawned on me that I was really alone. Totally alone. The first thing that I did was go to the church of The Virgin de Guadelupe, the patron of Mexicans. So, I asked her to protect me and my family, and to help me to stay safe. But I didn't have no problems as soon as I got into the cantina again. At first, the owner said, "What are you doin' here?" I told him that my mom said I could come and play. He said I needed a letter, because I was underage and they would put him in jail and close his place. I convinced him it was all right, because my mother was in San Francisco. Anyway, he told the guitar player to leave and I started playing. I stayed there for a year and a half. It was an experience. You learn in there to [snaps his fingers] *catch* the listener. Most people go there to get drunk, to find drugs or women. I learned in there that if you play the music correctly, you can make prostitutes stop hustling, you can make the hustlers stop hustling.

Bad for business, though…
Yeah, they didn't want me to do that too much. Just play the Top 40. If you couldn't play "Green Onions" and "Hideaway," you couldn't go on the bandstand. That's basically where I got my attitude as far as hitting the note. Here, here, and here [Carlos slaps head, heart, and groin]. Most musicians play from the fingers on out, so it's very hard for the music to go inside people. I learned in the cantina how to get inside the note, so when the audience is talking they even stop and listen. "Hold on—what?" One-on-one with the listener. I think that's where I got my first education on how to pinch the listener.

Elliot Scheiner, The Village, LA 1994

(L-R) Bruce Maddocks and Elliot Scheiner, Cups 'N Strings studios, LA 2004

Elliot Scheiner

Knob Boss

1998

How did you end up becoming a recording engineer?

I was a musician, playing in bands all over New York. Did some road tours as a sideman, and I just didn't want to do it anymore. My uncle was a studio trombone player, guy named Chauncey Welsh. He was doing massive amounts of work at the time and he introduced me to Phil Ramone. And that's how it all began. Shelly Yakus and I started the very same week at A&R Studios—what a great bunch of guys. But even then, you had to know somebody to get in that front door.

Are engineers getting more respect these days?

The ones who have been around are getting more respect, but the same problems exist for young engineers as 25 years ago. Unless you've got a name, you're just an engineer.

How do you get a name?

You get lucky. Hopefully you work on something huge and you take advantage of it.

Do you have any business tips for young engineers?

As an engineer gets more work, he acquires equipment that he needs for his projects. A lot of times they rent it back to their clients. I've never done that because I felt there might be resentment in the end. My philosophy is that when they hire me as an engineer, they get what I have.

What was the first music you recorded?

It was a Jimmy Smith record, in 1968. I was Phil's assistant, and it was the way many got started back at A&R. As an assistant, you set up the room for the engineer, miked everything. They really taught you mic technique. We knew how to mic stuff, we knew where these guys wanted it, and we knew what it would sound like. You got a chance to do rehearsals and stuff on weekends, or late at night.

We'd been working on this Jimmy Smith all week. There were daytime sessions, and then nighttime sessions. Jimmy Smith had the studio booked for a week or two at nights. So we'd have to break down the setup after we'd finished every night and set up again the next day. Phil walked in one day about five minutes before downbeat and said to me, "I got some stuff to do—you do it." I panicked, because it was the first time it would mean anything. It was such a shock. "You do it. I'll be up in my office." It made me an engineer.

Gallery III

Don Was, Center Staging, LA 2001

Producer Rick Rubin, Cello Studios, LA 2001

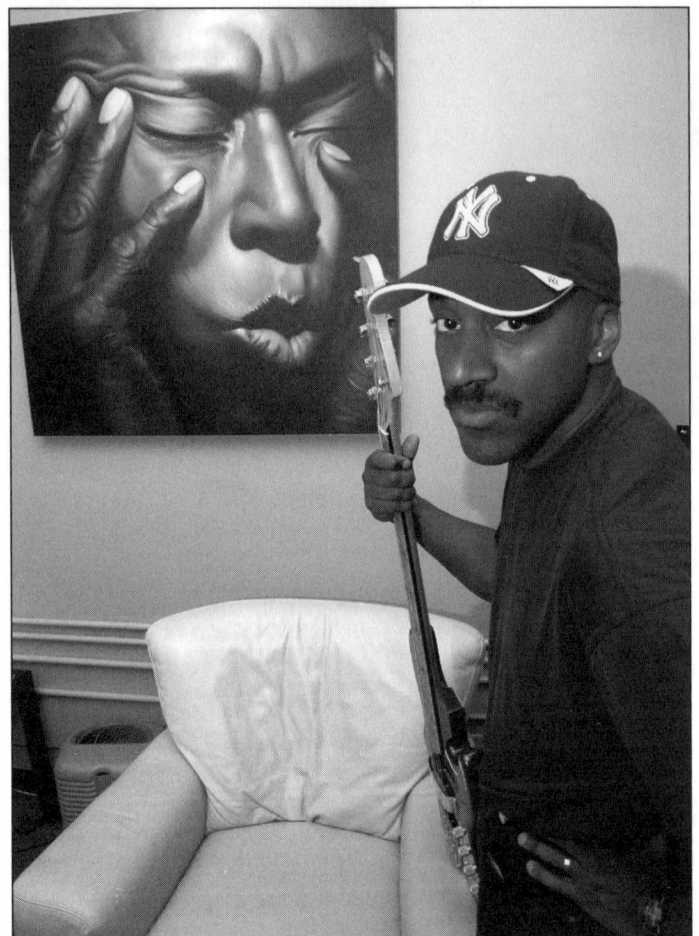

Marcus Miller, LA 2001

Producer Dr. Dre, Record One Recording Studios, LA 2001

(clockwise from lower left) Producer Rob Cavallo, Goo Goo Dolls John Rzeznik and Robbie Takak, Capitol Recording Studios, 2002

(L-R) Producer/mixer Jack Joseph Puig; John Mayer; Pro Tools engineer Lars Fox, assistant engineer Chris Stephen, bass player David LaBruyere, Ocean Way Recording Studios, LA 2003

(L-R) Jimmy Jam and Terry Lewis, San Francisco, 2004

Kitaro, Ocean Way Recording Studios, LA 2003

Joe Zawinul, LA 2003

Producer Glen Ballard, Hollywood, 2002

DJ Quik, Record One Recording Studios, LA 2003

Joe Cocker, Royaltone Recording Studios, LA 2004

(L-R) Tom McRae and engineer/producer Joe Chiccarelli, The Paramour, LA 2004

The Dust Brothers (L-R) John King and Mike Simpson, The Boat recording studios, LA 2005

Dweezil Zappa, Utility Muffin Research Kitchen, LA 2005

The Nervous Return (L-R) Jason Muller, Greg Gordon, Anthony Crouse, LA 2004

Al Schmitt, Capitol Recording Studios, LA 1993

Al Schmitt, Capitol Records mural, LA 1993

Al Schmitt

The Unforgettable Touch

So how do you like working with Mr. Sinatra?
It's been an incredible thrill—a huge undertaking, a 55-piece band—a *roaring* band with some of the best players around. French horns, harp, basses and celli and saxes, strings—and Frank.

It looked to me like he runs the entire show.
Certainly does [laughs]. He *is* the Chairman of the Board.

What comes next with the Sinatra project?
Well, it's similar to what we did with Nat Cole and Natalie. The other vocalists will come in and record, and we'll take Frank out in spots. Bono is supposed to do a cut, Natalie Cole, Willie Nelson, Gloria Estefan…

Can you name a few of your early hits?
One of my first big hits was with Connie Francis, "My Happiness," which was #1 for quite a while. I did some work with Jessy Belvin, Sam Cooke. Sam was really my favorite artist to work with—I was the engineer on "Cupid," "Another Saturday Night," "Bring It On Home," "Twistin' the Night Away," and all those records. The first Henry Mancini record, *Peter Gunn*, was started by Bones Howe and I finished it. I did *Breakfast at Tiffany's*, *Mr. Lucky*, *Mr. Lucky Goes Latin*, *Experiment in Terror*, and *Hatari*, which had "Baby Elephant Walk," my first Grammy®.

Can you think of anything about your style as an engineer that is unique to you?
Basically, I am an acoustical engineer. I like working with orchestras and the more players there are the happier I am. My big thing is microphone technique. I still use the old 67s, 47s, 49s, M-50s, with very little EQ. The assistants look at me and wonder sometimes. I use very little limiting. Maybe a little on the bass, sometimes on the vocal. I try to be in the studio, listen to what it sounds like there, and try to capture that. I don't have that Al Schmitt identifiable drum sound. It's the sound of the drummer I am working with.

Who has helped you the most in your career?
Well, I can't give enough credit to Tommy LiPuma. He gives me the freedom I like. Stu Levine is a producer I really enjoy working with. Great sense of humor, keeps the session light—one of the great guys who don't become overly impressed with their own importance. David Foster is a good musician, knows how to handle people, very pleasant to work with. Engineers who consistently do good work—Bruce Swedien, Bill Schnee, Elliot Scheiner, George Massenburg, Lee Herschberg, Kevin Killen, Allen Sides, Niko Bolas, Joe Furla… I'm sure there a lot of great ones I didn't mention.

Ken Scott, Total Access Recording Studios, LA 2002

Ken Scott

Mixing the Walrus   2005

❖❖

When did you first work with The Beatles?

I started out as a second engineer on *A Hard Day's Night* and continued on and off through *Rubber Soul*. During *The Magical Mystery Tour*, one of the engineers got sick, Geoff Emerick was on holiday, and I had just been promoted to first engineer. I had worked with The Beatles so much as a second engineer that I was assigned to record the orchestral sessions for "I am the Walrus." I continued working with them through the *White Album*.

Geoff Emerick had recorded the basics and vocal tracks for "Walrus." When I picked it up we did strings, and then we did the choir. I believe the parts were written out by George Martin, based on John's ideas. We also recorded the voices for the repeating phrase "Everybody's got one." At this point, everything was pretty terrifying for me because I was still learning on the job.

Was it surprising that you were mixing in a live BBC radio broadcast to the song?

Everything was a surprise with The Beatles. You could never tell what they would want you to do next. It was normal for everything to be unpredictable.

What was your relationship with John?

Well, you remember I wasn't doing much that night you were there—I was standing by. This was the first song I had ever mixed and at a certain point John wanted to take over. We were bringing the radio show in and out, and John had specific ideas. He would bring up the fader and decide which parts of the broadcast he wanted to bring in to the mix.

What other Beatles songs stand out in your memory?

"Yer Blues." We had been experimenting by recording vocals in the control room and during a playback I said to John, "The way this is going, the next thing you'll want to do is record next door." There was a tiny room attached to the control room which used to have the 4-track machines. John looked at me and said, "Great idea." The next song we did was "Yer Blues" and we had to cram all four of them into this tiny room. That's how we recorded it, and that definitely stands out in my mind. He wanted something different, and I guess that gave the song the sound of a small nightclub.

What was your last Beatles session?

That would be the all-nighter to finish up the *White Album*. We were using all of the studios at Abbey Road at the same time, because George Harrison was going to fly to the States the very next day to deliver copies of the album to Capitol Records. John was playing back some of his stuff for George Martin. One of the maintenance guys was finishing up some track with Paul. I was in Number 2 mixing "Savoy Truffle" with George. That was another first for me—my first 24-hour session.

Paul Shaffer, New York City circa 1995

Photo courtesy of Paul Shaffer/CBS Television/Worldwide Pants.

Paul Shaffer

The World's Most Dangerous Bandleader 1989

Tell me about your early musical education…

Mrs. Hardy was my first piano teacher. She encouraged me to play by ear, which I understand is rare with classical piano teachers. Most of them discourage it on the grounds that if a kid can play by ear, he will fake it and not learn how to sight read music. Mrs. Hardy said, "Well, you've got such a great ear. Don't worry about it. On the exam you'll make up in the ear training section what you lose in the sight reading section." She allowed me to play by ear. She was interested as I learned more and more chords, and she encouraged it.

In your daily role as bandleader on "Late Night," are you the raging tyrant type or the mellow spiritual guru figure?

Guru figure—that's funny. I think I may start referring to myself as a guru figure and try to get a few laughs out of it. I'm really neither of those things. I'm not a guru, I'm not a tyrant. I'm pretty loose with this band, as you can see. I picked the greatest musicians that I could find, who were suited to the particular characteristics that you have to have to cut this gig. Having them in place, I can be pretty loose. But they know that I am a stickler for detail and authenticity when it comes to the songs that we play in all the different styles.

I sense that you have a traditional musician attitude—very professional.

Well, you know, in the '70s everybody got hip to what a studio musician was. It seemed like a very hip thing to do for me. To be in the Muscle Shoals Rhythm Section was happening. You heard about people who played on everyone's records. I thought, "Boy, that's what I want to be." When I got to New York my first gig was in a Broadway show. I set out to become a studio musician, and I learned how to be that. It is still my attitude, and something that I like very much.

Any secret advice on how to survive in the cutthroat business of music?

No, but it's certainly the case that many musicians hate to think about business. They hate to admit that they love what they do and people are making money off them. Of course, they love it so much that they would do it for free and there is always somebody out there who will allow them to do it for free. I guess that's where we get in trouble businesswise.

How does one "Wang Dang Doodle"?

How does one pitch a wang dang doodle? To me, it means to have a helluva time. I would hope that there is some sort of sexual innuendo involved as well.

It sounds like you're sitting pretty—almost a charmed life.

It's a pretty good gig I have, I tell ya. It's nice to be working.

Artie Shaw, LA 1992

Artie Shaw

Art Rules

Did you have a teacher?

No, I studied with the guy next to me. As long as he knew more, I stayed there. When I knew more, I'd leave and find somebody else. Finally, I ran out of guys.

Why did you attract such beautiful women? Was it the music?

I think you'd have to ask the women about that. If you're a guy in the limelight and you're making a lot of money and you have power, there is a certain type of woman who is attracted to that. Look at Mick Jagger—he'd certainly win no beauty contests, but he's had a few women around.

You've sold about a hundred million records...

Last count was close to that.

So, if you got a buck a record, you must have over a hundred million dollars.

Me? You're talking about the record company. I quit the business every time I started to make any money. I've been told that if I had stayed in it, like Woody Herman did, I'd have been worth an awful lot of money. Either you save your money and lead a normal life, or you take the chance to live like an emperor. I thought, let's see what that's about—and I did. I gave orders and people jumped. One day I looked in the mirror and said to myself, "You're nuts." So, I quit. I realized I was losing what sanity I was born with.

Did you do everything you could possibly do before you quit playing?

No. I did everything I could up to then. If I could have lived that life and gone on, I would be playing quite differently today. But I've never looked back with regret. My career was taking too much of an emotional toll. They were begging me to play things I didn't want to play, over and over, like a monkey on a string. I have a low threshold for boredom. Some people thrive on it.

It's really a matter of "entertainer" versus "artist." I'm not saying that one is better than the other. An entertainer can be very serious, but the motivations are basically different. The entertainer is out to please people. The more people he pleases, the happier he is. The artist does what he has to do. He hopes people will be pleased and pay him so he can make a living. If not, he still has to do it.

What advice would you give to young musicians?

Do what you love and everything will follow from that. And remember, no advice is any good until you follow it. Do the best you can. Follow your deepest impulses, and if they are mistaken, you will make mistakes. If you don't make mistakes, you'll never learn anything. Nobody ever learns from success; you learn from failure. And don't follow me—you'll just make the same mistakes I did.

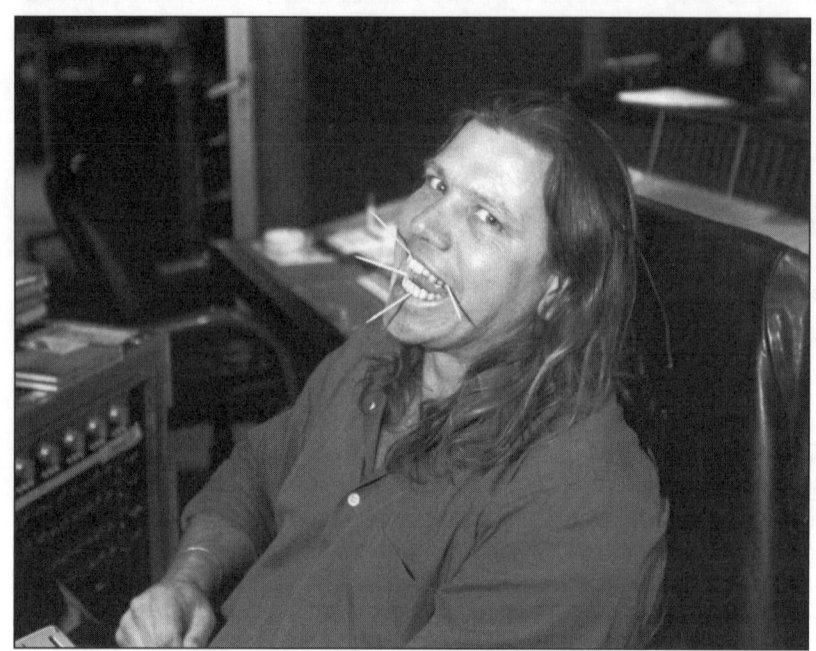

Kevin Shirley, Guillaume Tell Recording Studios, Paris 2000

Kevin Shirley

The Caveman

So why are you known as the Caveman?
Because I've always looked like this, I guess. Big, hulking Neanderthal with long hair.

What is the most important thing to remember when you are mixing?
To stop when it feels good.

Who were your musical heroes when you were getting started?
Jimmy Page, Trevor Rabin, James Patrick Page, Pete Townsend, Richie Blackmore, Ian Anderson.

Who do you respect and admire today?
Mutt Lange, Bob Clearmountain, George Massenburg, John Kalodner.

If you could go back in time before the birth of recording, what would you like to hear?
I think Beethoven's *Pastoral Symphony #6 in F major op. 68*—with original instruments, and him conducting. I'm sure you'd be able to hear the brook, the picnic, the storm, and the birds and insects of the meadow—his vision in music.

What did you learn from Iron Maiden?
I learned how to use Pro Tools, and bite my tongue. I also learned that not everyone hears things the same way, and it's all valid.

What music would you like played at your funeral?
"You Can Leave Your Hat On," as sung by Joe Cocker.

How would you like to be remembered in history?
Only as honest, diligent and a friend. I don't need to be a hero.

What was your most ridiculous experience in a recording studio?
Aerosmith, Journey, Iron Maiden—I have lots of stories. Every band has something amazing and then something ridiculous about them, but Aerosmith takes the cake. All of those guys just jamming on nothing for 30 minutes together, was unforgettable. And Steven is the greatest talent I've ever worked with, just a monster musician!

What old saying do you hate the most?
"Man, this is going to be huge—we're gonna take it to the top!"

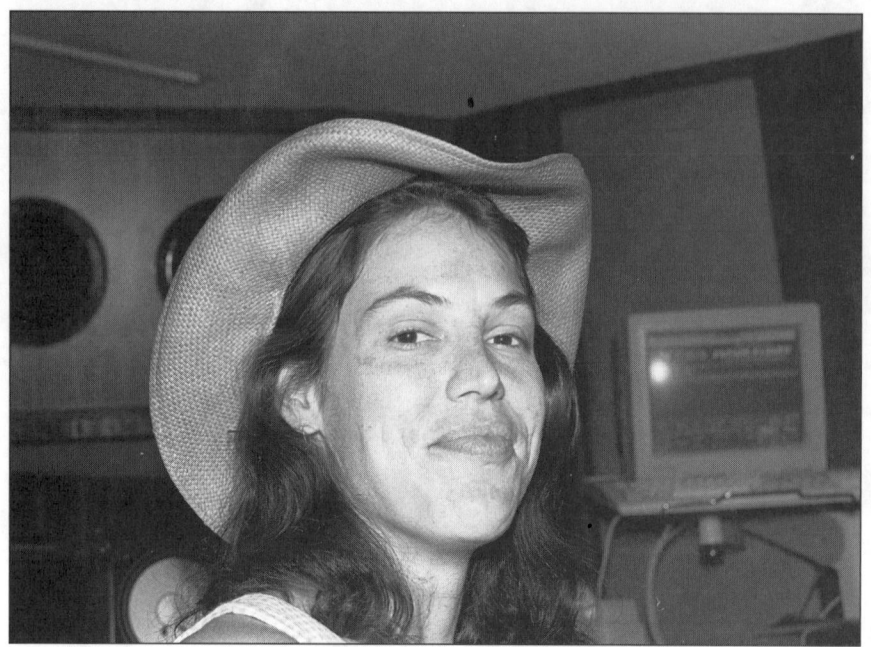

Trina Shoemaker, Sound Factory, LA 1997

Trina Shoemaker

Drive That Console   1997

xxxxxxxxxxxxxxxxxxxxxxxxxxxxxxxxxxxxxxxxxxxxxxxxxxxxxxxxxxxxxxxxxxxxxxxxxxxxxxxxxxxxxxxxxxxx

Why are you an engineer?

Because I wanted to make music, but I was afraid I wouldn't be able to make a living just as a musician. I always knew that I could record music because I was a smart little girl, took the stereo apart, looked inside the 8-Track, and listened to records with my dad's headphones. As a kid looking at album cover photos, I already had a concept of studio recording. At 19, I moved to California to be a record producer and ended up at Capitol Records as a secretary. But I wanted to work in that studio and drive that console. Now that I know how to do it, I can make my own records. This has been a long road, but not only can I make the records myself now, I can finance them, too.

Was progress tougher because you're a woman?

Not for me, because I have never perceived myself as all that womanly. I'm as feminine as they come, but I'm tall and extremely fit. I was raised by my father and I know how to operate in a world of men. It was easy for me to say, "I can lift that case." My physical strength matched most of the guys and my intellect was strong. I just moved straight on through.

But the thing that turned me into an engineer is my love for music. I can hear a person's song and memorize the form in one run through. Musicians like that—when they play it once and I say, "Let's go back to that bridge section." I know what the chord changes are, and I'm able to talk musically. I can memorize their lyrics immediately and can sing them back and guide them through their tracks. I'm much more musical than I am technical. I don't even know how to demag heads.

How did you hook up with Sheryl Crow?

I had just left Kingsway Studios as the house engineer in July of '95 and she booked into the studio. I walked in to pick up some of my DATs. Karen Brady, the studio manager, introduced me and said I knew the studio better than anyone. Sheryl said, "Will you just record me tonight?" and I said, "Sure." I set up a cozy little setup and ran the multitrack while they were jamming. The song "Home" was written that night and the cut on the record is the very first take. Sheryl said, "We need to start rolling multitrack because this is turning into a song." I told her that I'd been rolling, played it back, and she was blown away.

Do you have any good business tips?

Return all phone calls promptly.

If you could go back in time before the birth of recording, what would you like to hear?

The songs of the slaves in the fields, the old spirituals of the South.

Allen Sides, Ocean Way Recording Studios, LA 1990

Larry Klein, Joni Mitchell, Allen Sides, Ocean Way, LA 1999

(L-R) Ry Cooder and Allen Sides, Ocean Way, LA 1996

Allen Sides

The Ocean Way   1990

When you renamed United Studios as Ocean Way did you keep the rooms the same?

Oh yes—exactly the same. Bill Putnam built those rooms. All we did was build new control rooms. The studios were spectacular, and are really huge, with high ceilings and beautifully smooth decay. You walk in the room and you listen to a large orchestra playing live and the balance is perfect. You could put up a single pair of microphones, pull up two faders, and you'd almost have a mix.

You also have quite a collection of microphones…

Yes, in the last ten years, I've probably bought well over a thousand tube mics from Europe. About eight years ago a lot of the broadcast companies in Europe decided to update with transistor microphones and they bought the best available at the time. A tremendous amount of wonderful tube mics hit the market and I bought everything I could get my hands on.

The sad thing is that a lot of the studios here, as well as there, decided to get rid of their tube mics, not knowing what they were losing. In an English studio, it can be tough to find a couple of C-12s. I think they are more rare there than here now.

There is nothing currently made today that approaches the great tube mics. I probably have the largest collection in the U.S. If an engineer comes in to our studios and wants six C-12s, or eight 67s—we have virtually unlimited quantities of all the great microphones at no extra charge.

Were your sessions with Sinatra enjoyable?

Yes, a lot of fun, with Quincy Jones. We had large orchestras, and it was interesting for me as an engineer, because the whole band was rehearsed beforehand, and I had plenty of time to get a sound. I had a mic set up for Frank with a few baffles around the side, because he doesn't like to be in an isolation booth. I was very happy with the orchestra sound and I had some stand-ins for Frank to set the levels as close as I could guess.

Frank came in, walked up to Quincy and said, "Let's take it." He goes over to the mic and I haven't even heard him yet. No chance to set levels, no chance to set anything. And with Frank, it has to be right. We started recording and halfway through the first take, Frank said to stop, he didn't like what he was doing. "Quincy, let's just pick it up right here." They counted it off and finished the song. Frank says, "Next song." That's it.

Did you get it?

Yes.

Leland Sklar, LA 2004

Leland Sklar

First Bass

Your meeting with James Taylor was a pivotal point in your career, wasn't it?
Absolutely. After "Fire and Rain" was released we went out on the road with Danny Korchmar on guitar, Russ Kunkel on drums, myself, and Carole King was our piano player, before her album *Tapestry* had come out. We started touring, thinking it would be six weeks and it turned into 20 years.

What are you best known for?
I'm probably known for my beard more than my playing. Not intentionally, I have created a persona that carries me along without business cards. I'm that "guy with the big beard." Actually, I think I'm just known as a bass player. I don't see anything special going on—I'm just blessed with the career I have. You get up each day with as much insecurity as any other person who picks up an instrument.

Is there anything different about your playing technique?
There is one thing that I do that people have commented on over the years. Where a lot of guys are very articulate in the way they address notes, I tend to do glissandos more. I slide between notes, and play with a greasier style. Because of physical inadequacies caused by hand injuries, some of the articulation isn't that comfortable in my left hand. My middle two fingers really don't work that well, so most of my playing is my first and fourth fingers and sliding makes it easier to get to a note. If I have any signature, maybe that's it.

What do producers like about your playing?
One of the things that they generally like is that when I am involved in a project, they get the impression that I really care, and that I really work hard to play the best part I can. I contribute ideas and energy above and beyond the call of duty, which is what most of the players at this level do.

If you had to pick one recording of yours that captures your true nature as a bass player, which would it be?
It's hard, because there are songs like James Taylor's "Your Smiling Face" that everybody says, "Oh, I love that bass part."

Why does that stick in people's minds?
It's really difficult for me, as the performer, to really know what it is. There's something about it that feels good, it has a vibe that people like. When we play that live, in that section where it is just voice and bass, the audiences start waving their arms and singing along. People come up and they want to talk about that lick. I just say we were just working in the studio, and that part felt right. On that song, I think the lick is right, the song's right, the vibe of the whole thing is right—it's just one of those lucky moments that are few and far between.

(L-R) Derek Smalls and David St. Hubbins, Henson Recording Studios, LA 2000

Spinal Tap

Smell the Love

Have either of you ever had a spinal tap?
DEREK SMALLS: Never had a spinal tap myself, but "memorable and painful" seemed to sum up what we wanted to be as a band.

DAVID ST. HUBBINS: There's a sexual maneuver called a "spinal tap" and I procured one of those in Singapore. It burned.

How does it feel playing this dark metal music with one foot in the grave?
DAVID: I can think of no more appropriate place to keep one's foot.

DEREK: What do you mean by that?

Well, uh, you're not exactly kids anymore…
DEREK: But that doesn't mean you have one foot in the grave. To me, you've got a foot in the grave if they've got you hooked up to tubes and they put a catheter up your willie. None of us are in that situation, so we still feel that if you don't look at the calendar, and you don't look at the clock, and you don't look in the mirror, then it feels the same.

Could you compare the recording process today with that of yesteryear?
DEREK: Much quicker, much more focused, we're able to get much louder without being louder—I don't know how they do that. Much better take-out food and much better parking, really, to be truthful about it. Always had trouble finding a place for the Lamborghini in the old days.

DAVID: More snacks available in the studio these days. And the engineers are younger. And crankier.

If you could go back in time before the birth of recording, what would you like to hear?
DAVID: Al Jolson begging for work.

DEREK: I'd like to hear what it sounded like in Beethoven's head after he went deaf.

Do you know any interesting business tricks?
DAVID: Nothing like good old-fashioned theft!

DEREK: Buy low, sell soon.

What makes a great record?
DAVID: Three things: the hook, the hook, the hook. And the words.

DEREK: Variety, purity, body, and flavor.

Any advice for getting a good start in the music business?
DAVID: Be patient. Remember they're not going to like you automatically just because *you* do.

DEREK: Ignore all advice.

(L-R) Chris Stone, George Martin, John Burgess, Record Plant Recording Studios, LA 1987

(L-R) Al Kooper, Chris Stone, music producers Tom Werman and Bill Szymczyk, Record Plant Recording Studios "Last Jam," LA 1985

Photos courtesy of Chris Stone, Al Kooper photo by Ed Freeman.

Chris Stone

Growing the Record Plant

You've been a major studio owner for almost 20 years—how did it all start?

Well, in 1967, I was national sales manager for Revlon Cosmetics and met a very exciting fellow by the name of Gary Kellgren. We got together because my wife had just had our first child and his wife was about to have their first. A mutual friend introduced us so the ladies could talk about having babies. He and I had nothing to talk about—he knew nothing about my business and wasn't interested so I started asking about his work.

At the time he was working at Mayfair, a little recording studio off Times Square in New York City. He invited me down and at my very first session I saw a guy inside a grand piano with his legs sticking out—he was strumming the strings. It turned out to be Frank Zappa doing a Luden's cough drop commercial with backwards coughs. The second artist I met was Jimi Hendrix—Kellgren used to do all his work. I noticed that Gary worked very, very hard. He was one of the best audio engineers in the business.

Was this his studio?

No, but he was the only engineer. He worked six or seven days a week and made $200. I looked at the books and the owner was billing about $5,000 a week. I was getting bored with Revlon so we decided to start a studio. We borrowed $100,000, called it The Record Plant, and opened on March 13, 1968. We had everything covered because Gary knew the recording side of things and I knew the business side. Our first hit was "Electric Ladyland," our first big mixing session was for Woodstock, and our first remote recording was "The Concert for Bangladesh."

What was your essential role in the evolution of the recording industry?

I think Record Plant has made some big contributions. When we started out, studios were hospitals—fluorescent lights, white walls, and hardwood floors. Kellgren turned them into living rooms and the greatest compliment an artist could pay us was, "Goddamn, I'd like to live here!" And sure enough, he would. Our famous Jacuzzi room came about because Gary wanted to build a swimming pool in the back lot and I wouldn't let him. We were well-suited to each other, and from an aesthetic angle, we created the living room environment that is the norm today.

Andy Summers, LA 1988

Andy Summers

Police Yourself

How did you meet Sting?

The first time I actually met him was in a studio. We'd been brought together by someone else and halfway through the session, Sting said, "You know, I was on a bill with you once." I was getting quite well known in England at the time as a guitar player. While Mike Oldfield's *Tubular Bells* was popular, there was an orchestra going around England playing the music symphonically. Sometimes Oldfield would tour with them and sometimes he wouldn't, because he was a strange guy. One night in Newcastle, I was playing instead, and on the bill in this hall was a group called Last Exit, a Newcastle fusion group. Sting was the bass player. There we were on the same stage. At another time playing in Newcastle, I was staying in the same hotel as Curved Air. Stewart Copeland was the drummer. We had a long talk and two months later I found myself in a London studio with Sting and Stewart. We had all crossed paths in Newcastle and were brought together. I don't much believe in things like that, but there were undercurrents—of synchronicity.

Did you envision that the group would become such a monster?

Not really. Miles used to go on and on about how huge we were gonna be—"Bigger than The Beatles!" and all this stuff. We just laughed at him, but he did all right, actually.

What about the role of the producer—what qualities are important?

What I want from a producer is a safety net, in a way, so I can be free to flap around in the studio and know that some-one is there keeping things defined, holding the show together.

Do you know any really good business tricks you could share with the readers?

Yes, I do. Don't go outside your front door—that's where the trouble starts.

Would you consider yourself a gambler?

I would, definitely. I've taken plenty of risks. I've never been afraid to move anywhere and start a new life, or risk, financially. You don't always win, but I think it's extremely important to take risks in life and take your chance. Otherwise, life never moves forward. You've got to do it, especially if you are a musician or an artist of any sort. You have to take risks artistically, and risks in your life.

Is there any old saying that you really dislike?

Yes, "Have a nice day."

Ralph Sutton, Ocean Way Recording Studios, LA 1998

Ralph Sutton

The Miracle of Music   1998

How did you become an engineer?

When I was 15, I was a frustrated musician because I didn't have the patience to practice two or three hours a day. But I had always loved music. My mother bought me a Pioneer turntable and some components and I became an audiophile. I read the backs of albums and tried to understand the process as best I could. What really inspired me was the work that Rik Pekkonen did with The Crusaders.

Who was your mentor when you began engineering?

Ken Scott, the great European engineer of Beatles fame. I assisted Ken on two albums for Missing Persons and one for Kansas. I guess he really saw something in me that I didn't see myself. Ken is the drummer's engineer and during that time I feel like I perfected what is today my drum sound.

How do you get that drum sound?

The first thing is to communicate with the drummer and have him play a cappella without any mics up. I try to come up with the right mics for the particular style of playing.

Any complaints about the music industry?

I would like to see more live musicianship again. We're falling into a situation with a lot of producer/artists working in isolation, on their workstations with samples. I would prefer to see real musicians again, to see the cats come in. My best sessions were in a room with seven or eight guys all focused on the song. I think it would help society if a child could say "I'm going to be a musician when I grow up." Right now, no one can say that because it means nothing.

Any business advice for young engineers?

Pay your taxes. Work hard, ask questions, and don't let anyone smash your dream.

Have you ever witnessed a miracle?

Where I grew up in L.A'.s South Central, I once saw a little boy get hit by a car, which drove over him and tumbled him underneath. A storefront preacher ran out into the street, grabbed the little boy, and said something to him, and that little boy jumped up and ran home crying. I said, "Wow!"

I have also witnessed miracles in the studio—psychoacoustic phenomena. If you do this long enough, you will witness powerful physics at work in the creation and recording of music. I think we sometimes take this too lightly.

Bruce Swedien, Extasy Recording Studios, LA 2001

Bruce Swedien

The Platinum Viking   1998

Where did it all begin?

When I started in this business, the goal of recording a popular record, or any kind of record, was to present the music as though the listener was there, and to recreate the original soundfield with as much accuracy and clarity as we could. One record, in my estimation, is responsible for a major revolution in recording—Les Paul and Mary Ford, "How High the Moon." It was so successful and broke through just like a shining light. All of sudden it dawned on me, and perhaps subconsciously the public realized it as well, that it was no longer necessary to present popular music in concert-like form. I discovered that it was perfectly all right to bend reality. On that record there is only one instrument and one voice. Les Paul plays all the instrumental parts, and Mary Ford sings all the vocal parts. There isn't a shred of reality on that record. All of a sudden, with the tremendous popularity of this piece of music, pop music took a big turn. We realized it wasn't necessary to have reality in popular recorded music—maybe it was not even desirable.

From that point on, recording took a lot of turns—all of which are fascinating to explore. But that one record *forever* changed popular music. I talked to Les about it and he, of course, denies that there was any real pioneering being done by him. But that record was a turning point and we've never looked back.

What did you learn from Quincy Jones?

He told me once, "It's much easier to be done than to be satisfied." I drive everybody nuts with that philosophy, of course. I also learned about Quincy's kaleidoscopic approach to music—examining it from one angle, then you turn it and look from another angle.

What makes a great producer?

A great producer is like a great director in motion pictures—he knows how to cast the work at hand, and choose the right musicians, engineers, orchestrators, copyists. Then he gives them the freedom to do what they do well.

Any tips for people recording at home?

The musical values are always the same. The only difference in recording at home is that you have to keep the dogs quiet.

Do you have any interesting business tips?

Keep it in the family—someone you can trust.

Any advice for getting a good start as an engineer?

Listen to a variety of live music, a lot. Develop in your mind's ear a benchmark based on live music, real music. Learn how to identify a good musical balance in an acoustical situation—all music is conceived to be heard with acoustical support. By acoustical support, I don't mean reverb or echo. Then pick a good school. And finally, the most difficult thing for young people to learn: trust and follow your instincts.

Tommy Tedesco, LA 1988

Tommy Tedesco

The Man with the Golden Guitar

You play so many stringed instruments—how did you learn how?

I do it very Hollywood style. I tune 'em all like a guitar. If they want a truly authentic player, they'll hire that person. But generally, they run into problems, because they may not read, or aren't familiar with studio playing. You've got to be able to do exactly what is called for.

What about picking—what's your method?

I do what I call "economy picking." When you enter from one string to the next string, you always enter on a down stroke. It's worked for me. I can also do alternative picking, but this way I can play runs twice as fast.

How did you meet Frank Zappa?

It was funny, because I had heard about Zappa for many years. I'd seen pictures of him and thought he was the scariest person I'd ever seen in my life. When I got a call for *Lumpy Gravy*, I decided to do something different. I went in pajama bottoms and weird clothes—this was before it was hip to wear pajama bottoms. I walked in and Frank came over and introduced himself and said, "I like your costume." I told him I liked his, too.

The next thing cracked me up. He said, "You don't remember me, but when I was 15 I used to go to a bowling alley in West Covina and listen to you play." I 'bout died. I didn't realize he was a kid at one time. It was a whole different image. Since then, we've been together at times and he's unbelievable. After playing with him, I realized I shouldn't have been screwing around when we first met. I had to pay attention to what he wanted, because it was rough stuff to play. He's an incredible writer—one of the rare exceptions where you hear about someone and they live up to the stories. Dynamic music, but from a foreign place.

Can you recall any ridiculous sessions in your career?

I can remember some Phil Spector dates where Leon Russell would stand on the piano and start preaching.

And advice for young musicians interested in studio playing?

You have to be where there are sessions, like L.A., New York, Nashville. You have to be where the business is. Next step, people have to know you—you have to get a reputation. And never give up—as soon as you put the instrument in the corner, it's all over. Go to your own limit and maybe something will happen.

Toots Thielemans, Hittsville Recording Studios, LA 1991

Toots Thielemans

Man Bites Harmonica

Why did you choose the chromatic harmonica?

In the beginning I thought, play everything in C. I got good enough and friends would say I should sit in with the bands we went to see. I asked if they played the blues in C. "No, B flat." I studied for a week and came back. Then it was "Tea For Two" in A flat. I had studied all the original keys where the songs were written, but if I wanted to sit in, the bands would not transpose for me. It was survival. Play in their key or don't play. That way I learned to express myself fluently in all the keys. And each key has its problems and its advantages. Some runs, some effects are easier or sound more fluent, or *lay* better. That's a freak of an instrument, because some notes are blown and some are inhaled.

The harmonica strikes me as a very brave little instrument, like a voice.

It's a brave instrument, but also the harmonica is one of the few instruments that can create a mood all by itself. Okay, when a guy waits for the electric chair in the prison cell, you're not going to hear a violin playing all by itself, or a piano. That's almost too obvious an example, but the harmonica somehow can create a mood—I don't know how, but I'm happy it does, 'cause it got me a few jobs.

You're also known as a whistler.

My whole musical life, and maybe the rest, is a hobby that became a passion that became part of my life and my body. I bought a harmonica and then discovered jazz—that became my passion. I didn't go to school to play the harmonica or study jazz or guitar.

The whistling is the same thing. I'm not such a good whistler, in terms of whistling by myself, like Ron Macroby, who calls himself a "Puckerist." What I do is whistle together with the guitar, roughly speaking, like a flute on top, like a wind instrument playing the same runs.

I understand you were the first to really combine whistling and guitar?

Sure, nobody thought of it before. It may not be much, but it's something, right? Actually, it's a little like Slam Stewart. Nobody before him sang along with the bass. "Zoop zoop—Flat Foot Floogie." Slam did that. Twenty years after I did the whistling, George Benson underlined his scat singing with guitar.

What's the secret of your success?

Sweat. And each day, you know, doing my best, without believing in applause—having a rewarding feeling, but it's not because of a lot of applause that you play better.

photo by Tom Dubé

Richard Thompson, circa 2000

Richard Thompson

Burning Up the Road

How many guitars do you have?

Probably no more than eight—a modest total. I've got two Loudin acoustics, two Ferrington acoustics, a Ferrington acoustic baritone, a Ferrington electric, two Fender Stratocasters, and a couple of other things mucking around.

What music would you like played at your funeral?

Oh, I think I'd like the "Diwan" of Shaykh Muhammad Ibn-al-Habib, sung by the Tetuan Singers.

Is playing the guitar a form of exercise?

Depends on whether you play sitting down or standing up, I suppose.

A form of escape?

Could be a form of escape, but I think actually it's more a form of connecting with your inner being, your inner reality.

Aggression?

It can be a way that aggression is expressed. I think performance is a way of expressing aggression. I would broaden the idea to include the whole of performance. I find that you have to attack the audience sometimes—do a pre-emptive strike and get to the audience's airfields before they can start throwing tomatoes at you.

My Thompson theorem—you grew up singing the sad stories of other people, the folk troubadour with a fiery guitar and now tell tall tales of your own troubles with a resonance that reaches back through countless centuries. How did your folk days help you?

I think tradition is very important. To come from tradition gives you solidity, and a confidence to experiment and explore. As they say, those who don't know their history are doomed to repeat it. If you don't know what the past is, you can't invent the future. To be modern, contemporary, and forward looking, you have to know where you came from. There is such strength in traditional music. Compare a typical pop song with a Scottish ballad—no question which is the greater song by several hundredfold. It's been sung for hundreds of years, and all the bad verses have been dropped. The language is refined, and so strong, colorful, immediate. So much is conveyed in one verse, staggeringly good, and yet, it is popular music. If you study that, it can give you a strength, a wonderful base to build on.

Any inspirational words for those thinking of entering the music business?

Be honest. Tell the truth. Trust your instincts. And never eat at a restaurant called "Mom's."

Russ Titelman, LA 1994

Russ Titelman

✕✕

How did your producing career get started?

Well, I'd been a musician, playing on sessions and hanging out. The music business was entirely different in those days—I used to hang out at Metric Music with Lenny Waronker [now president of Warner Bros.], go over to Screen Gems where Brian Wilson would be working. Time went on, and I started taking sitar lessons at the Ravi Shankar School of Music in 1968. I met Lowell George there—he could play anything you could put into his hands, while everybody else was clunking away trying to pull the string correctly.

We all got together and did the *Performance* soundtrack, which Jack Nitzsche wrote. Ry Cooder, myself, and Randy Newman were the core of the band for the film. Interesting film, but bizarre. We went to a screening and do you remember when James Fox gets whipped? Randy leaned over and said to me, "Your mother will be *so* proud of you."

Did you play on "Memo From Turner"?

We played on all of it. That started as a track that Traffic had done and they didn't like the way it worked. We had a click track and Jagger's voice and we just played behind it. I played the Keith Richards rhythm part and Ry played slide. I think Bobby West played the bass, Gene Parson the drums. And the keyboard stuff was Randy.

Were things more flexible in those days?

Very flexible, and a lot of experimental stuff going on that soundtrack—we asked Lowell to come in and he played shakuhachi, I played the veena. We made all this crazy noise.

Anyway, Lowell was putting together a band—Little Feat. He was going to sign to Lizard Records and I had a friendship with Lenny Waronker. I took Lowell, and Billy Payne and we sat in Lenny's office on the Warner lot. Lowell and Billy played a couple of songs and Lenny said, "Great—go talk to Mo and let's make a record." That was the first album I produced—1969.

Then Lenny brought me in for Randy's live album, and then we made "Sail Away," and Ry Cooder's "Paradise and Lunch." In the meantime, I had signed Graham Central Station and made the album with Larry Graham from Sly and the Family Stone. I hate to use the word, but that was a *seminal* R&B record. Larry made up that whole slap bass style, and he had all these songs he'd been working on for years—so slimy, and smelly, and funky. You talk to any bass player—Marcus Miller, they all idolized him. Larry was the cat.

I'm of a different generation, but I think that the music that we loved—and still love to this day—is timeless. People will probably be listening to Eric Clapton records in 30 years, 50 years.

Tuck and Patti, Binky Studios, Menlo Park,
CA 2000

Tuck & Patti

Jazzical

How did you get your nickname?
TUCK: From "Little Tommy Tucker," because I used to cry when I didn't have food in my mouth. And from "Friar Tuck" because I was a fat little baby.

Who taught you how to play guitar?
TUCK: I'm pretty much self-taught. I played classical piano for seven years before I picked up the guitar, and then I had only a handful of lessons. I listened a lot, and played in bands, watched people, and got real good at figuring things out.

When you play, it sounds like three people playing—how do you do that?
TUCK: There's a lot of counterpoint and a lot of juggling going on. By juggling, I mean not necessarily playing all three parts at once. At this point, I am pretty good at playing two, three, or even four parts at the same time and keeping them going. It really comes from meeting Patti—I had heard other people do it before that, but I was just a straight ahead guitar player in soul and jazz bands when we first got together.

I play fingerstyle and keep a bass line going with the chords, plus some percussive action, and maybe some counter-melody—maybe even some inner motion with something that just developed. I had an ear for it from playing classical piano.

Patti, did you have a mentor?
PATTI: I had a really great teacher. I played violin starting in grade school and by the time I got to high school, I found a real teacher—Owen Fleming. I loved the violin, and then I started performing in school musicals and singing with the orchestra. He gave me a good classical foundation.

How would you compare now with the way it was when you first started out together?
PATTI: We are better musicians, and we continue to get better. We have relentlessly done this for 21 years—as time goes by, it just gets clearer and you get to the point much quicker. It's magical and we don't know where it will end up.

TUCK: Conceptually, it hasn't changed at all since we got together. The concept has evolved, just getting deeper and deeper.

Advice for the young musician?
PATTI: Play music from the bottom of your heart, as good as you can do it. Be true to yourself.

Leanne Ungar and Leonard Cohen, LA 2002

Leanne Ungar

Picturing Poetry

How and why did you become a recording engineer?

I had musician friends and the first time I walked into a studio for their demo session, I fell head over heels for the whole scene. Then there was a small recording studio at the publishing house where I had a temporary job. My friends and I started going in at night and making tapes. Eventually, the publisher hired and trained me.

Who were your recording heroes when you were getting started?

From the point of view of achievement, the women artists of the time, Joni Mitchell, Laura Nyro, and Bonnie Raitt. From an engineering perspective, I was inspired by the way Alembic was hand-making electronics gear for the Grateful Dead and knocked out by the Todd Rundgren records that he recorded by himself. That's when I really started thinking of the artistry present in the craft of recording.

Can you describe the mood in this workshop when Mr. Cohen steps up to your microphone?

Leonard is searching for a character who embodies the story of the song. I am waiting to meet that character, to believe him. Sometimes it happens right away, sometimes after much searching. In the past, working in various studios, there was a healthy dose of approach/avoidance in the process. On *Ten New Songs* a certain level of intimacy and comfort was achieved, due to his being able to work at home.

Sharon Robinson, who produced the record, and I would set up a rough mix and vocal sound he was comfortable with, and then we would leave. He was able to record whenever the mood struck, most often at 3:00 AM, his normal rising time. He would put down track after track on a 24-bit DA78, whispering into the mic alone in the quiet of night. This also worked well for me, as the studio wasn't really soundproof, and it cut down on the amount of dog barks and helicopter passbys I had to edit out. We would come back much later and the three of us would sift through, find the performance, and transfer it into Pro Tools.

Sharon collaborated with Leonard on the writing of all ten songs. He wrote the lyrics and she the music. She has a Pro Tools set up at her place, too. The hard drive would go back and forth for many revisions as the arrangements grew. Most of the sounds are samples that she played. When you listen to the backing tracks, you can hear that she created incredibly dense and complex rhythms that still are able to hang back and allow the lyric and voice to be the focus.

CJ Vanston, The Treehouse, LA 1998

CJ Vanston

Smoke on the Organ

What is the first music you remember hearing?
My dad, Paul Vanston, playing piano with a jazz trio in Saginaw, Michigan. Our apartment was above the nightclub and I had my ear glued to the floor every night. The jazz guys would come up after the gig, like the Kenton band when they were in town, and I could never figure out why all these successful musicians shared one cigarette.

Who is the most amazing artist you've worked with?
Hmmm… I remember being completely blown away by Dolly Parton—what a voice, what a woman. Joe Cocker's voice has never ceased to amaze me. Seeing Tina Turner tear up "Proud Mary" in the studio during the *What's Love Got To Do With It* soundtrack was a huge moment, because I had learned to hate that song from playing in wedding bands years ago. I finally "got it" when I saw her sing it three feet from me. Wow. Also, Christopher Guest, the film director and "Nigel" in Spinal Tap is completely brilliant and constantly inspiring. A truly sick man. My kinda guy.

What makes a great producer?
Picking the team, and finding the vibe.

Do you know any interesting business tricks?
It's all perception and marketing. When I first moved to L.A. I had no staff, but I would send faxes and letters signed with fake secretary names. I actually made phone calls with an English accent, posing as my own agent.

Performance highlight of your life?
Playing "Smoke on the Water" on the pipe organ in the Royal Albert Hall with Spinal Tap. I knew it right then that it could never get better than that.

What old saying do you hate the most?
"It's just a demo." Or, the producer says, "Yeah, it's a nice part, but we have to think about Ma and Pa K-Mart." I could frikkin' puke.

Any advice for getting a good start in the music business?
Surround yourself with great people and you can't go wrong.

What music would you like at your funeral?
A hundred bagpipes playing "Amazing Grace."

How would you like to be remembered in history?
CJ knew where to find the best restaurants.

Suzanne Vega, A&M Records, 1997

Suzanne Vega

Time to Start

You started performing at 16. Is it good to start so young?

In fact it felt late to me, because I'd started writing songs when I was about 14. I had been really interested in The Beatles and they were all massively famous by the time they were 18. I remember feeling that at 16 time was running out and I better get out there if I wanted to do anything with myself. I think 16 is a good time to start.

Had you been warming up?

Yes, by the time I was 16 I had about seventy-five, a hundred songs, so I was a very ambitious teenager. I was rejected in a lot of places because that was the '70s and folk music wasn't exactly in vogue. But it's good to be rejected, too, because you build character and you can take whatever life has to give you after that.

You have a degree in literature. Would you advise songwriters to pursue an education in literature and poetry?

No [laughs]. I wouldn't. I learned more from just reading. I loved to read, and had loved to read since I was five or six years old. That's really important—to read and figure out what you like for yourself. And working in the theater was very helpful. That probably helped me more than anything.

Do you know any good business tricks?

Yeah—get a lawyer and get a good one. And listen to him. Let him do his job. That's probably the best thing. You always need your own person to fight for you. And sometimes you need several to keep them in balance with each other. If you rely on one person too much, you can get into trouble. I think you always need a team of people with you.

Any advice for a formative artist?

You have to feel within yourself that you have something to offer. You have to be able to continue throughout being rejected or disappointed. If you don't feel that you really have something that you need to say, then you should try another profession. If you can make it through those times where you're rejected and depressed and you're not in fashion, you're not trendy, you're not hip—then you really know that you're cut out for it. Yet, you have to love it for itself. You have to love writing songs, and the rhymes and the guitar—you have to love those things for themselves. If you get into it because it's cool, or you want to be like whoever the current person is of the year, then it won't last and you're taking up everybody else's time.

(L-R) David Was and Don Was, Record Plant Recording Studios, LA 1990

David Was

What Was (Not Was) Is

This "Was (Not Was)" name has not been explained to me.
It's the distributive principal, actually. As in "Was (Not Was) = Was Not + Was^2." It's sort of algebraic.

What do you think Beethoven would be doing today in 1990 if he was alive and well, and not decomposing?
I would say a guy like Ludwig would probably be the equivalent in the pop music world of someone like Steve Vai. When I hear Vai, I hear that same architectonic sound.

You were once a jazz critic?
Yes, on my way to somewhere else. I really never meant to be one, and I apologize to the world for being one.

Was this to make money?
It was basically to not work and make money. I just continued the same lifestyle I had led throughout my adolescent years with Don Was. I met him when he was playing the junior high talent show doing a crude impression of Dylan. I had never heard of Dylan at 11 years old and took Don to be the real thing. Later on, naturally, I was bitterly disappointed. But I did fall under the sway of music and started studying and quitting every major instrument in the orchestra by the time I was 18.

How do you pay all the people who are on your records?
We're like a benevolent association. Sort of a soup kitchen. We've kept a lot of people alive. It's the most satisfying thing about our work.

And you are the main lyricist in the group?
Yes, but Don is my editor. He will edit a song from three pieces laying around in three different rooms. Bing, bing, bing—all of a sudden you've got "Yesterday," "Stardust."

1990—what a way to start out the decade, huh? You guys are on the top of the heap! I was just wondering. Do you ever wake up and fear that the ice is suddenly thin and the whole success will come crashing down?
There were so many times when we should have fallen through the ice and didn't. You don't expect the sky—but to even get to the top of a tree seems like gravy. You don't expect to drown anymore, and are constantly surprised by things working out. You begin to trust yourself a little more. We've been rolling for ten years like this, so I guess it could only get better.

Bonnie Raitt and Don Was, Record Plant Recording Studios, LA 1989

Bonnie Raitt, Ed Cherney, Don Was, Record Plant, LA 1989

Don Was and Bonnie Raitt, Record Plant, LA 1989

Don Was

Is   1990

⬥⬥

What is the first music you remember, the first song that got to you?
There is a great irony here. The first music I remember hearing was the Broadway cast album of *The Pajama Game*, which my mother played incessantly. It was John Raitt singing "Hey, there, you with the stars in your eyes" that first got me. When I first met Bonnie she had me call her dad's answering machine, where he sings that line and then says "Hi, we're not home now…" I got my mother to call long distance so she could hear it.

Who showed you that music could be fun?
Actually, I had a terrible music education, but there was one piano teacher in Detroit that I really liked. His name was Murray Jackman and he played the piano bar at the Playboy Club. He would come to my house and was very cool, and was always trying to pick up on my mother. He was a great influence on me.

I only took three lessons with him, but I didn't really like the discipline of learning scales. I only wanted to play what I felt like playing, and he was the one who said, "Okay, just do it." He explained that everything had chords and if you are going to play a C chord, you might as well be playing *West Side Story* as Mozart. He gave me that greater picture.

Where does your music come from?
I think it's a combination of having some R&B roots, and then being a little embarrassed being a white Jewish guy imitating it without hedging your bets. This is where you get a Bob Dylan, a guy who is essentially half John Lee Hooker and half Jewish intelligentsia. He's the genetic blend of the two. For second generation guys with a little consciousness of it, it's hard to throw these roots back, but you have the roots. You can't get around it.

As an example, "Yer Blues." The Beatles couldn't quite do a blues song. Lennon had to put his stamp on it; twist it around. Dylan's stuff is all that—essentially roots, blues and folk music with a contemporary twist on it. Zappa added this touch of humor, although I think you can find the humor in Bob Dylan. It's using roots music as a vehicle for rebellion.

Do you have a clear, distinct idea in mind when you start producing a project?
I'm loathe to go into something if I can't hear it first. It's like Hitchcock used to do elaborate planning. I don't go to that extent, where I have to hear every guitar part beforehand, but if I can't imagine what the overall texture will be, I figure I have nothing to offer. I think you go in as a fan. That's the best producer—someone who is a fan.

Jimmy Webb, circa 1988

Jimmy Webb

Captain Hook

What is a hook?

A hook is that *good* part of a song. The hook is the best part.

Does that come first?

Well, I don't give a lot of conscious thought to it. How could I set out to write a song like "Highwayman" and think about the hook? I'm so involved in telling the story that I'm not thinking about the hook. I'm dedicated to telling the story and somehow or other in the last verse the hook comes to me—God gives it to me. "Perhaps I may become a highwayman again." That's the hook in that song. But I don't go out consciously searching for these things. Sometimes they happen nicely of their own accord, and I tend not to contrive them.

When you're writing, what comes first—the lyrical nugget or the musical mood of the song?

When I first started writing, years ago, I almost always got things out of musical combinations: chords, melodies, musical elements that enthralled me and made me feel good, made me tingle a bit. That would get me started on a song. I started out from the musical side, and used the music, the playing of the chords, and the whole meditation of working with the piano. Down through the years, I have gradually become more of a lyric writer. I think I'm at my best when I sit down and work out a lyric and start working the real idea in advance of the music.

Do you see songs cinematically? Your work seems so visual.

Well, I do relate to music visually and I do see things. For instance, "Wichita Lineman" came to me when I was driving along one of those flat Oklahoma panhandle roads up by Kansas. You can see for 50 miles and the telephone poles just receding into the distance, getting smaller and smaller. As I was driving, I saw a man working on the top of one of these tall poles. There he was, suspended between heaven and earth.

"Macarthur Park" is another—I conjure up very clearly what that love affair meant to me. It's encapsulated in a picture of a Sunday afternoon lunch, walking through the park with my girlfriend then. All those images are little snapshots that I keep.

Can you remember the first song you ever heard?

One of the first things I remember is riding along in the back seat of my dad's '52 Plymouth at night and hearing "Tara's Theme" from *Gone With the Wind*. It was cozy in the back seat and I remember the green glow from the instruments on the dashboard. My folks were talking and I drifted off to sleep listening to them and the music on the radio.

Max Weinberg, LA 1990

Max Weinberg

Boss Beat

✕✕

How tough was it for The E Street Band in the early days?

It was tough on the road, but we always had a great band. All my life I wanted to be in a great band, a band that left people blown away. When I first went on the road with Bruce I was 23—I'm 38 now—and the only thing I had was a set of drums. No car, no place to live. For me, it was the greatest life in the world. I was getting 50 to 75 bucks every week, playing six shows a week. I loved it. We rode the buses for ten years—long rides. Eight or ten hours on the bus was nothing to me. But it was tough, because physically you got worn down.

Now, I feel very privileged to have gone through such an experience, because if you make it today you don't do that kind of thing anymore. There are still bands on the road, but not like it was then. Now you make your first record and if you're successful you go straight to the arenas. We played for six years before we played an arena show.

We did every kind of gig imaginable but I never thought of it as hard. I never lost sight of the fact that I was very lucky to have joined the band at *that* particular time, to experience everything from driving ourselves around, playing small clubs to riding the hottest jets going to the biggest stadiums. It was a progression and every night I was able to get up there and blow it completely out. I never had any trouble sleeping.

After all these years, has it become intuitive, subliminal working with Bruce?

Absolutely, and it actually became intuitive very early on. We're street musicians, schooled in the bars and the joints of New Jersey where there is not a lot of technical prowess. You could find better players—more technically proficient guys—but you would never find any musicians who play with more feeling, or who believe as strongly in the music they are playing. That's what comes across. The rehearsals in Bruce's living room are as intense as it is onstage. Nobody lays back in this band. It's a band about heat.

What is your strangest characteristic as a drummer—the odd twist in your style?

I can hold a single stroke roll longer than just about anybody—right-left, right-left as fast as you can go. "Miami" Steve always insisted that the drummer follow through to the downbeat. It isn't used very often, but Bruce calls it the "Weinberg Roll." I guess my strongest point is my feeling for rock-and-roll.

How old were you when you started playing?

Four years old—a cousin gave me an old drum and one stick and I was good on that thing. I could bang on that drum and get rhythms going. At four you are able to do that kind of thing. I could play the drums from the first time I picked up a pair of sticks and I started taking drum lessons when I was seven years old. I got paid to play when I was eight, and since then I've considered myself a professional drummer.

(L-R) Lisa Coleman and Wendy Melvoin, Sound Factory, LA 1997

(L-R) Lisa Coleman and Wendy Melvoin, Sound Factory, LA 1997

Lisa Coleman, Tchad Blake, Wendy Melvoin, Sound Factory, LA 1997

Wendy & Lisa

Girl Brothers

Who is responsible for the lyrics, and who is responsible for the music?
WENDY: Depends—sometimes Lisa goes away and comes back with a finished piece; sometimes I do the same. She'll put the frame around mine, or I'll frame her song. Other times we sit down with a couple of guitars and start from scratch.

If you were a musical instrument, what would you be?
WENDY: I'd be that mixing board at the Sound Factory and Tchad Blake would be using it.

LISA: I would be the first piano I played as a kid, an upright Yamaha, which I still have. It helped raise me, and is responsible for the way I am.

What's wrong with the music industry?
LISA: It's run by people who aren't musicians—sort of upside down.

Is it getting better or worse?
WENDY: Worse. A horrifying experience.

Which came first, music or the musician?
LISA: Music. Musicians take sounds and put them where they want them. It's very interesting that with sampling and the more advanced our technology becomes, the more we are able to use the natural sounds of nature.

Who inspired you two to be musicians?
WENDY: My parents. My father was a professional, of course, but my mother was the ultimate musical fan—she really loved listening and experiencing music. I loved the idea that someone might appreciate my music as much as my mother enjoyed it.

LISA: Same here. My father playing the piano inspired me, and my mother would play me records she loved.

What music would you like played at your funeral?
LISA: Carousel music—a circus atmosphere.

Do you have any interesting business tips?
LISA: Don't trust anybody.

WENDY: Take risks but don't be stupid. Don't let your ego make your decisions.

What old saying do you hate the most?
WENDY: "Not bad for a girl." I hate that.

LISA: But I think girls should always be bad. As Mae West said, "When I'm good, I'm very good. But when I'm bad, I'm better."

Any advice for getting a good start in the music business?
WENDY: Find a good therapist.

LISA: Talent would be helpful.

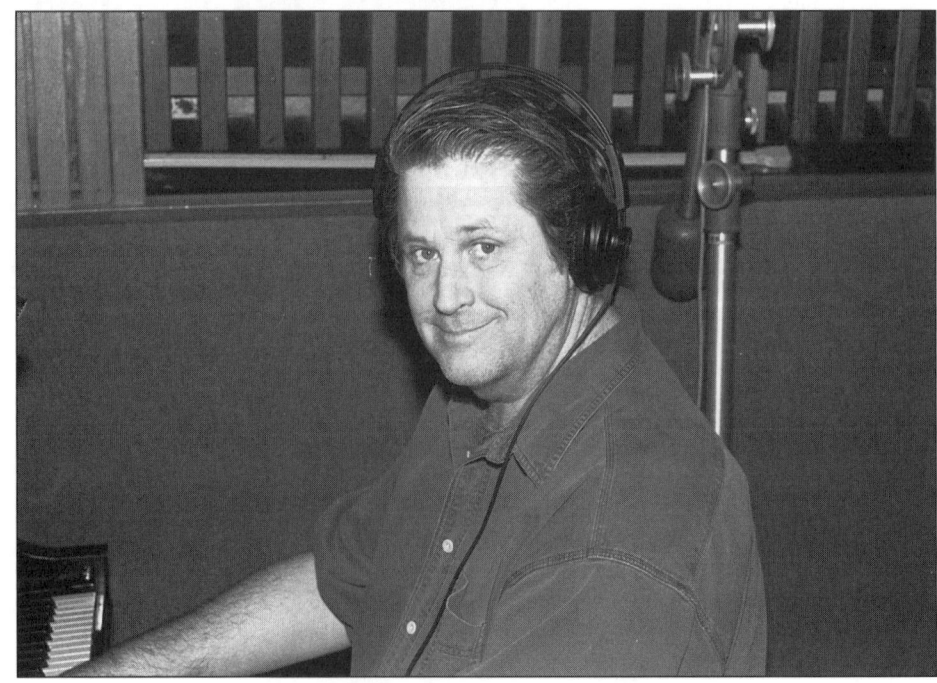

Brian Wilson, Ocean Way Recording Studios, LA 1995

Brian Wilson

American Original

Do you know how to surf?
No. I tried once and the board shot by my head—almost hit me. Scared me so bad, I never tried again.

Can you imagine what your life would have been if you hadn't become a musician?
No. Maybe hell.

What was the first song you produced?
I think it was "Surfin' USA."

How did it change for you when you began producing and taking charge?
Well, when you have the production in your hands you are able to do something that you can control and it could be a smash. Sometimes I feel like I didn't have all the control over the records I produced. I thought there was somebody up there in heaven that would pull my strings, but that's okay. I could be that person who surprised God with all my talent. I think God liked The Beach Boys because of their ability.

Can we talk about Pet Sounds?
That was the love album. It had love in it, and I think people need that. A lot of people don't want to admit it, but they need that kind of a spiritual love that we put out there in our records.

"God Only Knows" is supposed to be the first pop song that had God in the title…
For a while there, no one got away with that, but we got away with it, because—we got away with it [laughs].

As time goes by, I think I'm beginning to understand your voice more and more.
Right. Well, that's very personal. You could tell the difference between "Surfer Girl" and "Sloop John B." Two different kinds of voices. Now how did those come out of this one throat? I don't know.

And the album finishes with "Caroline No."
"Carol I Know." It's "Carol I Know."

Through some of the ups and downs in your life has music helped you carry on?
Well, it's just peace for me. I heal from it. I thrive on it. I need it really badly, I really do.

Your first song?
"Surfer Girl" in 1961.

Not a bad place to start. What's the biggest success?
Probably "Good Vibrations." Went to #1. Everybody said "You're a great genius, Brian." And I'm thinking to myself, "Wow, how the hell did that happen anyway?" That record happened, but I'm not sure it was produced. Could be just the place, you know? I wasn't really able to explain it to anybody [laughs]. Kind of personal, you know?

Stevie Wonder and producer Quincy Jones, Wonderland Recording
Studios, LA 1987

Stevie Wonder

Love With It

What was the first song you wrote?
"Lonely Boy"—never recorded.

Your first instrument?
Harmonica, and then piano.

How did your parents contribute to your life as an artist?
Well, my mother sang in church, and both of my parents were singers. They were never recorded, but they could hold a note.

What have you gained from your long relationship with engineer Gary O?
Most of all, I think he's a person who has been eager in creating a marriage between music and technology—being able to record it on tape. He has the ability to understand what I come up with musically and I can share my ideas with him—he knows how I imagine it sounding and can make it a reality. It's like him watching my ears. And, of course, he's been a very best friend. We've grown a lot together and a lot of the time has been the most significant and precious time.

You spoke to me once about some dark premonitions you had—do you often have flashes of the future?
Yes, I do, and I'm sure they'll continue. The interesting thing about the future is that even with premonitions, you live with faith and trust that whatever you perceive it as being, it is only a change to move onto another place for yourself, and those around you—loved ones, friends, acquaintances.

What fulfills your heart the most?
I love people. I love meeting people and I love knowing that those people who are special to me—those that are very close, but also just about everybody I've met—I love bringing a smile, a positive feeling. I have been fortunate to do many things in this profession, which is something that I cherish very highly. And yet, as much as I love it, I want others with talent to have the opportunities. It's just not enough for me alone—I want it for other people as well.

When did the picture of your life come together and you knew your destiny?
I think I'm still learning about my voice and my talents. I'm still growing and I hope to grow until the day I die. And then I hope that what I leave behind will grow through someone else and become better than where I was able to take it.

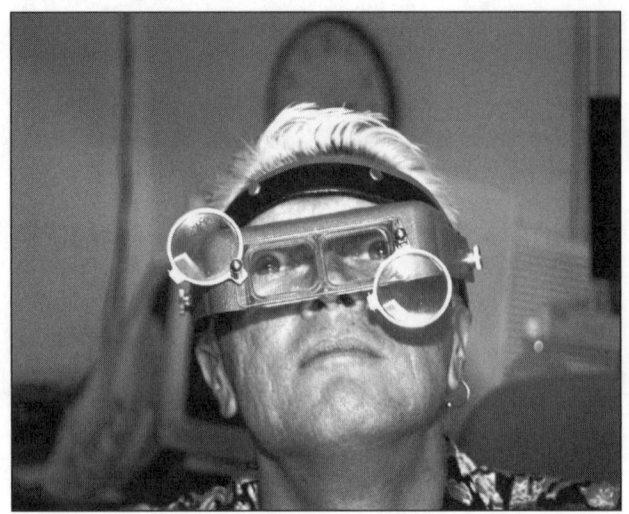

Geza X, LA 1998

Geza X

Punk Pioneer

1998

What was your role in the band The Bags?
The Bags was one of L.A.'s first punk bands, along with The Germs, Weirdos, Screamers, Controllers. I was lead guitarist and we all wore bags on our heads.

Did you enjoy being one of The Deadbeats?
Yes, it was one of the best musical experiences of my life. Back in the '70s, I idolized Frank Zappa, Captain Beefheart and loved '60s underground music. The Deadbeats played jazz-punk—really rude, loud, and rowdy, with power chords off flat 5s in a primitive rhythmic setting. At one gig at The Whisky, I threw seaweed at the audience. We were either loved or hated by the punk audiences.

Were you the boss in The Mommymen?
Yes, I was a total totalitarian. I thought we were going to be huge, my version of Beefheart meets The Knack, with nasal vocals courtesy of me as the lead singer known as "Victim," a whining psycho kid. Socially aware but very neurotic.

Did you ever lose anything?
Yes, I lost my mind for about eight years. I haven't done any drugs for years, but I used to be a speed freak and by 1980 I was walking down Hollywood Boulevard in a trenchcoat with my hair sticking out a foot from my head. I was gone, real gone.

Do we really need to make gods out of musicians?
There was a time when musicians really were gods, a distillation of the counterculture. The values of the culture crystallized in these individuals, during the '60s and '70s, and then it was co-opted and the record industry learned how to operate the star-making machinery and create stars artificially. The artists were no longer a reflection of the culture, but a fabrication.

What was your first recorder?
I had a machine made by Wilcox-Gay called "The Recordio," which belonged to the family. You opened the top, flipped out the speaker, it used ¼" tape and had a 78 rpm record player. You could cut records, use it as a PA, plug a guitar into it, and record on tape. It was a mad scientist's do-anything box.

Have you ever witnessed paranormal phenomena?
Yes, once in a while I turn the key in my car's ignition through sheer mind power.

Do you know any interesting business tricks?
Yes, keep your hand on your wallet, because people in the music business will try to skin you alive.

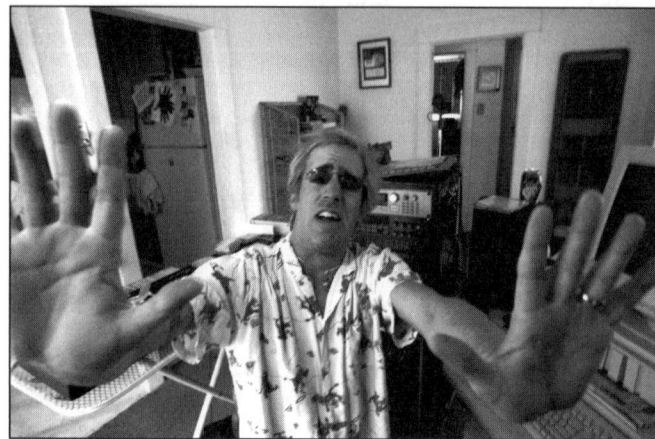

John X, LA 1999

John X

Mixologist

What about this rumor that you and Mick had a little fling?
There was nothing little about it!

If you were a musical instrument, which would you be?
There's a Bulgarian bagpipe made from a sheep, called a Gida. It makes one of the most horrible sounds I've ever heard—sounds like a baby getting a Shiatsu massage.

What music would you like played at your funeral?
The theme from *Sesame Street*.

Garbage—what do they do for fun?
I don't know—they were on tour when I was mixing their remix. I did a remix with Butch Vig for U2, and I love him. He's quite a character.

What is the first music you remember hearing?
Traditional Greek music—you know, get up and throw some plates around. Scare the neighbors.

What did you learn from Danny Saber?
He taught me how to get better hotel rooms when you're out of the country.

Who were your heroes when you were a little snotnose?
My formative inspirations were Todd Rundgren and Brian Eno. And I'm still a little snotnose.

You've worked with Ice Cube—is he any relation to Ice T? Mr. T? Vanilla Ice? What's with all the Ice shit, anyway?
I don't know, but Ice Cube is definitely his own man.

Do you know any interesting business tricks?
I've always found that blackmail works the best.

What old saying do you hate the most?
Can't we just be friends?

Who is the most amazing artist you've worked with?
Of all the unbelievably talented people who have just knocked me out, the most awesome sight was seeing Tom Jones walk into the studio to sing Prince's "Kiss" for the *Art of Noise*. He had laryngitis—no voice, could barely speak, but he went out there and belted it out in one take. That's the vocal that's on the record. It took me longer to set up the microphone than the actual entire session did.

Shelly Yakus, A&M Recording Studios, 1994

Shelly Yakus

Golden Ears

1994

What did you learn from Phil Ramone?
How to use echo, and when you hear something you don't like—you go out to the room and move the microphone, instead of moving the equalizer. You go out and listen in the room.

Was Roy Cicala your main mentor?
Yes, Roy was the engineer who did most of the rock-and-roll at A&R Studios and he began requesting me as his assistant. He was also producing his wife's records at night after the rock sessions. I learned how to get vocal sounds because if he didn't come up with a great vocal for his wife there would be trouble at home.

Basically, what these guys taught me was that anything goes. Don't be afraid. There are no rules. One time we put a prophylactic on a long thin mic, put it into a milk bottle filled with water, and then put headsets on the bottle to send a sound through. We tried everything, especially after The Beatles showed everyone how far you could take it. One time Roy got a great kick drum sound by taking the cardboard liner from a tape box, which had a metal center, and adding a block of wood and taping it to the drum head. Then he hung the mic in surgical tubing so that there was no vibration from the floor.

There were no holds barred in getting sounds, because we didn't have the equipment we have now to make instant sounds. You had to go out there and work your ass off to make it sound exciting.

Who is the most amazing artist you worked with?
So hard to say, because I've worked with so many great people. But it was amazing working with John Lennon on *Walls and Bridges*. Jim Keltner was the drummer, Klaus Voorman on bass, Jesse Ed Davis on guitar, Ed Mottau on acoustic guitar, and Nicky Hopkins on piano. John was producing. He was the kind of person that even if you didn't know who he was, and he was standing in a crowd of a thousand people, you would pick him out first. He just had this aura, and he was also a very kind person. He'd come in after each take and look at the musicians and say, "Anybody have any mistakes they want to tell me about before we play this, so I know what I'm listening for?"

During one take I had the Fairchild on the overhead tom-tom mics and somebody kicked the plug out of the wall in the middle of the song. When the tom-tom part came during the break it sounded like they were down at the end of the street. But it worked, just one of those lucky things. John was definitely an amazing person to work with.

331

"Weird" Al Yankovic, LA 1997

"Weird" Al Yankovic

True to the Original

Al, what is the first music that you remember hearing?

One of my earliest musical memories is a song called "Boa Constrictor"—sung by Johnny Cash and written by the brilliant Shel Silverstein. The recording ends with the boa constrictor belching—which to a five-year-old is, of course, the pinnacle of cerebral humor. The first pop song I remember hearing was "These Boots Were Made for Walkin'" by Nancy Sinatra. And even as a small child, I could play that guitar solo.

Who were your heroes when you were getting started?

The artists that influenced me the most were Spike Jones, Allan Sherman, Stan Freberg, Tom Lehrer—people that I came to appreciate through my weekly exposure to the Dr. Demento radio show.

How do you emulate the exact sound of the records you parody?

The secret to producing parodies is working with people that know what they're doing. My recording engineer is as good as they get, and my band is extremely accomplished and versatile. They all pay incredible attention to detail, so I never really have to crack the whip on them. Oftentimes, all I really need to do is to pass out CD singles to the band and say, "Here… learn this!" Depending on the song, sometimes we have to track down an obscure make of guitar or rent an archaic piece of gear or utilize a prehistoric baffling technique. We try to be as authentic as possible.

What was your most thrilling experience in a recording studio?

I was called in to do some session work on a Brian Wilson album a few years ago. Brian was producing, Van Dyke Parks was hanging out (along with Dr. Landy, who was still handling Brian at the time), and there I was, playing the accordion! I don't think that album was ever released—at least the cut I worked on wasn't. All I remember is that the song was in waltz time, and Brian just had me doing the most ridiculously simple oom-pah-pah part. I kind of wanted to show off my chops to him, but I guess it wouldn't have been appropriate in the context of the piece.

What's the biggest mistake of your life?

Turning down the role of Indiana Jones. Oh, and getting that tattoo of John Tesh on my butt.

Do you have any advice for getting a good start in the music business?

Kids, just practice, practice, practice. I don't want any of you having to sleep your way to the top like I did!

Dweezil Zappa, Utility Muffin Research Kitchen, LA 1997

Dweezil Zappa

Son of Invention

Why are you a guitarist?

I enjoy the guitar, I gotta say, just because it's the most versatile instrument. You can make it sound almost any way you want. You can torture it, you can bend the strings. There's just so much that can be done with it.

Did you once change your name?

I never did. I had the fortunate experience of being in a shoe store when I was four years old and this big kid came over and was threatening me. He said, "What's your name?" I told him "Dweezil" and he said it was a stupid name. I said, "What's your name?" He said "Buns." At that point I never questioned the validity of my name. I thought my name was cool—compared with Buns. I thought, "I don't have a problem."

Both Ahmet and Moon wanted to change their names. When Moon was little she wanted to change her name to one she considered to be normal, which was "Beautyheart."

Ahmet was tired of being called "Ahmet Vomit" at school. There was a construction worker at our house who Ahmet thought was cool. He had a motorcycle and his name was Rick. So, Ahmet wanted to be "Rick Zappa." The next day he went to school and told everybody he'd changed his name. "I'm now Rick Zappa." Everybody goes, "Rick the Dick." He went right back to Ahmet Vomit.

If you could go back before recording gear was invented, what would you like to hear?

I like the Baroque period, full of melody. The Renaissance period would be a fascinating thing to witness. The best ideas were just being made up back then.

How would you sum up your experience as a TV sitcom star?

Oh, it was absolutely brutal. The TV show that we did bore no resemblance to the concept that was the original idea for the show. We were put through the TV wringer. Frank told us, "You really don't want to be involved in this industry." He was talking to me and Moon. "I know that you guys want to be excellent at what you do, and you're not allowed to be excellent at anything on TV."

Any business insights for musicians?

I'm still trying to find them myself. It's hard enough to make a living doing anything, and doing something you enjoy doing may be the hardest. For a musician, it depends on the instrument. For guitar players, there are very few opportunities because the instrument is not looked at in the same way it used to be. There used to be an interest in playing rock guitar, but now it's all about learning a few chords. Guitar is almost the kiss of death right now. It's all keyboards, sampled guitar, loops, and manipulation. They don't need guitar players. Bass players may have an easier time finding jobs.

Frank Zappa and Mr. Bonzai, Utility Muffin Research Kitchen, LA 1985

Frank Zappa

Big Mother

What is your strongest characteristic as a human being?
Probably stubbornness.

Have you ever witnessed a miracle?
Well, I think I heard my band play this certain bar in my "The Black Page" correctly one time.

If you hadn't become a musician, what would you be doing now?
I would probably be a chemist, or a physicist.

Who is your best musical friend?
I don't have any friends in any category—I try to avoid them.

Who has musically affected you the most?
Probably Varese—and also Webern and Stravinsky.

Are you as successful as you would like to be?
I would say that the basic characteristic of my life is failure. If there is one thing that I excel at, it's failure—I manage to fail at 100 percent of the things that I do. Since most of the things that I set out to do are theoretically impossible, it's very easy to fail. I've learned to live with it. In terms of machinery and personnel, there never seems to be enough to get things done exactly right.

What's the most outrageous thing a fan has done to you?
I was knocked off the stage by some bimbo in London—broke my leg, a rib, put a hole in the back of my head, broke my nose. I was in a wheelchair for a year.

If you were to star in a film, what would your dream role be?
I never liked the idea of acting. I have trouble identifying with things that are "make-believe," where people pretend.

Do you have any idiosyncrasies?
I smoke a lot of cigarettes, drink a lot of coffee, and do a lot of work.

Why do people have pets?
That varies from person to person. I have pets because I like them better than humans. Some people have pets because they think they're furniture.

How would you like to be remembered in the distant future?
I would rather not. I'd rather just skip it. I think that people who build an aspect of remembrance into their work habits, like "If I don't do this, then how will I be remembered?"—that's really bad. You should just plan for The Big Blotch.

Was there anything wrong with this interview?
No, it was perfect.

Hans Zimmer, Media Ventures, LA 1995

Hans Zimmer

Scoring King 1995

In the pop music world, you were a member of The Rutles?
Rutles? No, the ill-fated Buggles. Nobody got that joke. You got it, because it's the same as The Rutles. Buggles? Bugs are little Beatles. Nobody got it. Oh well. We had a hit with "Video Killed the Radio Star" and all hell broke loose.

How did you break in to film scoring?
It came about because I was scoring commercials for a company which belonged to George Martin. George actually gave me my first job.

What was the big challenge of Crimson Tide?
Trying to do an action picture and not making it like an action picture. Not going over the old ground that other people have done. That's the idea of the choirs, the idea of becoming very still without virtually any movement. And I was forever trying to create this muddled underwater sound. There are very few hard edges in the soundtrack of *Crimson Tide*. Everything seems to be muffled; nothing really seems to go above G above Middle C. I was purposely trying to have the weight of the ocean above me.

Do you enjoy pulling the emotional strings, do you like to scare people?
Oh, I love to scare people. I love to scare myself. I try to be very careful, though, because there's a Hollywood way of scoring pictures I notice more and more. Something happens and as it happens the music will tell you everything that's happening. What I try to do most of the time is to have a reaction.

In *The Lion King* it was the big stampede. At a certain point I went, "No more action, no more hitting cuts. I'm going to write this requiem here and even though the father lion is still running around, I'm going to tell you he ain't gonna make it." And I get slow and quite sad. What I like to do is a reaction to the scene as opposed to the music either signaling what is going to happen or simultaneously doing the same thing. I try to wait until the end of the cut and then do that other thing you can't describe in words or pictures, the emotional thing. I think that if you do it at the same time, it's like telling a joke twice. It's not as funny; it's meaningless.

Why did you get involved in film?
I can't think of anything else that's as close to magic. I'm totally useless in the real world. I don't drive a car; I don't play tennis or any of those things. I read books and I love films. My whole life takes place in some sort of imaginary place and I worked bloody hard to never have to grow up. I'm an extreme escapist.

Appendix

Biographical information and selected credits.

Adante, Gary
Engineer, producer, widely known for his many albums with Stevie Wonder.

Alagia, John
Producer/engineer/mixer. Credits include Dave Matthews Band, John Mayer, Liz Phair, Lifehouse.

Allen, Steve
Comedian, composer, author, founder of The Tonight Show *(1921-2000).*

Allison, Mose
Composer, pianist, performer. Songs have been recorded by The Who, Leon Russell, Bonnie Raitt, etc.

Alpert, Herb
Composer, trumpeter, co-founder of A&M Records.

Apple, Fiona
Singer, songwriter, pianist.

Asher, Peter
Composer, producer, performed/recorded as Peter and Gordon with Gordon Waller.

Barresi, Joe
Engineer, producer, mixer. Credits include Buckcherry, Fu Manchu, Queens of the Stone Age, Loudmouth, Catherine Wheel, Monster Magnet, Veruca Salt, Anthrax, Bauhaus, The Jesus Lizard, Alanis Morissette, Loudermilk, Fastball, Powerman 5000, Hole, Weezer, Kyuss, Beth Hart, The Rentals.

Baxter, Jeff
Producer, composer, guitarist. Credits include Steely Dan, The Doobie Brothers.

Becker, Terry
Engineer, producer. Credits include Bonnie Raitt, Jackson Browne, The Crusaders, The Band.

Becker, Walter
Guitarist, bassist, songwriter, producer, co-founder of Steely Dan.

Benson, Ray
Hailed as the Post-Modern King of Western Swing, founder of Asleep at the Wheel.

Bishop, Stephen
Singer, songwriter, composer. Credits include "On and On" and music for Animal House, Roadie, Tootsie, The China Syndrome, Unfaithfully Yours.

Blaine, Hal
Recording and performing drummer. World's most recorded musician. Credits include The Beach Boys, Tijuana Brass, Frank Sinatra, Elvis Presley, The Mamas and the Papas, John Denver.

Blake, Tchad
Producer, engineer, musician. Credits include Los Lobos, Richard Thompson, Crowded House, Bonnie Raitt, Peter Gabriel.

Böhm, Martin
Engineer, producer, Vienna's MG Sound studio owner. Credits include U2, Marianne Faithfull, Jose Carrera, Placido Domingo.

Botnick, Bruce
Engineer, producer. Credits include The Doors, The Beach Boys, Love, The Buffalo Springfield, The Turtles, Tim Buckley, scores by John Williams and Jerry Goldsmith.

Brion, Jon
Producer, engineer, songwriter, multi-instrumentalist. Credits include Fiona Apple, Aimee Mann, David Byrne, Rufus Wainwright, Eels, scoring Magnolia, Eternal Sunshine of the Spotless Mind, Punch-Drunk Love, I Heart Huckabees.

BT
Brian Transeau. Producer, engineer, re-mixer, composer. Credits include Britney Spears, NSYNC, scores for Monster, The Fast and the Furious.

Buckingham, Lindsey
Producer, songwriter, guitarist, renowned as a member of Fleetwood Mac.

Buffett, Jimmy
Singer, songwriter, author, sailor, pilot.

Carlton, Vanessa
Singer, songwriter, pianist, ballerina.

Cheech & Chong
Comedians, musicians, actors, filmmakers.

Cherney, Ed
Engineer, producer. Credits include The Rolling Stones, Elton John, Kris Kristofferson, Jann Arden, The Manhattan Transfer.

Ciani, Suzanne
Composer, pianist, electronic music pioneer.

Clearmountain, Bob
Engineer, mixer, producer. Credits include Bryan Adams, David Bowie, Roxy Music, INXS, Simple Minds, The Pretenders, Crowded House.

Cohen, Leonard
Singer, songwriter, poet, author.

Connick, Harry Jr.
Composer, pianist, singer, actor.

Copeland, Stewart
Composer, drummer, film scorist, founding member of The Police.

Coppola, Carmine
Flautist, film scorist, father of Francis Ford Coppola. Credits include The Godfather: Parts, I, II, and III, Tucker: The Man and His Dream, The Outsiders, Gardens of Stone, The Black Stallion, Apocalypse Now *(1910–1991).*

Crenshaw, Marshall
Singer, songwriter, actor, author.

Criss, Peter
Drummer, songwriter, founding member of KISS.

Cropper, Steve
Guitarist, songwriter, member of Booker T. and the MGs.

Crosby, David and Nash, Graham
Singers, songwriters, producers. Crosby was a founding member of The Byrds and Crosby, Stills, and Nash. Nash was a founding member of The Hollies.

Crowded House
Australian band co-founded by Neil Finn.

Crystal Method
Dance-based electronic duo influenced by rock, hip-hop, soul, and pop.

Devo
New Wave band renowned for pioneering music videos.

Douglas, Steve
Sax player, worked with Duane Eddy, Phil Spector, The Beach Boys, Jan & Dean, Bob Dylan, Ry Cooder, The Ramones (1938 – 1993).

Dr. Demento
Barret Hansen, master's degree in music from UCLA, radio producer and announcer, record collector and compilation producer.

Dr. John
Mac Rebennack. Pianist, singer, songwriter, New Orleans legend.

Duke, George
Producer, pianist, music director. Credits include work with Jean-Luc Ponty, Don Ellis, Frank Zappa, Cannonball Adderley, Sonny Rollins, Billy Cobham, Stanley Clarke.

Eddy, Duane
One of the most successful instrumental rockers, known for his low, twangy guitar sound.

Eels
E aka Mark Oliver Everett. Singer, songwriter, multi-instrumentalist.

Elfman, Danny
Scoring composer and founder of Oingo Boingo. Credits include Charlie and the Chocolate Factory, Chicago, Men in Black, Spider-Man, Mission: Impossible, Batman.

Emerick, Geoff
Engineer, producer. Credits include The Beatles, The Zombies, Badfinger, Split Enz, Elvis Costello.

Fair, Ron
Producer, engineer, mixer, record company executive. Credits include Slayer, Vanessa Carlton, Christina Aguilera, Lisa Loeb, Big Mountain.

Finn, Jerry
Producer, engineer, mixer. Credits include Green Day, Rancid, Blink-182, Sum 41, Fastball, Bad Religion.

Finn, Tim
Singer, songwriter, guitarist, pianist, founding member of Split Enz.

Firesign Theatre
Comedians, writers, performers, recording artists. Founded in 1966.

Fleetwood, Mick
Drummer, co-founder of Fleetwood Mac.

Foster, David
Producer, composer, keyboardist. Credits include Celine Dion, Chicago, Whitney Houston, John Lennon, Barbra Streisand, Diana Ross, Rod Stewart.

Froom, Mitchell
Composer, producer, arranger, keyboardist. Credits include Los Lobos, Crowded House, Elvis Costello, Richard Thompson, Suzanne Vega, Ron Sexsmith, Sheryl Crow, Bonnie Raitt.

Gabriel, Peter
Singer, songwriter, film scorist, co-founder of Genesis.

Galuten, Albhy
Guitarist, keyboardist, arranger, songwriter, producer, engineer. Credits include The Allman Brothers, Bee Gees, Eric Clapton, Rod Stewart, The Eagles, Jellyfish, Kenny Rogers, Diana Ross, Barbra Streisand.

Gardner, Brian
Mastering engineer. Credits include Dr. Dre, Eminem, 50 Cent, Blink-182, Queens of the Stone Age, Christina Aguilera, Beck, Ray Charles, Creedence Clearwater Revival, DJ Quik, Destiny's Child, Eazy E, ELO, Funkadelic, Marvin Gaye, George Harrison, Ice Cube, Janet Jackson, Linkin Park, Ricky Martin, No Doubt, Prince, Smash Mouth, Snoop Dogg.

Grundman, Bernie
Mastering engineer. Credits include Michael Jackson, Quincy Jones, Stevie Wonder, Van Halen, Prince, The Carpenters, Steely Dan, Herb Alpert, Barbra Streisand, Jack Johnson, Outkast.

Hancock, Herbie
Composer, keyboardist, film scorist, producer. Credits include work with Miles Davis, Donald Byrd, Tony Williams, Wayne Shorter, Freddie Hubbard, George Benson.

Hayes, Gemma
Irish singer, songwriter, guitarist prodigy.

Holland, Brian and Edward
Hall of Fame songwriting and production brothers teamed with Lamont Dozier. Credits include "Where Did Our Love Go," "Baby Love," "Reach Out I'll Be There," "Standing in the Shadows of Love," "Nowhere to Run."

Horn, Paul
Flautist renowned for his recordings in The Taj Mahal, The Great Pyramid, exotic locales in China and the Soviet Union.

Hudson, Mark
Singer, songwriter, producer, actor, member of The Hudson Brothers. Production credits include Ringo Starr, Aerosmith, Hanson.

Hutchence, Michael
Lead singer of the Australian group INXS (1960 – 1997).

Isaak, Chris
Singer, songwriter, actor. His "Wicked Game" from the David Lynch film Wild at Heart *secured his stardom in the early '90s.*

Isham, Mark
Recording artist, film scorist. Credits include Crash, Moonlight Mile, Rules of Engagement, Men of Honor, Blade, The Moderns, Quiz Show, The Majestic.

Jarre, Maurice
Film scorist. Credits include Lawrence of Arabia, Ghost, Fatal Attraction, The Man Who Would Be King, Ryan's Daughter, Topaz, Doctor Zhivago.

Jones, Booker T.
Composer, keyboardist, leader of Booker T. and the MGs.

Jones, Rickie Lee
Singer, songwriter, producer, poet.

Ka'apana, Led
Hawaiian singer, songwriter, arranger, slack key guitar master, proficient on ukulele, steel guitar, autoharp, bass.

Kantner, Paul
Singer, songwriter, founding member of Jefferson Airplane and Jefferson Starship.

Keltner, Jim
Drummer. Credits include John Lennon, Traveling Wilburys, Bob Dylan, Joe Cocker, George Harrison, Willie Nelson, Ry Cooder, Harry Nilsson.

Killen, Kevin
Engineer, producer. Credits include U2, Jewel, Elvis Costello, Peter Gabriel, Tori Amos, Mister Mister, Bryan Ferry, Talking Heads, Laurie Anderson, Sophie B. Hawkins, Paula Cole, Maureen McKenna, Jude Cole, Kate Bush.

King, B.B.
Singer, composer, electric guitar virtuoso, self-styled legendary Bluesman.

Kitaro
Composer, film scorist, electronic music pioneer. First gained international fame for his Silk Roads *score.*

Kooper, Al
Singer, songwriter, keyboardist, bandleader, engineer, producer, scoring composer. Co-founder of The Blues Project; Blood, Sweat & Tears. Plays Hammond B-3 on Bob Dylan's "Like a Rolling Stone." Discovered and produced Lynyrd Skynyrd.

Kortchmar, Danny
Producer, songwriter, guitarist. Credits include Carole King, James Taylor, Linda Ronstadt, Warren Zevon, Harry Nilsson, Jackson Browne, Don Henley, Neil Young, Billy Joel.

Kottke, Leo
Singer, songwriter, acoustic guitar virtuoso.

Kramer, Eddie

Engineer, producer, photographer. Credits include Jimi Hendrix, The Beatles, The Rolling Stones, Led Zeppelin, Bad Company, David Bowie, Eric Clapton, Joe Cocker, Peter Frampton, KISS, Santana, Traffic, Vanilla Fudge.

Kristofferson, Kris

Singer, songwriter, actor. Compositions include "Me and Bobby McGee," "Help Me Make It Through the Night," "Sunday Mornin' Comin' Down."

Kunkel, Nathaniel

Engineer, producer. Credits include Lyle Lovett, Sting, James Taylor, Kenny Loggins, Linda Ronstadt, Dolly Parton, Emmylou Harris.

Kunkel, Russell

Drummer, producer. Credits include Stevie Nicks, Aaron Neville, James Taylor, The Bee Gees, Dolly Parton, Jimmy Buffet, B.B. King, Bob Seger, Carly Simon.

Ladanyi, Greg

Engineer, producer. Credits include Toto, Fleetwood Mac, Don Henley, Jackson Browne.

lang, k.d.

Singer, songwriter, innovator, musical icon, vegetarian.

Leary, Timothy

Writer, lecturer, recorded spoken word/sound montages.

Lindley, David

Singer, songwriter, string instrumentalist, founder of Kaleidoscope and El Rayo X. Credits include Bob Dylan, Rod Stewart, Linda Ronstadt, Ry Cooder, Warren Zevon, James Taylor, Ziggy Marley, David Crosby, Graham Nash.

Los Lobos

Distinctive LA-based band known for their expertise with rock, Tex-Mex, country, folk, R&B, blues, traditional Spanish and Mexican music.

Lovett, Lyle

Singer, songwriter, producer, film composer, Large Band leader.

Lukather, Steve

Guitarist, songwriter, producer, member of Toto. Credits include Elton John, Herb Alpert, Warren Zevon, Chicago, Lionel Richie, Joni Mitchell, Neil Diamond, Larry Carlton, Bob Seger, Rod Stewart, Spinal Tap, Van Halen, Yardbirds.

Lynch, David

Filmmaker, musician. Films include Mulholland Dr., The Straight Story, Twin Peaks: Fire Walk with Me, Wild at Heart, Blue Velvet, Eraserhead, The Elephant Man. *Recorded music with John Neff as "Blue Bob."*

Mancini, Henry

Composer, film scorist. Credits include "Moon River," "Dear Heart," "Charade," "Days of Wine and Roses," scores for Breakfast at Tiffany's, The Pink Panther, Peter Gunn, Hatari, Victor/Victoria, Mr. Lucky *(1924 –1994).*

Mann-Cherney, Rose

Recording studio manager, president of Record Plant recording studios.

Manzarek, Ray

Composer, keyboardist, producer, founding member of The Doors.

Marley, Ziggy
Singer, songwriter, guitarist, keyboardist, drummer, eldest son of Bob Marley.

Mars Volta
Musical group known for explorations in hard rock, psychedelic rock, jazz.

Martin, George
Producer. Credits include The Beatles, America, Peter Sellers, Gerry & the Pacemakers, Billy J. Kramer & the Dakotas, Peter Gabriel, Celine Dion.

Massenburg, George
Engineer, producer. Credits include Linda Ronstadt, Randy Newman, Jimmy Webb, Lyle Lovett, Journey, Phil Collins, Little Feat, Earth, Wind and Fire, Toto, Kenny Loggins, Bonnie Raitt, Carly Simon, Herbie Hancock, Weather Report.

Miller, Steve
Singer, songwriter, guitarist, founder of The Steve Miller Band.

Moog, Robert
Electronic music pioneer, creator of the Minimoog synthesizer.

Mothersbaugh, Bob
Guitarist, composer, founding member of Devo.

Mothersbaugh, Mark
Composer, guitarist, keyboardist, film scorist, founding member of Devo. Credits include scoring Pee-Wee's Playhouse, Rugrats, Bottle Rocket, Happy Gilmore, Rushmore, The Life Aquatic with Steve Zissou, Thirteen, Lords of Dogtown, Herbie: Fully Loaded.

Nash, Graham
Singer, songwriter, producer. Founding member of The Hollies; Crosby, Stills & Nash.

Neff, John
Engineer, producer, composer, guitarist. Credits include numerous David Lynch film scores, Steely Dan, Willie Nelson, Buffy St. Marie, Ry Cooder, David Lindley, Kris Kristofferson, Jimmy Buffett.

Nelson, Willie
Singer, songwriter, founding member of The Highwaymen with Waylon Jennings, Johnny Cash, and Kris Kristofferson. Songwriting credits include "Night Life," "Crazy," "Hello Walls," "Funny How Time Slips Away."

Neve, Rupert
Recording equipment designer and engineer. Credits include revolutionary mixing consoles, pre-amplifiers, compressors, automated mixing systems.

Nilsson, Harry
Three-and-a-half octave range singer, songwriter, named favorite American singer by John Lennon and Paul McCartney. Credits include "Without You" (1941 – 1994).

Nitzsche, Jack
Composer, arranger, producer, songwriter, keyboardist. Credits include The Rolling Stones, Neil Young, numerous Phil Spector hits, Tim Buckley, Bobby Darin, Marianne Faithfull, The Monkees. Films: Performance, The Exorcist, One Flew Over the Cuckoo's Nest, An Officer and a Gentleman (1937 – 2000).

O'Keefe, Danny

Enduring singer, songwriter, composer of "Good Time Charlie."

Offord, Eddy

Engineer, producer. Credits include Yes, Emerson, Lake and Palmer, Pink Floyd, The Police, John Lennon, Todd Rundgren, Thin Lizzy.

Padgham, Hugh

Engineer, producer. Credits include Phil Collins, Peter Gabriel, XTC, The Police, Paul McCartney, Genesis, Sting, Michelle Shocked, Melissa Etheridge.

Paley, Andy

Singer, songwriter, keyboardist, producer. Credits include Jonathan Richman, Jerry Lee Lewis, Brian Wilson, John Wesley Harding, Madonna.

Parks, Van Dyke

Composer, arranger, lyricist, keyboardist, actor. Credits include Sonny & Cher, Paul Revere and the Raiders, The Beach Boys, The Byrds, Judy Collins, Tim Buckley, Harpers Bizarre.

Parsons, Alan

Engineer, producer, keyboardist, composer. Credits include The Beatles, Pink Floyd, Alan Parsons Project, Al Stewart.

Paul, Les

Engineer, producer, guitarist, arranger, musical and recording equipment designer renowned for his pioneering work in solid-body electric guitars and multitrack recording machines.

Paul, Stephen

Singer, songwriter, engineer, producer, renowned for his modified vintage microphones (1951 – 2003).

Payne, Bill

Singer, songwriter, keyboardist, founding member of Little Feat. Credits include Beck, Jackson Browne, Shawn Colvin, The Doobie Brothers, Bonnie Raitt, Linda Ronstadt, Robert Palmer, Bob Seger, Rod Stewart, Carly Simon, James Taylor.

Ramone, Phil

Producer, engineer, violinist. Credits include Billy Joel, Paul Simon, Kenny Loggins, Barbra Streisand, Frank Sinatra, Elton John, Liza Minnelli, Rod Stewart.

Red Hot Chili Peppers

Funk and punk rock group formed in the early '80s. Current lineup: Anthony Kiedis, Flea (Michael Balzary), John Frusciante, Chad Smith.

Reitzas, Dave

Engineer, mixer, producer, drummer. Credits include Madonna, Ricky Martin, Celine Dion, Michael Bolton, Natalie Cole, Barbra Streisand, Frank Sinatra, Kenny G, Gloria Estefan, Babyface, Jimmy Page.

Ria, Gaetano

Engineer. Credits include Paul Anka, Neil Sedaka, Stevie Wonder, Jose Feliciano, The Supremes, The Four Tops, scores by Ennio Morricone and Henry Mancini. Ria's work has contributed to more than 100,000,000 records sold.

Robertson, Robbie

Singer, songwriter, guitarist, producer, actor, film scorist, founding member of The Band. Film scores include Raging Bull, The Color of Money, The Hustler, The King of Comedy.

Rosas, Cesar

Singer, songwriter, guitarist, founding member of Los Lobos.

Rundgren, Todd

Singer, songwriter, engineer, producer. Credits include Badfinger, Meat Loaf, Grand Funk Railroad, New York Dolls, XTC, Bad Religion.

Rzeznik, John

Singer, songwriter, founding member of The Goo Goo Dolls. Credits include songs for City of Angels, Treasure Planet.

Saber, Danny

Producer, songwriter, re-mixer, guitarist, programmer. Credits include Seal, Black Grape, U2, The Rolling Stones, David Bowie, Public Enemy, Jesus Lizard, Garbage, Marilyn Manson, Megadeath, Madonna.

Santana, Carlos

Singer, songwriter, guitarist, founder of the band Santana.

Scheiner, Elliot

Engineer, producer. Credits include Van Morrison, The Eagles, Steely Dan, Jimmy Buffett, John Fogerty, Beck, Sting, Fleetwood Mac, Aerosmith, B.B. King.

Schmitt, Al

Engineer, producer. Credits include Sam Cooke, George Benson, Jefferson Airplane, Toto, Steely Dan, Jackson Browne, Diana Ross, Michael Franks, Ray Charles, Natalie Cole, Frank Sinatra.

Scott, Ken

Engineer, producer. Credits include The Beatles, America, Jeff Beck, George Harrison, Duran Duran, Elton John, Harry Nilsson, David Bowie, Supertramp, The Tubes, Devo.

Shaffer, Paul

Composer, arranger, keyboardist, musical director of Late Night with David Letterman *and leader of The World's Most Dangerous Band.*

Shaw, Artie

Composer, author, clarinetist, bandleader, renowned for his renditions of "Begin the Beguine," "Stardust."

Shirley, Kevin

Engineer, producer, mixer. Credits include Aerosmith, Silverchair, Jimmy Page, The Black Crowes, Journey, Billy Joel, Iron Maiden, The Divinyls, Cold Chisel.

Shoemaker, Trina

Engineer, producer. Credits include Sheryl Crow, The Dixie Chicks, Patti Scialfa, Steven Curtis Chapman, Victoria Williams, Midnight Oil, Iggy Pop.

Sides, Allen

Engineer, producer, Ocean Way recording studio owner. Credits include Eric Clapton, Alanis Morissette, The Goo Goo Dolls, Beck, Ry Cooder, Emmylou Harris, Phil Collins, Natalie Cole, Trisha Yearwood, Kenny Loggins, Little Richard, Aretha Franklin, Linda Ronstadt, Etta James, Bobby McFerrin, The Pointer Sisters.

Sklar, Leland

Bass player, composer, arranger. Credits include James Taylor, Hall & Oates, Jackson Browne, Phil Collins, Willie Nelson, Clint Black, America, Jimmy Buffett, Vanessa Carlton, Ray Charles, Cher, Neil Diamond, Julio Iglesias, Kris Kristofferson, Linda Ronstadt, Rod Stewart, Warren Zevon.

Spinal Tap

Fictitious band comprised of David St. Hubbins (Michael McKean), Derek Smalls (Harry Shearer), Nigel Tufnel (Christopher Guest).

Stone, Chris

Founder of Record Plant recording studios, World Studio Group, co-founder and executive director of the Music Producers Guild of the Americas, co-founder and former president and chairman of the Society of Professional Audio Recording Services (SPARS).

Summers, Andy

Guitarist, composer, producer, co-founder of The Police.

Sutton, Ralph

Engineer, producer, sound designer, remixer. Credits include Stevie Wonder, Michael Jackson, Babyface, The Temptations, The Four Tops, Rick James, Smokey Robinson.

Swedien, Bruce

Engineer, producer. Credits include Michael Jackson, Quincy Jones, Duke Ellington, Count Basie, Stan Kenton, Woody Herman, Jennifer Lopez.

Tedesco, Tommy

Reputedly the most recorded guitarist in history. Credits include The Beach Boys, The Monkees, Elvis Presley, Jan & Dean, Frank Zappa, The 5th Dimension, Van Dyke Parks, Frank Sinatra, Ella Fitzgerald, Barbra Streisand.

Thielemans, Toots

Harmonica virtuoso, whistler, accordionist, guitarist, composer. Credits include work with Charlie Parker, George Shearing, Quincy Jones, Oscar Peterson, Ivan Lins, commercial for Old Spice.

Thompson, Richard

Singer, songwriter, guitarist.

Titelman, Russ

Producer. Credits include Randy Newman, Eric Clapton, James Taylor, Paul Simon, Chaka Khan, Steve Winwood.

Tuck & Patti

Tuck Andress and Patti Cathcart, duo known for inventive jazz, R&B.

Ungar, Leanne

Engineer, producer. Credits include Leonard Cohen, Cat Stevens, Loudon Wainwright III, Janis Ian, The Temptations, Fishbone, Holly Cole, Joe Henderson, Adam Cohen, Willie Nelson, Big Mountain, Luther Vandross, Natalie Cole, Vonda Shepard, Tom Jones, The Paul Winter Consort.

Vanston, CJ

Keyboardist, arranger, composer, producer. Credits include Joe Cocker, Spinal Tap, Tina Turner, Barbra Streisand, David Foster, George Michael, Prince, Ringo Starr, Celine Dion.

Vega, Suzanne

Singer, songwriter. Credits include "Luka," "Tom's Diner," "Caramel," "Woman On the Tier."

Was, David

Co-founder of Was (Not Was), flautist, lyricist, composer, scorist, producer.

Was, Don
Co-founder of Was (Not Was), bassist, producer, filmmaker. Credits include Bonnie Raitt, The Rolling Stones, Bob Dylan, Willie Nelson, Bob Seger, Paula Abdul.

Webb, Jimmy
Singer, songwriter. Credits include "By the Time I Get to Phoenix," "Wichita Lineman," "Up Up and Away," "MacArthur Park."

Weinberg, Max
Renowned drummer with Bruce Springsteen and the E Street Band, bandleader for the TV show Late Night with Conan O'Brien, *leader of The Max Weinberg 7.*

Wendy & Lisa
Guitarist Wendy Melvoin and keyboardist Lisa Coleman, famous for their work with Prince, duo recording career, and scores for feature films and episodic television.

Wilson, Brian
Producer, composer, singer, songwriter, bassist, keyboardist, co-founder of The Beach Boys.

Wonder, Stevie
Producer, composer, singer, songwriter, social activist.

X, Geza
Engineer, producer, programmer, arranger, songwriter, guitarist. Credits include Germs, The Dead Kennedys, Black Flag, Redd Kross.

X, John
Engineer, remixer, producer. Credits include Ice Cube, Black Grape, The Rolling Stones, Garbage, David Bowie, Barry White, X, Marilyn Manson, Jesus Lizard, Michael Hutchence, Korn, U2, Black Sabbath.

Yakus, Shelly
Engineer, producer. Credits include Van Morrison, The Band, Tom Petty, Stevie Nicks, Bob Seger.

Yankovic, "Weird" Al
World's leading humorous song parodist. Hits include "Beat It," "King of Suede," "Like a Surgeon," "Smells Like Nirvana," "Amish Paradise."

Zappa, Dweezil
Composer, guitarist, actor, TV host, voiceover artist.

Zappa, Frank
Prolific and influential composer, producer, performer (1940 – 1993).

Zimmer, Hans
Scoring composer. Credits include Gladiator, Pirates of the Caribbean, The Lion King, The Last Samurai, Crimson Tide, Rain Man.